I Once Was Lost

by

William Delia

Copyright © 2016 William Delia

All rights reserved. No part of this book may be used or reproduced by any means without written permission of the author except for brief quotations used in critical articles or reviews.

I Once Was Lost is a work of fiction. Any similarities to persons living or dead is unintentional and coincidental. The views expressed in this book are solely those of the author.

Books by William Delia may be ordered through booksellers or by contacting www.wmdeliabooks.com.

Cover images provided by 123RF.com

ISBN: 978-1539325475 (softcover)

Printed in the United States of America

DEDICATION

We live in a world that is dangerous and troubled at times. Our safe journey through this world depends on those among us who selflessly give of themselves to help people in need. First responders, second responders, people who do not run away from trouble but summon the courage to run toward it. Search and rescue personnel are prominent among this group of courageous people and their work never fails to inspire me. This book is dedicated to all those who see someone in need and willingly offer their time, their talent and their caring. They make our world a better place.

Prologue

The camera zoomed in, filling the screen with the director's requested "money shot". The extreme close-up had become the trademark of *Up Close and Personal;* a shot so close viewers could count the freckles on the young man's cheek. However, counting freckles was not the point. The unstated, but accomplished, objective was to capture the first tear as it formed on his lower eye-lid and then slowly trickled down the side of his nose.

"I suppose it is ironic, isn't it?" he said. "I mean, what I do – searching for people who are lost and here I am, like some pathetic lost soul myself. I don't know who my parents were, I have no family, and my best friend is my dog. I have a nice place to live, but it seems like I'm never there. We are on the road so much of the time, now, trying to help others find their way home that I'm seldom home myself. The Bible speaks of the blind leading the blind; I guess my version of that passage is 'the lost seeking the lost'.

Don't get me wrong: I'm not complaining. I've been blessed in so many ways. I do wonder, though, if my own story has something to do with why I do what I do. I wonder if helping others who are lost somehow makes up for being lost myself. Does that sound crazy?"

The interviewer smiled a scripted smile, then brushed an unscripted tear from her own eye and shook her head, "No – that doesn't sound crazy at all."

The Priory – 1972

From a distance the call of a loon

Softly floats across a purple sky.

In harmony, a coyote howls at the moon

Oh hear them sing

An Adirondack lullaby

Chapter One

  The solitary figure moved along the tree line, in and out of darkness, traversing elongated moon-shadows of bare-limbed trees, while creeping steadily toward the weathered stone building at the head of the path. Clad in black from head to toe, the figure defied description; male, female, old, young, slender or stocky all indecipherable. Only a distinct limp on the left side offered any clue to the figure's identity. The vaguely human form seemed little more than shadow itself, weaving among the slender pine tree silhouettes that striped the silver October frost glistening on the ground.
  A full Fisher Moon hung low in the sky; a brilliant silver-white disk set against an eternally deep blue backdrop flecked randomly with sparks of starlight. On any other night, the sight would have been something to behold and admire, but this silent specter appeared not to notice. It moved forward purposefully, stealthily, head down, picking each step with care to avoid crackling downed branches or rustling autumn leaves scattered beneath the trees. Although a wide, open path led toward the

building, the figure held close to the tree line, fending off low hanging branches with one arm while cradling what appeared to be a bundle of rags with the other.

When the building was no more than a few steps away, the figure stopped and stood motionless against the trunk of a large white pine. The night offered no sound at all, as if the universe was holding its breath waiting to see what would happen next. The building, too, stood silent offering no sign of life; its tall arched windows staring like dark and empty eyes fixed on the mountains in the distance; its double door a gaping maw ready to swallow anyone bold enough to enter.

Apparently satisfied by the stillness, the figure stepped into the open and advanced the toward the building moving even more deliberately than before; step, shuffle, step, in near-waltz time. Approaching the doorstep from the side partially covered by an overgrown box elder, the intruder suddenly froze in mid-stride and stood motionless, not even breathing. A low growl rumbled from the blackness on the other side of the stoop. Then nothing; only impenetrable silence. The figure in black hesitated, close enough to reach the door but apparently fearful that whatever beast lurked on the other side of the steps would arrive there first. A second growl, longer and even lower than the first settled the matter. Moving in slow motion the figure bent low it's right arm extended toward the door and placed the bundle on the top step. Still moving in slow motion the figure straightened up and backed away from the building. Step, shuffle, step, shuffle, step repeated three, four, five times – no sound, no movement, nothing. Suddenly another growl echoed in the darkness, louder this time, accompanied by something big rustling in the bushes. The figure turned away from the building and hurried frantically down the path.

A large dog bounded out of the bushes with yet another menacing growl. It followed the figure a few yards down the path then it stopped abruptly and turned toward the bundle on the steps. In the dim light, the rags appeared to move ever so slightly. The dog cocked her head to one side and lifted her nose to the air, her mouth slightly open as if tasting the scent. Cautiously she circled toward the stoop, positioned her two front paws on the step and stretched her neck toward the bundle, now clearly twitching with life. The dog nuzzled the cloths open and a tiny face looked back at her with the unseeing eyes of a newborn baby. The dog nuzzled the rags some more, pushing aside the blood stained blanket that covered the child. Her inquisitive tongue began licking the still moist birth fluids from the tiny body. The dog nuzzled the child, then the rags again pushing them aside as she opened her mouth to its fullest aperture, then bared her teeth and bit down hard.

∞

Brother Clement grunted as he pushed open the thick oaken door letting the first dim light of morning trickle into the chapel. Since being elected Prior two years ago, he had begun each day the same way: by faithfully preparing the chapel for morning worship. He arose before dawn, dressed in his usual blue jeans, flannel shirt and work boots and then made the short walk down the hall from his quarters to the chapel. There, he would light the candles and sit in the pew nearest the altar to complete his personal devotions in silence. When his prayers were finished, and the altar set with chalice and paten, he would open the doors to welcome the new day. No matter the season, even in the cold of the mountain winters, he would stand on the stoop with his arms thrown wide as if embracing the morning, and intone aloud the words of Psalm 118: "This is the day the Lord has made, let us rejoice and be glad in it!"

His words were heartfelt; he truly rejoiced in each new day. It had not always been like this; the years before he came to the Priory had tested his faith and his mettle. Now in his late fifties and having lived more than twenty years in the community, those hard times lingered only as a distant recollection, something more visceral than remembered. On difficult days, he could still feel the empty ache in his soul that had been his constant companion for much of his life before. While he never wanted to live that way again, he hoped that feeling would never leave him. Each time it reverberated in the depths of his spirit, he remembered why he had chosen this life. At times, however, he wondered if he had chosen this life or if he had been chosen for it. Either way, he had been blessed by the choice and he was confident he would live out his days in this place.

Clement stood on the front step of the chapel gazing at the mountains still faintly wrapped in a fading blanket of stars as the glow of the dawning sun began to light the eastern sky. As he lowered his eyes earthward, he noticed the dog lying on the grass near the shrubbery.

"Good morning, Serena. What is this all about? Usually by this time of day you are lurking around the kitchen waiting for a handout."

The dog, a large yellow Labrador, stared at him without moving; even her tail remained motionless. She was curled up in a half-circle with her back to the doorway where Clement stood.

"Are you alright, girl?" Clement said as he approached her. "What have you got there?"

As he came closer, he saw that she was curled up around something that appeared to be a ball of rags. Her eyes followed him as he approached but she did not move. When Clement bent down and reached his hand toward her an almost inaudible growl rumbled deep in her chest.

"Serena," he said with a gentle but firm voice, "leave it. Leave it."

The dog submitted to the familiar command. The muscles in her flank twitched then relaxed and her tail wagged slightly.

Clement, reached out and stroked her head as he examined the rags cuddled within the half circle of her body and legs.

He pulled the top rag away and gasped, "Holy Mary, mother of God!"

Over the years, the dogs of Good Mountain Priory had brought many trophies home from their forays into the mountains but nothing like this. A newborn baby snuggled against the dog's warm underbelly. At first, he could not tell if the baby was alive or dead. Clement put his hand to the child's face; the baby squirmed, screwed-up its face and opened its mouth wide, as if to cry, but no sound came.

"Brother Clement?"

Clement snatched back his hand, startled by the voice behind him. He turned quickly around to see Marcel in the doorway.

"Is Sister Serena alright?" Marcel asked.

"Brother Marcel – yes, Serena is fine, but look at this – she has brought us a child. A newborn baby, I think."

"A baby?"

"Yes. Quickly, go find Sister Hannah and bring her here."

"Shouldn't we call someone – an ambulance, the police?"

"Yes, in due time, but first Sister Hannah – now, please."

A short while later, Hannah hurried into the chapel and found Clement sitting on the step by the altar, humming and rocking the baby in his arms.

He smiled at her and said, "All I could think of to sing to the child is the Doxology, but he seems to like it." He turned back to the child and began singing again, "Praise God from whom all blessings flow..."

"Brother Clement, may I..." Hannah spoke in little more than a whisper.

Hannah took the child, "O my – he's not more than a few hours old. Whoever cleaned him up did not do a very good job." Hannah paused and said, "I'm sorry, Brother, I didn't mean – "

Clement raised his hand, "I didn't do it – I think Serena did."

"Sister Serena? Well that explains a lot. She must have treated him like one of her own puppies. She licked off some of the birth fluids and here, you can see where she bit off the umbilical cord. I need to examine him more thoroughly." She glanced up at the altar and said, "Perhaps this is not the place."

"No, Sister," Clement replied, "this is precisely the place. What better place could there be for a newborn baby than the house of God? I will bring you whatever you need. You can rest him here, on the altar."

"Oh, no! I can't examine him on the altar table!"

"Sister, the altar is where we place our gifts and where we consecrate God's gift of the Bread of Life. A newborn child is one of God's greatest gifts – please do as I say and please work quickly. Brother Marcel has called the authorities so we don't have much time."

Twenty minutes later, the Sheriff's patrol car pulled up in front of the chapel followed closely by the one ambulance operated by the Colvin Valley Volunteer Ambulance Corps.

"Good morning, Sheriff! I didn't expect you to come yourself," Clement called from the steps of the chapel. He recognized the two ambulance volunteers but did not remember their names so he simply nodded in their direction.

"Good morning, Brother Clement. I had to come myself when I heard a call about an abandoned baby. Where is the child?"

"He is being cared for, Sheriff. Before I take you to him, I need to know what you intend to do. If you take him, what will happen to him?"

"What do you mean, '*if*' I take him? The ambulance is right here; we need to be sure the baby receives proper medical care, then we need to try to find out who he is, where he came from and what crimes have been committed."

Brother Clement smiled, hoping to reassure the Sheriff, "Of course, I understand all of that. What I mean is where will the child be taken? Who will care for him?"

"That is not my call, Brother. Child Protective Services will step in and place him in a proper facility. I have never had to deal with an abandoned infant before, so I don't really know their protocol. Now, where is the child?"

"Sheriff, I don't mean to be a problem, but there are conflicting duties here. You have your duty and I have mine," Clement intentionally smoothed his cassock and adjusted the cincture around his waist as he spoke. "This child was not left by the side of the road; he was left in our Chapel. Because of that, we have an inviolable responsibility to care for and protect him. Are you familiar with the principle of religious sanctuary?"

"Yes, I am familiar with the notion, but this is not 18th century England, and this baby is no criminal begging church protection from the government. Brother Clement, I must insist that you turn over the baby immediately. If he is truly newborn, he needs proper medical attention. By denying him access to medical care you are endangering his welfare and that is a crime."

"Sheriff Hansford, how long have we known each other – at least 12 years, yes? Have I ever done anything to make you believe I would allow a child to be endangered? Have I ever done anything to make you believe that I do not respect you and your authority? But this is an unusual situation for both of us. You need to fulfill your responsibilities and I need to fulfill mine. After all, we have both taken vows and pledged ourselves to higher authorities."

"So, what are you suggesting?"

"We called you because we wish to be cooperative and to allow you to do the necessary investigation. I suggest you and the paramedics come in and examine the child. Be reassured that he is alright and being properly cared for. Once you see that the child is in good hands, I suggest that you leave him in our care while you conduct your investigation. I promise we will abide by the outcome of that investigation. If you are able to locate a family member to care for the boy we will gladly release him to your custody. If you do not locate his family, then we will work with you, Child Protective Services, and whoever else is involved to place the child in a good home. I know this may be a bit unorthodox, but this solution allows both of us to keep our vows: we shelter a child in need of sanctuary and you fulfill your obligations to the law."

The Sheriff took a deep breath and blew it out before answering. "Brother Clement, I appreciate your concern –"

"It is more than concern, Sheriff. It is a sacred obligation imposed by our religious vows."

"Understood. But this is not my call. The State of New York is very clear that Child Protective Services has jurisdiction for any child that is abandoned, unidentified, or in any other way left without parental care. My duty is to notify them and place the child in their care. I'm sorry, Brother Clement, but I have no choice..."

"Sheriff, it is Saturday morning. Child Protective will have to respond from some distance, right? Probably from Indian Lake – a trip that will take some time and we all know how overworked their caseworkers are, they may not even make it here until Monday or even later next week. What would you do in the meantime with a newborn baby – lock him up in a jail cell, or ship him off to the hospital in Glens Falls? Let me suggest this: after you examine the child, leave him in our care while you return to your office and file the necessary mounds of paperwork. Tell Child Protective he is being cared for until they arrive and let us deal with the caseworker when he or she comes for the baby. That way, you have fulfilled your duty and we have fulfilled ours."

Shaking his head, the Sheriff replied, "This is a whole new side of you, Brother Clement; one I haven't seen before. But you do make a good point – my department is not equipped to care for a newborn. We'll try it your way, BUT only if the baby is healthy and well when we examine him. Now, where is he?"

"He is in the sanctuary, of course. Come with me."

Sister Hannah sat rocking the baby in the celebrant's chair behind the altar in the front of the sanctuary. Brother Clement smiled when the Sheriff removed his hat and both of the ambulance attendants made the sign of the cross as they entered the chapel.

"Sister Hannah, you know Sheriff Hansford. He and these good people from the ambulance squad need to examine the child."

Hannah handed the baby over to the paramedics and self-consciously brushed back her hair and straightened her bathrobe. Unlike Clement, she had not taken time to change clothes.

While the paramedics examined the child the Sheriff took a formal statement from Clement about where and how the baby was found. He also examined the rags the baby was wrapped in and placed them in a plastic evidence bag. Hannah had washed the child, trimmed the bite marks from the stump of his umbilical cord and wrapped him in clean linen cloths from the sacristy. She explained to the Sheriff what she had done, omitting the part about Serena's bite marks, and explained she had acted in the baby's best interests knowing that the rags held ample DNA evidence if the Sheriff needed it for his investigation.

The paramedics conferred with Sheriff Hansford and then began packing up their equipment. The Sheriff signaled to Brother Clement to come with him as they left the chapel.

Outside in the full sun of morning, the Sheriff said, "I probably should have my head examined, but I'm going to do it your way. The baby can stay here with you until Child Protective responds. Frankly, I don't understand why you are pushing so hard on this, Brother. It seems to me that you are not much better prepared to care for a newborn than is my department. But if you have any notions of this baby staying here permanently, I suggest you lose them right now. I doubt that you will find the Child Protective caseworker to be as cooperative as I am. They just hired a new worker, a woman who took an early pension from New York City Social Services and bought a retirement place outside of Speculator. I hear she is battle-hardened and takes no grief from anyone. So consider yourself warned. I'll let you know if our investigation turns up anything, but I'm guessing that whoever left the child here like this has no intention of being found."

Hannah stood in the doorway cradling the baby. After the Sheriff and the ambulance had driven away she said to Clement, "Brother, I have to agree with the Sheriff. I don't understand, either, why you insisted on the baby staying here. We are not prepared to care for this child."

"Nonsense, Sister. Last month, Sister Claire's new granddaughter was here for a visit, remember? Sister Clair was so excited she stocked up on all things baby – diapers, baby bottles and formula, clothes, even one of those portable cribs. She will be delighted to share her supplies and to help care for him."

"But why? Why not let the child go?"

"Sister, how many years has our Good Mountain Priory been here?"

"I don't know – maybe thirty?"

"Thirty-one – the monks fled the Languedoc after the Germans invaded France in 1940 and they arrived here less than two years later. In all those years, have we ever had a day like this one? Have we ever discovered a lost soul on our doorstep? Have we ever heard a newborn baby cry out for sanctuary, for compassion and shelter here in our chapel? No! I tell you, God is doing something new here today. I don't know what it is, or why it is happening but I can see the hand of the Almighty moving in these early morning hours. We are called to be God's presence in this place; to do the work of God's hands as we are given that work to do. We have no choice. This is not a chance happening – it is a blessing!"

Clement thought for a moment of telling Hannah about the vision he had in prayer that morning, but he decided against it. This morning's vision, like the others of recent weeks, would remain between him and his God.

"Sister Hannah, I will ask Sister Claire to bring her baby supplies to the chapel. You can set up a nursery for the child in the nave to the side of the altar."

"Brother, the chapel is cold and drafty, wouldn't the baby be better off –"

"The baby is not to leave the chapel, even for a moment. Is that clear? He remains here. I will ask others to help you, but as our community's medic you need to lead the way for the next few days. Please, Sister, do as I request."

"Of course, Brother, I will do as you say. I trust that you will explain all of this to me when the time is right." She turned back toward the chapel and said over her shoulder, "Please ask Sister Claire to bring me some proper clothes when she comes."

Chapter Two

The next day, the entire Good Mountain Priory community gathered for Sunday morning worship in the chapel just as the sun appeared in full glory over the eastern peaks. Nineteen men and eight women sat in a semi-circle praying, singing, reading from scripture and reflecting on Brother Clement's message for the day. They shared all the usual elements of worship, but in a way none of them had experienced before. Sister Adina played the old pump organ but with such a light touch that every tune sounded like a lullaby. Prayers spoken aloud bore conviction but in a volume barely above a whisper. Even Brother Clement, whose powerful voice often reverberated throughout the small chapel, spoke with a gentleness that gave a new dimension to the Gospel. All of this was accomplished between furtive glances toward the corner of the nave where the baby boy slept in Hannah's arms. After a long and restless night, she sat rocking him afraid he might wake if she put him back in Claire's portable crib. Hannah's own eyes, heavy with sleep, glistened with an unmistakable contentment.

When worship ended, everyone crowded around Hannah and the baby, smiling, whispering and pointing out the child's endearing qualities. After a few moments, Clement herded them out of the chapel leaving only Claire and Hannah with the baby.

Outside, Clement said to Marcel, "Isn't it amazing how a baby can become the center of attention for an entire room full of people without speaking a word or doing anything more than breathing in and out?"

Marcel nodded, "We are all fascinated by God's miracle of new life in the flesh."

Before Clement could respond he was distracted by a car, a dark late-model sedan, coming up the driveway toward them. They often had visitors to the Priory, but seldom on Sunday mornings and never this early.

The woman who stepped out of the car bore the unmistakable presence of authority. Even though she was casually dressed in a long woolen skirt and baggy sweater, the way her gaze scanned the scene before her left no doubt: she was here on business. Instinctively, she zeroed in on Clement and walked directly to him.

"Brother Clement? I am Miriam Fossler, County Child Protective Services. I'm here to pick up the baby." Her level voice matched her businesslike demeanor.

Clement extended his hand, "Welcome, Ms. Fossler. I didn't expect you so early on a Sunday morning." The woman took his hand and held his gaze, but said nothing. "We just finished morning worship services and are on our way to breakfast. Please join us."

"Thanks, but I don't eat breakfast. If you will bring the baby to me, I will be on my way."

"Perhaps coffee, then, or some juice? We have fresh apple juice pressed yesterday from our own orchard..."

"Brother Clement," she spoke his name as though the words left a saccharine taste in her mouth. "I know from the Sheriff's report that you have other ideas about this baby, but let me be perfectly clear. The State of New York will take custody and decide what is best for this child and it is my job to act on behalf of the State. Frankly, I cannot believe that Sheriff Hansford left a vulnerable newborn baby here, in this monastery, instead of securing proper medical attention. No matter, I intend to correct the error in his judgment; that is why I am here so early on a Sunday morning, instead of sitting on my screened porch reading the New York Times. So, again, if you will produce the child I will be on my way."

"Ms. Fossler, I can assure you that the baby received proper medical attention. I can also assure you that he has been very well cared for and he will continue to be very well cared as long as he is in our custody. Furthermore, Good Mountain Priory is not a monastery and certainly not the archaic medieval institution you are imagining. We are not chanting, cloistered monks retreating from the world to transcribe illuminated texts by candlelight. We are a community of lay people with diverse gifts and graces who have been called to a communal life of service."

Fossler softened slightly, "I meant no disrespect. I know very little about religious institutions. In fact, I know nothing of your priory other than your reputation as breeders of exceptional service dogs. Of course, that hardly qualifies this as a place to care for a newborn baby."

"Perhaps, we should find a better place to talk, so you might come to understand what does qualify us. Please come with me."

Without waiting for a response, Clement nodded to Marcel and then led the woman toward a low building adjacent to the chapel.

Sunlight streamed through a set of large bay windows giving the room a welcoming glow. The walls were covered with photographs of Priory dogs, each one seeming to be smiling for the camera at least as much as the happy people in the pictures with them. Each of the dogs was dressed in working gear – harnesses and service dog vests with first responder insignia of all kinds. A couple of the dogs wore medals hanging around their necks. The people with them in the photos were dressed in matching gear – firefighters, rescue personnel, law enforcement officers and therapy dog handlers of all kinds. Miriam Fossler scanned the pictures and spotted many familiar faces including two state governors and one former President of the United States.

As they took their seats at a small oval table, Marcel entered carrying a tray of coffee, apple juice and muffins still warm from the oven. He placed the tray on the table and left without a word being spoken.

Clement poured juice and coffee for both of them and the woman took a tentative bite of a muffin. Her face revealed no reaction, but she devoured the muffin in three quick bites.

"They are good, aren't they?" Clement said. "Please have another; I can never stop with just one."

As if to illustrate his remark, Clement placed two muffins on his own plate. "Our cook is really remarkable – a classically trained chef who worked in some of the finest restaurants in Boston."

"And he gave it all up to serve the Lord, here..." Fossler's words dripped with sarcasm.

"Actually, after more than ten years of acclaim he couldn't get a job. Even as talented as he was, no one would entrust their restaurant to a meth-head."

"Oh, I, uh, I'm sorry," the woman stumbled.

"No need to apologize. Things are not always what they appear on the surface, are they? At first the drugs were just a little pick-me-up to get Brother Seth through long demanding days in the kitchen. But I imagine you have heard this story a hundred times before, working as you do with families in crisis. The drugs soon became his entire life. Thank God, he got out alive."

"So he came here to kick his habit?"

"No – I wish we could take credit for that, but Seth was forced into rehab by the courts. He was arrested for possession in a large federal sting operation and given the choice between jail and rehab. He chose wisely and the treatment worked for him. When he got out he knew he could not go back to his old life. His parole officer suggested using his skills in service to others and got him a job cooking for the rescue mission down in Schenectady. The mission staff came here on retreat a couple of years ago and Seth found a home."

"So now he cooks for you," she said.

"Yes, for us and for a consortium of homeless shelters throughout upstate New York. He develops recipes and techniques – tested on us – to help the shelters put out good-tasting, nutritious meals using local inexpensive ingredients. Those muffins are probably being served in half a dozen homeless shelters this morning."

"I suppose there is a story behind the apple juice, too," her voice held slightly less sarcasm than before.

"As a matter of fact, there is, but I will save it for another time. I know you came for the baby and you are probably anxious to fulfill your responsibility."

"Yes, I am."

"Please understand we, too, are anxious to fulfill our responsibilities – our obligations. We did not ask for this child to be left in our chapel but once he arrived it became part of our sacred duty to care for him. We may not be monks, but we take our vows very seriously."

"Surely, you don't expect the State of New York to say 'finders-keepers, you can have the baby!' A newborn child belongs in a safe family environment where he can be loved and cared for, given medical attention, nurturing, the opportunity to grow-up healthy and strong."

"Ms. Fossler, I have no doubt you believe every word you just spoke. But you know, as well as I do – probably better than I do –

that most children placed in foster care by the benevolent State of New York never find that kind of loving home. Being totally honest, do you have a home like that ready and waiting for our little boy?"

"Honestly," she hesitated for a moment, "no I don't. But that is my job – not yours – and I will see that he is properly placed. Please don't make me force the issue. If necessary, I will call the Sheriff and have him forcibly remove the child. By the way, he told me about your sanctuary ploy. Really, Brother Clement? Clinging to an arcane and archaic notion like sanctuary seems beneath you."

"Actually, several recent court rulings have upheld religious sanctuary in both state and federal cases dealing with draft resisters and undocumented immigrants. Our lawyer has already found a judge willing to receive our petition. If you attempt to take the child by force, we will seek an injunction."

For the first time, Miriam Fossler's confidence appeared shaken. She stood up and walked around the room, gazing once again at the photographs. She stopped in front of one that appeared recently hung. The photo was taken at the State Capitol and showed the current governor of New York scratching a large yellow lab behind the ears. Several men in black robes stood smiling behind him; she was certain that she recognized one of the robed men as a State Supreme Court judge.

She turned back to face Clement, "And I thought this was friendly conversation over juice and muffins, but you are playing hardball aren't you? The Governor – and the State Supreme Court?"

Clement smiled beneficently, "The governor was quite taken with Serena after she assisted State Troopers with the rescue of a kidnapped child."

Miriam Fossler sighed deeply and returned to the table. "So, let's try a different approach. What would you suggest I do? Just ride off into the sunset and forget any of this happened?"

Clement shook his head, "Of course not. You have a job to do and I am hoping that we can help."

"Help? How?"

"Since we don't know who the child is and whether or not he has family members willing and able to take him, you will need a temporary foster family until the investigation is complete and the court rules on custody."

"So, Brother Clement you have done your homework."

Clement smiled. "Why not leave the child here with us while the Sheriff conducts his investigation. Perhaps he will succeed in finding the boy's family and all of us – even the State of New York – will be happy to have the boy raised by his own relatives."

"I can't just leave the boy somewhere, anywhere. Regulations require that if the child cannot be suitably placed with family that he must be placed in a designated institution or with a licensed foster family. I'm afraid your priory is neither designated nor licensed."

"So license us! You have the authority, don't you, to issue a temporary license for thirty days pending further review and approval? We will cooperate in every way. If, after the review, we are not deemed appropriate for licensing we will surrender the child. Meanwhile, the baby will be cared for and you will have thirty days to find a more permanent placement."

"I can't license an institution. I can only license a married couple – how many of those do you have living here?"

"Three, actually, but there is one couple that would be perfect."

"You have married couples living here in a monastery – a priory – whatever!" the woman said with obvious surprise.

"I can see you are still struggling with who we are, Ms. Fossler. Why don't I show you around and introduce you to some of our community? We can even check in on the little boy at the center of all this controversy."

Clement began the tour without leaving the room, pointing to a painting hung prominently between the two windows. "That is Serrabone Priory in the Pyrenees Mountains of France. It is our namesake – Serrabone means good mountain – and the brothers who founded our Priory originated there. Serrabone was established by Cistercian Brothers in the 12th Century and many of the buildings still stand today including the one in the painting. Brother Bernard, one of the founders of our Priory, painted this picture from memory. I've seen photographs of the Priory; he captured the scene perfectly.

In France, Brother Bernard and five others had begun breeding and training sheep dogs for the Basque sheep herders in the Languedoc. Apparently, their initiative had not been well received and the Prior had forced them to take the dogs and live outside the Priory itself. They reluctantly went, hoping they would find success and earn their way back. Before they could prove their worth, World War II intervened. When the Germans invaded France in 1940, Bernard and the others fled to America leaving behind their beloved Serrabone and all but one breeding pair of their dogs.

When they arrived in New York City, they were told they were welcome but their dogs were not. Since they had no registration papers or veterinary records, the dogs would have to be put down. The brothers could not bear the thought of the dogs being euthanized. A local priest who was acting as interpreter for the brothers suggested they go to Canada instead. He told them the dogs would be permitted to enter there and suggested they might be more comfortable among the many French speaking Quebecois.

How the brothers arrived here is a little vague. Apparently a wealthy Canadian logging family owned this land and when the last of the family died, the land became part of an estate left to a church in Montreal. The rules of the bequest, however, did not allow the church to sell the property and specified that if they could not make use of the land, ownership would pass to the State of New York to become part of the Adirondack Park. The church was ready to surrender the land when someone – perhaps Brother Bernard – suggested establishing a mountain priory. So, two years after fleeing the war in France, the brothers found themselves here in the Adirondack Mountains of New York."

Clement led the woman outside and continued the story as they walked around the grounds. "When the brothers arrived they found only a primitive saw mill and a small bunkhouse that had housed lumberjacks. The bunkhouse still stands today as part of our kennel. It took some time, but the brothers built most of the other buildings you see here today. Of course, the chapel came first, then the residence, over there. The common rooms – kitchen, dining hall, library, meeting rooms – all were added as time passed."

Clement introduced her to Marcel at the kennel entrance, and Marcel picked up the story. "The brothers began breeding dogs again, but they quickly discovered that sheep dogs were in little demand in the Adirondacks. They tried two or three other breeds before some of their Canadian contacts sent them an excellent breeding pair of Labrador retrievers. They knew right away that these were the dogs for them. Labs are good at so many things. They are working dogs but they also make great pets and they are outstanding as service dogs. Of course, as you know, today our dogs are best known as search and rescue specialists."

Marcel led them into the kennel where a gaggle of eight puppies, less than a month old, swarmed around their ankles yipping, jumping and wagging their tails so hard that their whole bodies swayed from side-to-side. Miriam Fossler knelt down and let the puppies clamber over her. Her whole demeanor changed and suddenly she was smiling and laughing. She stood up, holding one puppy squirming in her arms as he licked her neck and face.

"Maybe, I should have introduced you to the puppies first," Clement said.

She laughed, "Who could resist these little guys? Look at the size of those paws! He's going to be a big boy!"

Outside, again and puppy-less, she said to Clement, "OK, the dogs are adorable but everything else seems like a monastery to me. Where do the lay people come in?"

"Many Cistercian Orders have lay communities attached to them, so the idea was familiar to the brothers. Frankly, once they were established here, they became rather disconnected from their order, even from the church in general. They established a full communal and spiritual life here, but they attracted few converts interested in taking the vows of the order. They did, however, gradually attract a thriving lay community drawn, in large part, by the dogs. Men and women came here seeking a more spiritual life style, one based on principles of faith and service to others. Those who came were comfortable living the communal life but not prepared to make a lifelong religious commitment."

"So, how many of you are brothers and how many are lay people?"

"We are all lay people; we have been for nearly seven years now. The last of the brothers left us in 1965."

"Even you? You are the Prior, aren't you? I don't understand – you wear the robe of a monk and all of you call one another 'Brother This' and 'Sister That'."

"I imagine it is confusing for someone coming from the outside world. As I said before, things are not always what they appear to be. I am the Prior, elected two years ago by the members of the community. Being Prior is a calling from God, but one that must be affirmed by the community. I wear the robe for liturgical and special occasions as a sign of my calling as Prior. Most of the time we dress in ordinary work clothes.

The use of Brother and Sister is very intentional. It is not meant as a title; it describes our relationship for we try to live as members of one human family. When we are joined to the community we take a name of meaning and significance to our community and we no longer use the name we were given at birth. My name for example, Clement, means mercy or merciful. It was given to me when I joined the community more than twenty years ago."

"I guess I need some time to digest all of this."

Clement said, "I understand. Let's walk over to the chapel. There is someone there you should meet."

Hannah and Claire were sitting together talking as the baby slept. When Clement and Miriam Fossler entered they stopped talking and reached for one another's hands. Their faces showed both fear and resignation.

All four of them stood around the crib for some time, watching the baby sleep. Finally, Clement signaled to the others to follow and they crossed to the opposite side of the nave.

Clement whispered introductions and then said in a low voice, "Sister Hannah, please tell Ms. Fossler something about yourself and your husband Brother Adam."

Hannah nodded and spoke, slowly at first, "Well, we came to the Priory about four years ago. We had been living in Albany since we got married. I worked at the medical center and Adam was teaching at an alternative school for at-risk kids. We both loved our work but it took a toll on us and on our marriage. We recognized what the stress was doing to us, but when Adam's doctor prescribed tranquilizers for him, we knew it had gone too far; we had to do something. We had hoped to start a family but we couldn't imagine bringing a child into the chaotic lives we were leading."

Hannah appeared to relax as she spoke and her words came more freely, "We decided that we weren't ready for a child, but hoped a dog might be good for us. A friend told us about the Priory. She said they had the most wonderful dogs here so we came for a visit. It was love at first sight – with the dogs, the

Priory, the community, everything. We began coming to visit on our days off.

On one of our visits, Brother Marcel was very ill. I noticed right away that his symptoms were consistent with appendicitis and I called for an ambulance. They got him to the hospital just in time; his appendix was ready to burst. Brother Clement was so appreciative and mentioned how they had been praying for God to send them someone with medical skills to be part of the community. Adam and I had never talked about moving here permanently, but right at that moment we both knew. A month later we moved in and have been here ever since."

Clement interjected, "Sister Hannah, you didn't mention what you did at the medical center."

"Oh, sorry. I worked in Pediatric ICU. I'm a Nurse Practitioner, with a specialization in early childhood care."

"A Nurse Practitioner," Clement repeated while looking straight at Miriam Fossler. "Duly licensed and registered by the state of New York, and her husband is a teacher."

The baby began to cry and Hannah said, "Excuse me, it's time for Jesse to be fed."

"Jesse?" Miriam Fossler said looking at Clement.

"At the community meeting last night, we decided he needed a name. Someone suggested Jesse – it means "gift"."

"Did you give him a surname, too?"

"No, just Jesse."

"Well, you're going to have to work on that. For now, I will put just 'Jesse' on the temporary foster placement forms," she said as a hint of smile appeared at the corners of her mouth.

"Ms. Fossler –"

"Brother Clement, we are going to be seeing each other a lot in the next thirty days, so maybe you should call me Miriam."

"Miriam," Clement said warmly, "thank you."

Chapter Three

Miriam Fossler proved true to her word. She not only secured the temporary foster family license in the names of Adam and Hannah but she became a regular visitor to the priory, sometimes coming as often as twice a week. Her visits always included time with Jesse and his foster parents, an update for Clement about the search for Jesse's family and a lengthy stop at the kennel.

Jesse appeared to be thriving in his temporary home. Hannah and Adam doted on him as did the other members of the community. Depending on the time of day, the baby might be found with Hannah in the clinic, sleeping in a warm corner of Seth's kitchen, or being soothed by Adina's music in the chapel. At first, Miriam questioned the wisdom of such shared child-care, but as the days passed she realized this was yet another unique quality of Priory life.

As day thirty approached, Clement and the others wondered what would happen next. Miriam had little to say other than she was working on a permanent placement, since the search for Jesse's family had, so far, produced nothing.

On Jesse's one-month birthday Miriam arrived at the Priory and, breaking her routine, went straight to see Brother Clement. The others, watching her arrive and noticing the ominous change in her visitation pattern, feared the worst. She found Clement in the chapel.

"I spoke with Sheriff Hansford, yesterday," Miriam began, "and he has nothing; no leads of any kind. Clearly, whoever left Jesse on your doorstep does not want to be found."

"So where does that leave us? Our temporary license expires tomorrow."

"I have arranged for a more permanent foster placement for Jesse. I know you had hoped, as I did, that we might find someone in his own family to take him, but that seems unlikely at this time. The Sheriff will keep looking, but we need to move ahead with what is best for the child. I think the home I have found is the next best thing to his own family."

"Are you sure? Perhaps if we worked together we could –"

"Brother Clement, it's time to move on. You and the others have done a wonderful job providing temporary care for Jesse, but now we need to make more permanent arrangements."

Clement began to say something but Miriam interrupted, "So, I have arranged to place Jesse here, with you, if you are willing to sign-off on the forms making the Priory a designated institution."

Clement's mouth opened, but no words came out. He nodded his head and without thinking wrapped his arms around Miriam and embraced her.

He held the embrace for just a moment and then stammered, "Everyone will be so pleased. Thank you."

Clement let Miriam tell the others the good news and one by one they all embraced her as he had done. In a few short weeks, Jesse had become an important part of their lives and their community. All of them had hoped, and many had prayed, that Jesse might remain with them even though they knew that would be unlikely.

"God is good," Marcel said to no one in particular.

With one voice, the community answered, "All the time."

The entire community gathered in the chapel for the big moment. Miriam placed the paperwork on the altar next to Jesse's infant seat.

"The only blank left on the form is a surname for Jesse. I don't know what to put there. Did you come up with anything or should I use –"

"Tobias," Marcel said, without hesitation.

"Tobias," Clement repeated. "Tobias means God is good. Yes - our little boy will be Jesse Tobias – a gift from our good God."

Miriam filled in the name on the form and then handed the pen to Clement for his signature.

"First, a prayer," he said. "O God of us all, our hearts are full of gratitude for the life of this child. We know you have great things in store for him and we pray that in our loving care he will flourish and grow and become the person you have created him to be. Help us to be good stewards of this gift you have placed in our care so that everything we do in raising this child might bring honor and glory to you. And all God's people said:"

"Amen," the community said with one voice.

Clement signed the papers and handed them to Miriam.

"Jesse Tobias – I like that," she said.

"Miriam, thank you. You have become a good friend in these past weeks. I hope you will continue to visit us."

"I'll be here, alright, for official reasons and for unofficial reasons. I'm looking forward to watching our boy grow. Of course, if his family should be found..."

Clement nodded, "I understand, but if you look around this room I think you will see all the family Jesse will ever need, and that includes you." He paused for a moment, then added, "I don't know your own faith background but do you know about your Biblical namesake?"

"Miriam – sister of Moses," she replied. "Why is it that Biblical women are always defined by the men in their lives?"

Clement said, "It's an unfortunate vestige of Middle Eastern patriarchal societies. But, of course, Miriam was much more than Moses' sister. She was a prophetess and a revered leader of her people in her own right. When the Hebrews crossed safely through the Red Sea on the Exodus and escaped from the Pharaoh's army it was Miriam who led the celebration. She was much more than just Moses' sister. She was a formidable woman."

"Well, I guess I need to know more about her."

"The book of Exodus in the Old Testament," Clement said. "It's interesting reading on many fronts."

Over the next few months, Jesse and his new family fell into a comfortable routine. Watching the boy grow became the favorite pastime of the Priory community. Mealtime conversations invariably included the latest stories of Jesse's day and his rapid growth and development.

When Jesse began crawling, the other members of the Priory community, the dogs, began to take an active role in his rearing. Serena took the lead, perhaps because she had found the boy or perhaps the other dogs simply deferred to her because of her status in the community. Serena's position was apparent to all but the most casual observer; if these had been sled dogs, Serena would be the lead dog. The human members of the community treated her similarly. They allowed her to go where she wished in the Priory, even into places where dogs were not usually permitted. They spoke to her as if she was one of them, all but Clement calling her Sister Serena. Clement often said that Serena stood as his biggest competitor for the position of Prior.

Serena had also become the "face" of the Priory to the outside world after the dramatic rescue of a kidnapped child last year. The yellow Labs of Good Mountain Priory had built a solid reputation as service dogs working in many different roles, but German Shepherds had long been the preferred breed for search and rescue work. Law enforcement, especially, preferred working with Shepherds but other first responders had begun using different breeds, including Labs, with some rather high profile success stories.

Then came the kidnapping of Heather Soames, eleven years old and snatched from the school bus stop in front of her rural central New York home. Every law enforcement agency in the state worked around the clock for four days until finally they cornered their prime suspect in an abandoned hunting camp in Herkimer County. Police, fire and ambulance personnel surrounded the camp hoping to find some trace of the girl before closing in and risking that she might be hurt or even killed in the assault.

Serena was there on loan to a volunteer rescue squad trying to acclimate a new dog having a hard time settling into its new surroundings. Several agencies at the scene had dogs with them, but only Serena picked up the scent of the girl who had been buried alive by the kidnapper in a make-shift wooden bunker two hundred yards from the cabin. While everyone else focused their attention on the building where the suspect had holed-up, Serena incessantly indicated in a different direction. Finally, she broke free from her harness and bolted directly to the freshly turned earth where the girl had been hidden and sat staring at the ground just as she had been trained to do. Normally, the handlers would have waited for a second dog to confirm Serena's indication, but two State Police K-9 handlers realized what she was doing and ran to where she was indicating. In moments, it was all over. The girl was rescued alive and the suspect, realizing his only bargaining chip had been lost, surrendered without a shot being fired.

Serena was a hero. Photographs of her with the Troopers appeared in papers nationwide the following day. A week later, when the kidnapped girl was released from the hospital, her first request was to hug the dog that had found her. Again, Serena's photo made headlines. She returned to the Priory a star and the Priory suddenly had more requests for search and rescue dogs than they could handle. Agencies endured long waiting lists especially if they hoped for a puppy born of Serena's own bloodline.

Serena, however, took it all in stride and these days was much more interested in following Baby Jesse around the Priory than in having her picture taken. She followed him as he crawled, sometimes nudging him along and other times lying down in front of him to block his way when she decided it was necessary. Her patience had no bounds. Jesse climbed on her, pulled on her ears, her tail, her whiskers – anything he could grip in his tiny hands. He especially enjoyed pulling up her jowls and poking at her teeth. Serena never complained. The day Jesse took his first steps without an adult helping him, he did so holding on to Serena's ear. When he plopped down after four tenuous steps he held fast to her ear and pulled Serena down with him. Hannah and Adam gleefully applauded his accomplishment and Serena wagged her tail in celebration.

Miriam brought the balloons and a box full of presents for Jesse's first birthday party. The whole community celebrated with cake and ice cream. Jesse spent the entire party tearing open the wrapping paper on his gifts more interested in the giftwrap than the presents inside. As the party wound down Miriam took Clement aside.

"I thought you should know that the investigation into Jesse's abandonment has been officially discontinued. The case will remain open, but no further action will be initiated unless someone comes forward with new information. It looks like you are stuck with Jesse for the long haul."

"That is the best birthday present you could bring us. Thank you."

"When I first came here, a year ago,' she said, "I never could have imagined how this would turn out. In all my years working with at-risk children, I've never seen a place like this or met people like you. I still worry whenever I let myself think about most of the placements I've made in my career, but when I look at Jesse and this place I don't worry, at all."

"Miriam, I think Jesse was meant to be here. The very first moment I saw him something moved in my heart and I knew, no matter what, Jesse belonged here and it was up to me to see that he stayed. He became part of our community at that first moment – its newest and youngest member."

"Speaking of new members, I don't think I know the young man over there talking with Marcel. Is he just visiting or do you have a new member of the community."

"A little bit of both. His name is Ryan Eastwood. He started coming a few months ago volunteering to help in the kennel. He's a local boy, apparently at loose ends since finishing high school. College seems out of reach, right now, so he's been working odd jobs when he can find them and spending the rest of his time helping Marcel. Jesse took to him right away, which along with Serena's inspection and approval, amounts to our new preliminary screening process. We may have to do some more serious investigation, however, as Ryan has been talking with Marcel about joining the community permanently. He's quite a bit younger than we usually see, so we'll have to do some soul searching about what is best for him and for the community. He's a nice young man; you would like him."

"What do you mean, 'investigation'?" Miriam asked.

"Well, we don't just take in anybody who shows up on our doorstep."

Miriam laughed, "You took Jesse!"

Clement chuckled and shook his head, "Let me rephrase that. Except for abandoned babies and stray puppies, we don't take in just anyone who shows up on our doorstep. Joining the community is a serious commitment. Our vows may not be as binding and as demanding as the religious vows taken by monks, but they still represent a serious commitment. For the most part, those who join the community make a lifetime decision. We have only had three people choose to leave us in more than thirty years and each one of those resulted from extenuating family circumstances.

When someone wishes to join the community we put them through a pretty vigorous screening process. We ask them for a detailed personal history and then we confirm as much as we can through criminal background checks and other investigations. As you already know, a criminal record does not preclude someone from coming into the community, but concealing a criminal record would be a huge red flag for us. We also require them to undergo a six-month spiritual assessment to help them examine, for themselves, the motivations behind their decision to join us. We want them to be absolutely sure about what they are doing. For many people, this spiritual assessment process is the first time in their lives they have truly tried to discern God's will for them; the first time they have examined in detail who they believe God created them to be. Throughout this assessment they spend individual time with each member of the community getting acquainted and experiencing more of the communal life. After all of this is completed to our satisfaction and to the satisfaction of the potential member, then and only then do we decide whether or not the person belongs in the Priory community."

"So, what, do you vote? Thumbs up or thumbs down?"

"We try to reach all our decisions by building consensus. It takes more time and effort, but produces better choices. I can only remember one time when we actually resorted to a vote; that was when Seth came to us. His history with drug addiction was a big hurdle for one of our members who had lost a brother to a heroin overdose. Even though we voted in secret, when we had only one person vote no, we immediately understood who and why."

"So she was outvoted?" Miriam said.

"No. We honored her objection and did not accept Seth into the community. To his credit, he remained with us until he earned her trust. It took more than a year but we finally welcomed him into the community. When we held our new member dedication service for Seth we included a time of remembrance for all those who had lost their lives to addiction and for their loved ones who were also victims of their compulsion. The service proved to be a time of healing for our community and for Seth."

Miriam shook her head slowly, side to side. "The more I hear from you people the more I think maybe you folks have it right and the rest of the world has it wrong. By the way, I reread the book of Exodus. You were right, interesting reading; so I kept going. Except for some of the weird customs, the obsession with numbers and the incessant genealogies I found it very helpful. I've never been a religious person, before, but I've started going to synagogue. My friends think you are a bad influence on me, but I'm withholding judgment."

"Sounds like it's time for some new friends. Better yet, bring your friends along for a visit."

"Maybe I will; I bet they would be as surprised as I was when I first came here. I think they are afraid you are trying to recruit me – that I'm going to end up spending my golden years holed up here with a bunch of religious fanatics and a pack of proselytizing pooches."

"Miriam, you could do worse…"

Chapter Four

The Book of Jesse
November 12, 1973
Dear Jesse,
I began writing this book, your book, today because we now know you will be staying with us here in the Priory. I expect that one day you will come looking for answers about who you are and how you came to live such an unusual life. Unfortunately, I won't have all the answers for the questions I imagine you will ask, but I hope this journal will fill in some of the blanks and serve as a tangible reminder of how much you are loved; loved by all of your Priory family and most of all loved by God who, in wisdom only God possesses, decided to bring you to us. For us, you are and will always be our Jesse – a gift from God.

With love and blessings
Clement

Clement always read that first page and thumbed through several other pages of the book each time he wrote a new entry. He paused randomly to read a paragraph or two and remember how Jesse had grown and changed over his years in the Priory, and how Jesse's being there had changed all of them.

The first several pages read like the pages in any parent's baby book: snippets of life with an infant. Notes describing how Jesse smiled at anyone who lingered over his crib, about how he tried so hard to communicate in his own baby language and how he could wrap anyone around his little finger before they knew what had happened. Remembrances of the first time he sat up by himself, of the comical wrestling matches between Jesse and whatever puppy was within reach of his tiny arms, of his first steps and of Serena's boundless patience with him. It was all there in cryptic but heartfelt prose.

The pages about his toddler years described a healthy, happy and somewhat precocious child exploring the world around him with intrepid abandon. Of course, he got into everything that toddlers get into especially in the kitchen and in the bathrooms. He also insisted on being an active and vocal part of worship services, so much so, that Clement looked for every opportunity to appease Jesse by giving him a role in worship. Sometimes he stood next to Adina and helped lead the music. Other times he sat watching the candles as if afraid their magical flickering would stop if he turned away. His favorite worship activity was to sit with Clement in the big chair behind the altar and smile and wave at all the others sitting in the pews. Sometimes when Clement stood to speak, Jesse would stand behind him and imitate his gestures in a comical pantomime.

Clement paused at the entry in the book describing the day Ryan Eastwood joined the community. Reading about and remembering that day always brought a smile.

September 24, 1977: "This afternoon, Jesse, you stole the show again. Today the entire community gathered in the chapel to welcome Brother Reuben (formerly Ryan Eastwood) into our community. Even though you are not quite five years old, you seemed to understand we were doing something significant. Brother Reuben is clearly one of your favorite people, maybe because he works with the dogs, maybe because he lets you take naps in the puppy room, or maybe because he seems as happy to be around you as you are to be around him. Whatever the reason, you have chosen to spend time every day with Brother Reuben.

In today's service, when we invited Brother Reuben to come and stand before the community to take his vows of membership, you never hesitated. You climbed down from the big chair behind the altar, walked over to where Brother Reuben stood and took hold of his hand. You stood there with him, looking very serious, as he took his vows and when he knelt down before the altar, you knelt beside him, never letting go of his hand. Brother Reuben had waited a long time to join our community and the ceremony moved him deeply. He managed to hold his emotions in check, except for the times he glanced at you close beside him. Each time he looked at you a tear would spill out onto his cheek. He clearly loves you and appreciates the love you demonstrate for him.

No one who attended today's ceremony will ever forget the wonderful way you welcomed Brother Reuben into our Priory family. Yes, we offered the prayers and blessings, and we were the ones to affirm Brother Reuben's new name, but you welcomed him in love in a way far more genuine than anything we could do. We may be raising you but you teach us new lessons every day and we are all better people because of you.

Growing up as the only child in a priory hardly qualifies as a normal childhood. Still, Jesse appeared for all intents and purposes to be rather ordinary in every respect, save one: Jesse possessed an uncanny ability to communicate with the dogs. Even as a toddler, he seemed to understand what the dogs were thinking and before he had many words of his own he could order the dogs around and even help with their training. Marcel joked that Jesse spent so much time in the kennel that the dogs thought he was one of them. Serena clearly related to him as one of her puppies. She would cuddle with him but nudge him away when he monopolized too much puppy-time. She always seemed to be nearby when Jesse headed for trouble. She was quick to position herself between Jesse and the woodstove that warmed the puppy room. She blocked the way when an open door might have tempted Jesse to stumble into trouble and when he did bump his head or stub his toe, Serena was the one he turned to and she would lick away his tears. Without other children around him, the dogs occupied much of his play time and in their own way, they taught him about how to get along with others.

Clement flipped through the pages of the book until he came to his most recent entry: *Tonight you wandered away as everyone was cleaning up after supper. You are six years-old and quite independent but it was unlike you to go off alone at night. After a few harried minutes of searching, Marcel and Reuben found you in the kennel. Apparently, you had squirreled away a few bites of pork roast from your dinner and you were feeding them to Serena. Marcel and Reuben quietly listened as you explained to her that you would not be around as much once school started. But, you promised to come to the kennel every day as soon as you got home to tell her everything that happened while you were gone.*

Clement smiled as he pasted into the book a photograph of Jesse's first day of school. Jesse stood at the steps of the school bus bearing a green and blue backpack, half as big as him. His smile was the one he put on when he knew he had to smile before someone would let him go and do what he wanted to do. In this case, Jesse wanted to get on the bus with the other children but he understood getting his picture taken was the price he had to pay. So he smiled that smile then waved at Clement who held the camera and said goodbye to Serena who paced nervously and barked twice at no one in particular. Then Jesse disappeared up the steps into the school bus.

Jesse's first weeks of school did not go well. Sister Hannah had taken responsibility for getting him ready to go each morning and she noticed, as the days went by, that Jesse became more and more unhappy about going to school. By the end of the second week she had to take him by the hand and walk him to the bus stop. When the bus arrived, Jesse would climb the steps with his shoulders slumped and his head down, the same body language she had seen on the rare occasions when she had punished him for misbehaving. The other children on the bus seemed happy to see him; she couldn't hear what they were saying, but the chatter on the bus certainly increased as Jesse boarded.

At the end of the second month of school, Jesse's teacher called and asked Brother Clement to come to the school for a parent-teacher conference. When Jesse registered for first grade, Clement had met with the school to explain his unusual living conditions and all had agreed Clement would act as Jesse's parent in dealing with the school.

Jesse's teacher, Ms. Mitchell, explained that Jesse's school work was above average, even though he had not attended kindergarten. However, Jesse was having some difficulty socializing with the other children. She did not discover the problem until the children were asked to draw a picture of themselves with their families. Most of the children drew a picture of their mother, father, brothers and sisters standing in front of their house. She showed Clement the picture Jesse had drawn. It was quite artistic and showed a stick figure of a boy standing in front of a building with a cross on top. There were several stick figures in the background by the building, but the most prominent figure in the picture was a large yellow dog. Clement smiled at the picture, especially the very nice drawing of Serena until Ms. Mitchell explained the problem.

"Apparently some of the other children have been teasing Jesse, pretty much non-stop. I didn't know what was going on until the children began laughing at his picture."

Clement nodded his head, "Children can be cruel, especially to others who they think are different than they are. Jesse doesn't have a normal family – a father, mother, brothers and sisters – and he lives in Priory instead of a house. I can understand –"

The teacher interrupted, "They call him dog-boy. Apparently they make up stories about him and how he lives in a kennel with a pack of dogs. They say he smells like a dog, and not in a good way. When they saw his drawing, they laughed at him and said the dog was his mother."

"What did Jesse do?" Clement asked.

"He looked like he wanted to cry, but he didn't. He looked right at the class and told them the dog, I think he called her Sister Serena," the teacher swallowed hard, "he said the dog was his mother. Did he tell you about any of this?"

"No. When did it happen?"

"A week ago."

"Jesse never mentioned any of it. Not a word about the teasing or the picture; nothing."

"Yesterday, at snack time, I noticed the children giggling and pointing at Jesse. When I looked closer I saw Jesse was snacking on dog biscuits. That was when I decided to call you."

That night, after supper and not long before bedtime, Clement found Jesse sitting in front of the television and sat down next to him. Without a word, he set a glass of milk in front of Jesse along with a small bowl of dog biscuits. Jesse stared at the bowl.

"I've never tried them, myself," Clement said, "but I hear they are pretty good."

Clement picked up one of the dog biscuits, dunked it in the milk and took a loud crunching bite.

Jesse looked at him with an odd mixture of surprise and sadness, "Who told you?"

"I had a meeting with your teacher today. She is very nice and she is worried about you and the other children. Jesse, why didn't you tell me?"

"What's wrong with me? Why, didn't my mother want me? Why did she leave me here?" Jesse's questions came fast and with a trembling voice Clement had not heard before.

"Jesse, nothing is wrong with you –"

"My mother didn't want me! She gave me away!" Jesse's tears flowed freely now. "What's wrong with me? I don't have a family; I don't live in a house like all the other children. All I have is you and the dogs."

Clement wrapped the boy in his arms and held him close while he sobbed.

"Jesse, I don't have all those answers, but I can tell you what I think. Is that OK?"

Jesse nodded.

"I think your mother loved you so much that she made the hardest decision in the world. She brought you to us so you would be safe; so you would grow up healthy and happy and loved – not just by a mother and a father but by a whole priory full of people. Jesse, your family may not be like the families the other children have, but you have a huge family that loves you. Why do you think Sister Hannah and Brother Adam take such good care of you? Because they love you! Why do you think Brother Seth always makes your favorite macaroni and cheese even when the rest of us would rather have something else for dinner? Why do you think Brother Marcel and Brother Reuben spend so much time with you? Because they love you! Why do you think Sister Adina and I ask you to help us lead worship every Sunday? Because we love you and we know how much God loves you, too."

"Do you know my mother?" Jesse whispered.

"No, son, I don't know who she is or where she went after you were born. But I know things about her."

"Like what?"

"Like she has blue eyes, brown hair and she is very pretty. She's smart too and one of the nicest people you could ever know."

"How do you know that?"

"Because, I have seen her in you. You can learn a lot about parents by looking at their children. You are the smartest six-year-old I have ever seen and you have such a kind heart that everybody loves you the moment they get to know you. Where do you think you got all that?"

"From my mother?"

Clement nodded at him and smiled warmly, "The other children may not see it yet, but give them time and they will. One thing, though, maybe you should spend a little less time with the dogs, just so the children –"

"No. The dogs need me. I'm not going to stay away from them just to make friends at school. Besides, being a dog-boy isn't really so bad."

Chapter Five

As Jesse grew older, it became clear the school children were right – Jesse was, in fact, a dog-boy. His skills – his gift for working with dogs – could no longer be overlooked. Marcel and Reuben ran out of things to teach him by the time he was nine years old; after that, Jesse taught them. He knew things. How he knew them was a mystery, but Jesse understood dogs inside and out. By the age of twelve he had delivered more litters of puppies than most adult breeders. Marcel no longer bothered calling the veterinarian to examine the newborn puppies. Jesse quickly found any with potential problems and he seemed instinctively to know what to do about them.

Reuben still did most of the training, especially for Search and Rescue dogs. The U.S. Rescue Dog Association regularly consulted with Reuben about standards for dog training; he was highly respected in SAR (Search and Rescue) dog circles. As good as he was, Reuben knew that Jesse would be better, much better.

Jesse worked the dogs every day, except Sunday. After school, weekends, school vacations Jesse spent all his free time in training. Clement tried to get him involved in sports and to join clubs at school but nothing could compete with Jesse's passion for the Priory dogs. Finally, Clement accepted reality. Maybe it was a phase, maybe not, but the dogs were the center of Jesse's world.

Breeding and training dogs provided the primary source of income for the Priory. Marcel and Reuben loved the dogs, but they also knew raising them was a business. Each new litter was thoroughly examined and each puppy evaluated. The best dogs trained for Search and Rescue while others completed basic obedience training and then were sent to a trainer in Massachusetts to become service dogs working with persons with disabilities. Puppies that showed little aptitude for training were made available for family pets. Marcel and Reuben made the decision about each puppy with help, of course, from Jesse. Most often the three of them agreed but there were times that Jesse saw things differently.

Of all the Priory dogs, Serena's puppies were the most prized; the stuff of legends. Every SAR group in the Northeast had a story to tell about the exploits of one of Serena's offspring. Phenomenal finds, unbelievable rescues, relentless determination all attributed to Serena's bloodline. Each time she had a litter of puppies, SAR people across the country practically climbed over one another to get on the waiting list for one of Serena's pups. When Serena had her final litter, Marcel selected the best female, Sabella, to carry on the line.

Sabella had her last litter when Jesse was ten. Of the seven puppies, only six would be placed. The seventh, and the only female, was a runt. Marcel sadly knew Serena's line ended here. If the little one survived, she would be unlikely to have the temperament necessary for anything more than being a family pet and she would certainly be of no interest for breeding. It was a truism of dog training – runts seldom had the capacity for work and should never be bred. No one disputed the facts except, in this case, Jesse.

From the moment Sabella gave birth, Jesse adopted her runt. He named her Sarajevo after the city hosting the 1984 Winter Olympics, but most of the time he called her Sara. She did not make a good first impression; she was small with stumpy legs too short for her body and her yellow coat was paler than most except for dark splotches on her ears. Still, Jesse saw something in her. He hand-fed her for weeks since she could not compete with the other puppies when nursing. He kept her moving constantly to exercise and develop the muscles in her legs. When the other puppies shoved her aside, Jesse pushed her back among them to reinforce her right to a place in the litter. He was gentle but firm. Most children his age would have simply cuddled a cute fuzzy ball of fur. Although, Jesse allowed Sara to snuggle with him and to nap curled up under his arm, he never lost his focus on helping her grow and progress.

When the puppies were a few weeks old Reuben began their basic training, but he refused to include Sara.

"Jesse, I have people waiting for these dogs. I can't waste my time on a runt. Sara will never be more than a pet. Even if she were trained, no one would take the chance on a runt – even a runt born of Serena's bloodline. They won't invest the time and money it takes to fully prepare a SAR dog."

"Fine," Jesse said. "I'll do it myself."

And he did. Jesse knew the routine; he had helped Reuben many times before. So he ran his own basic training for Sara shadowing what Reuben did with the other puppies. If Reuben worked the pups for an hour, Jesse worked Sara for an hour and a half. If Reuben had the puppies do three finds each, he had Sara do five. Jesse was determined that Sara would not only be trained like the other puppies, she would be better trained at the end.

Weeks went by and the puppies – all of them – completed test after test. Each puppy had to be rated by the trainer as to suitability for search and rescue work. Bloodline, aptitude, personality and willingness to work with humans were tested first at about six weeks and then again at ten weeks. Traits essential for SAR dogs emerge early; if the puppy doesn't have the make up by three months of age it will not happen later. Serena's puppies invariably tested well and this litter of Sabella's passed with flying colors. Sara showed positive results, but she lagged behind the others; still Jesse remained undeterred.

At three months, Reuben and Marcel determined that all six of Sabella's puppies should begin serious SAR training. They decided Sara should be made available for adoption as a family pet.

"Jesse, you did well with Sara. She learned a lot and she will make someone a wonderful companion," Marcel said.

Jesse listened without showing any emotion and then pulled a folded piece of paper from his pocket and handed it to Marcel.

"What's this?" Marcel asked.

"An adoption form for Sara," Jesse said.

"You found a home for Sara, already? You knew she wasn't going to make the grade, didn't you?" Marcel looked at the form and then back at Jesse. "*You* want to adopt Sara?"

"Yes. I don't have the whole fee, yet, but here is seventeen dollars. I will give you the rest when I get it." Jesse handed several crumpled bills to Marcel.

"Jesse, I don't know –"

"I do. Sara isn't like the others, but she is a good dog and she will be a great SAR dog, just like Serena. I'm going to train her myself. Brother Reuben you are a good trainer, but you are wrong about Sara."

"Jesse, I don't think I can agree to this," Marcel said handing the paper and the money back to the boy. "I think we need to talk to the others about it."

"Keep it," Jesse said. "When everybody meets on Saturday, they will say it's OK."

Jesse was right. No one at the community meeting spoke against him after he and Sara demonstrated what she had already learned. They were impressed with Jesse and with Sara and, even though most agreed with Reuben's evaluation, they could not say no to the boy.

The Priory offered extended SAR training as an option, and given Brother Reuben's reputation, many handlers took advantage of the opportunity. Two of Sabella's six brothers were placed with handlers and left the Priory, but the other four continued training with Brother Reuben. Their new handlers came to the Priory for training events each weekend. Jesse continued to observe from a distance and mirror Reuben's training techniques with Sara. When the dogs did their lost-person finds Jesse recruited others to hide for Sara. Hannah, Adam and Seth were always willing to help. Seth was usually the choice of last resort since finding him was too easy; his clothes always carried the aroma of the day's dinner.

Sara grew stronger and healthier and her SAR skills quickly caught up with her brothers. Jesse noticed one big difference, however. For Sara's brothers a successful find, and the reward they earned for that success, was all that mattered. They would work for anyone: Reuben, Marcel or one of the weekend handlers. They always performed; they found their target and waited breathlessly for their reward. Sara, however, showed little interest in working for anyone else. She would do anything for Jesse, but when he tried having someone else give her commands she responded half-heartedly. While the other dogs worked for rewards like play time with a favorite ball or an energetic tug-of-war, Sara only wanted a good belly-rub and words of praise from Jesse.

When the day arrived for Reuben's group to receive their final evaluation, Jesse observed from a safe distance. Four people were sent out to hide in various places. And one by one, the dogs were asked to find only one of them – the one whose dirty t-shirt they sniffed at the starting line. In some searches, such as following a natural disaster, finding someone, anyone, is good work. But most search and rescue events are looking for a specific victim and the dogs have to distinguish that person's scent from many conflicting scents. It is not good enough to find someone; they have to find the right someone.

SAR dogs are scent trained, taught to follow the raft of human scent left on the air by a passing person. Tracking dogs, like bloodhounds, search for points of physical contact, places where footsteps land on the ground or clothing brushes against undergrowth. Scent dogs, however, follow the airborne trail of dead skin cells people shed at the rate of about 40,000 cells per minute. Those lost cells waft on the air trailing behind a person in a cone shaped pattern. Depending on the terrain and conditions, a scent dog can pick up a specific trail from hundreds of feet away.

Each of Sara's brothers completed their final exam successfully in just a few minutes. One of the handlers noticed Jesse watching and said something to Reuben. At first, Reuben shook his head but after a few more words with the handler, he motioned to Jesse to come over.

"Jesse, Mr. Carlson wonders if you would like Sarajevo to take the test. He's seen you working with her over the past few weeks and thought you might like to see how she could do. What do you think? Is she ready?"

"I think so; I mean she's passed all the other tests so far," Jesse hesitated only a moment. "Let's try it."

The volunteer victims headed back to their hiding places out of sight over the ridge, while Jesse walked Sara in the other direction. When the time came, Jesse gave Sara the scented t-shirt, unsnapped her lead and said, "Find more!"

Sara stood motionless for a moment, nose in the air, and her mouth slightly open. Her tongue twitched a couple of times, as if tasting the air, then she bounded off. She moved quickly back and forth across the field in the classic zig-zag pattern.

Mr. Carlson said to Jesse, "She already works off the lead? Aren't you afraid you will lose sight of her?"

At that moment, Sara stopped and stood unmoving, her nose again in the air.

"She's lost the scent," Carlson said.

Sara turned her head toward Jesse. The boy nodded and the dog leaped forward breaking into a run, heading over the hill and toward a stand of small pines.

Reuben said, "Well, I'll be…"

By the time they caught up with Sara, she was sitting and staring at a small mound under the low-hanging branches of a spruce tree.

Reuben called, "OK, John, you can come out now. You have been rescued."

The victim threw off the camouflage tarp that had covered him from head to toe and crawled out from under the tree, "Wow, that was fast!" he said.

Jesse clapped his hands twice, "Sara! Good girl!"

The dog jumped up and ran to Jesse with her tail wagging and an expression that looked like a smile of pure joy on her face. She flopped at his feet, wriggling on the ground, all four paws waving in the air as Jesse rubbed her belly.

Carlson watched Jesse and Sara for a moment then turned to Reuben and said, "I think I picked the wrong dog."

"Maybe the wrong trainer, too," Reuben said with unmistakable pride.

That Sunday, Jesse and Reuben took one of their usual Sunday afternoon hikes in the mountains surrounding the Priory. Sabella and Sara trotted ahead of them as they made their way to the top of Cougar Mountain. The familiar trail led to a spectacular view looking over Pasco Lake toward the High Peaks. Jesse and Reuben sat on a huge boulder admiring the view and snacking on leftover pancakes from breakfast smeared with Brother Seth's homemade apple butter.

Reuben turned to Jesse, "I was wrong about Sara. She has all the makings of an outstanding SAR dog. I'm so impressed with how you trained her. I've never trusted a puppy that young to work off the lead."

Jesse listened and smiled, but said nothing.

"Jesse, Mr. Carlson was so impressed, he wants to buy Sarajevo."

"No, she's mine! She's not for sale, at any price!"

"Easy. Relax. I told him she belonged to you and that she was not for sale. I just wanted you to know how impressed he was with Sara and with you." Reuben said.

Jesse nodded, "I'm sorry –"

"It's OK; I understand. I do have a favor to ask, however. When Sara is old enough, what would you think about breeding her; keeping Serena's bloodline going?"

Jesse thought for a moment and said, "I don't know. Maybe."

"It won't be for a couple of years, yet, so you have time to decide. But when the time comes, I want you to know it will be your decision. Sara is your dog."

As they returned to the Priory, Brother Adam jogged across the meadow to meet them.

He spoke to both of them, but looked only at Jesse. "It's Sister Serena; she's had some kind of stroke."

All the members of the community stood in small clusters outside the kennel. As Jesse and Reuben approached, the crowd parted lining a path directly to the door. Inside Clement, Hannah and Marcel knelt over Serena who lay motionless on her side on a bed of straw and old clothes.

Jesse and Reuben dropped down next to the others. Serena's eyes were glassy, unseeing, but her nose twitched and her tail stirred slightly from side to side. Clement put his arm around Jesse's shoulders.

"She knows you are here; I think she's been waiting to say goodbye to you," Clement said.

"Is she dying?" the boy whispered.

Marcel nodded, "She had a seizure earlier this afternoon outside the chapel. She recovered enough to come out here and then she had another one – much bigger. She's lived an amazing life, Jesse. Fourteen is old for a Labrador. We need to let her go but we waited so you could say goodbye. She loved you most of all."

Jesse bent low and buried his face in Serena's neck while gently scratching behind her ears. He whispered something only the dog could hear and ran his hand along her side, smoothing her coat one last time. When he raised up again, his cheeks were wet.

Those who had been standing outside crowded into the kennel forming a multi-layered circle around Serena and the others. Tears flowed freely.

"I want to stay with her," Jesse said to no one in particular.

Marcel turned to Hannah and took the syringe.

"Wait!" Jesse said. Turning to Clement he said, "Please say a prayer for her."

Everyone standing joined hands; Hannah, Marcel, Reuben, and Clement each placed a hand on Serena and Jesse stroked her head as Clement softly prayed for all of them. When he finished, Marcel injected Serena with such a gentle touch that she did not react to the needle. No one moved or spoke until several moments after Sister Serena let go of her final breath.

Later that night, as Clement sat in his study reading the Psalms, Jesse knocked softly on the door.

"Brother Clement, I need to ask you a question."

"Of course, Jesse."

"Do dogs and other animals go to heaven?"

"What do you think?"

"What I think doesn't matter. I need to know what God thinks and you know God better than I do."

Clement smiled slightly. "Jesse, what happens after this life is over is one of the great mysteries of faith that God has chosen to keep secret even from those who know God best. Jesus spoke beautifully about God's promise of eternal life but even Jesus chose not to share the details, and as far as I know Jesus never said anything about dogs and other animals going to heaven.

But here is what I think – I think God's love is big enough for all of creation. God created us and God created all the animals and put the same spark of life inside all of us. The Bible tells us about God's love for the animals in the story of Noah's ark and in the poetry of the Psalms. Jesus, himself, teaches about God caring for the life of even the tiniest sparrow. What's more, the Bible calls Jesus the Lamb of God – God's only son compared to an animal – a sheep! So, yes, I think God loves all of us and loves the animals too.

When I think about how much love Serena had for you and for everyone I have no doubt that God created that love and gave it to Serena because he knew she would share it willingly. Sometimes I wish people would learn to love others the way our animals do. Maybe that's why dogs don't live as long as we do – it takes us a lot longer to learn how to love that way. I trust God to do what is best with my own eternal life and I trust God with Serena's life, too."

"What am I going to do without her?" Jesse's voice cracked and dissolved into tears as he buried his face in his hands.

Clement put his arm around Jesse's shoulders and felt his own eyes begin to fill up.

Chapter Six

  Autumn comes to the mountains early. In the waning days of August, cold nights and sunny days bring the first golds and reds to the trees. By Columbus Day weekend in October, an insurrection of color swarms over the mountains overrunning the habitual verdant greens and granite grays crafting a fantasy landscape only an artist could imagine.
  Lured by the season, hikers, climbers and leaf-peepers from all over the world come to gawk at the Fall colors, to breathe deep of the crisp mountain air and to trek the Adirondack foothills and mountains. Many of them, dog lovers mostly, found their way to the Priory, curious about this enclave of gifted dog trainers and their four-legged protégés. Television coverage of several high-profile rescues brought national exposure to the Priory and attracted visitors, expected and unexpected, nearly every day in the autumn. On weekends they came by the busload, hoping to see the dogs in action. Reuben and Marcel often appeased their visitors by incorporating rescue demonstrations into their daily training routines. However, with increasing frequency, visitors found the dogs and their handlers engaged in actual search and

rescue missions searching for seasonal hikers, lost, disoriented, or simply guilty of over-estimating their own abilities or underestimating the Adirondacks. Most of these lost souls were easily retrieved, but not all.

Snow is a fact of life in the mountains; when it comes it often comes fast and heavy burying the countryside, blurring the lines between familiar and unfamiliar and leaving behind a new and unrecognizable landscape. Even experienced winter hikers easily become disoriented and lose their bearings in an Adirondack snowstorm. Occasional visitors out for an autumn stroll stand little chance against these same elements.

The foliage was nearing peak color on the first weekend of October 1984 when the sky turned an ominous gunmetal gray and the first flakes began to fall. In only a few hours, snow piled thigh-high in open meadows and weighed down branches to the breaking point along highways, roads and hiking trails. Snow that usually filtered gently through bare winter branches instead nestled against pads of brilliantly colored foliage on branches high above the ground. Sounds of cracking and splintering wood echoed through the hills like gunfire as branches, limbs and entire trees crashed to the ground under the weight of the snow. Nearby towns and cities found themselves isolated and in the dark as roads, littered with fallen trees and downed power lines, quickly became impassable under nearly two feet of snow. In the mountains a muffled stillness surrounded anyone caught outside in the elements, as if the earth had sighed and resigned itself to being draped and muted by a cold white blanket.

The residents of the Priory took the storm in stride. Life in the mountains demanded vigilant preparation. Coping with the early arrival of winter, after so many years, held few challenges for them. The buildings and kennels were well insulated and two industrial-sized generators powered lights, heat and well pumps whenever outside power went down. In this storm, as in several before it, the Priory not only carried on its own life but also offered gracious hospitality to stranded travelers – more than a dozen by mid-afternoon.

Late in the day, when the snow began to wind down, a pair of college students trudged up the driveway. Snow clung to every inch of their bodies and piled high on their backpacks.

"They look like snowmen," Jesse chuckled to Reuben.

"Very cold snowmen," Reuben replied as he waved and motioned to the hikers to come to the chapel.

The chapel had been transformed into a shelter with cots and a small dining area where people huddled together over coffee and hot chocolate. The two hikers joined others clustered around the wood stove and soon thawed out sufficiently to join in the conversation. Stories of the storm passed among the visitors and seemed to become more dramatic with each telling.

Jesse brought refills of hot chocolate to the two newly arrived hikers and overheard them asking others about a minivan they had seen parked at a nearby trailhead. The van apparently did not belong to any of the Priory's visitors.

"Which trailhead?" Jesse asked.

"I'm not sure, there is so much snow out there, but we passed it just before we saw your sign and turned up the road to come here," the shorter one answered.

"Was there a porta-john in the parking area?" Jesse asked.

"Yeah, I'm pretty sure there was."

"That sounds like the trailhead for the backside approach to Sagatuck. Day-hikers like to use that trail; it's longer but a lot easier than the frontal approach from Cold River."

Jesse went looking for Brother Clement and found him in his office. He was talking to Sheriff Hansford on the radio.

"We've got fourteen, so far. We'll be fine tonight. The forecast sounds better for tomorrow."

"Brother Clement," Jesse interrupted. Clement put up his hand, signaling Jesse to wait, but Jesse persisted, "Brother Clement! I need to tell the Sheriff something."

"Hold on, Sheriff," Clement said and turned to Jesse. "What's so important?"

"Two hikers saw an abandoned car at the backside trailhead for Sagatuck Mountain. It doesn't belong to anyone here, which means there could be people still out there."

Clement turned back to the phone, "Sheriff, did you hear that? Maybe one of your guys could check it out…"

An hour later just as the last light of day yielded to heavy darkness, Sheriff Hansford walked into Clement's office and plopped down, his expression a mix of weariness and worry.

"Jesse was right. We found a minivan at the trailhead. The log book has a family of three – husband, wife and seven-year-old little girl signed in for a day hike this morning. If they are still up there, well, it's not good. We can only hope they know what they are doing and found someplace to hunker down for the night."

Clement nodded, "You want us to go up there at first light?"

"Only if you think it's safe. I don't want to have to come looking for you, too."

Clement gathered the community after supper and told them about the family stranded on Sagatuck Mountain. "Roger McKinley, his wife Maureen and their seven-year old daughter, Lulu, signed in at the trailhead early this morning and planned to be out by two o'clock. Sheriff Hansford confirmed a few minutes ago that the van is still there, so we assume they are still on the mountain. We need to see what the conditions are in the morning, but the Sheriff would like us to take the lead and find these folks."

Reuben spoke first, "Skipjack is ready, but we should have a second dog team go with us."

"Sara and I will go," Jesse volunteered.

Clement quickly said, "No, Jesse, this is too risky for you. Even if the weather clears, the snow is too deep and the conditions will be brutal. You will stay here."

Jesse tried to argue but Clement would not hear it. In the end it was decided that Reuben and Skipjack would take the lead with Adam and Stonewall as their second team. It was agreed that they would leave at dawn, weather permitting. Jesse asked permission to sleep in the kennel that night, so he could help get the dogs ready in the morning.

The storm lifted during the night having done its worst. When Jesse awoke two hours before sunup, he dressed quickly and stepped outside. A million stars sparkled against the sky's blackness but the light of a full moon gave the newly fallen snow an eerie glow. He looked toward the residences but all was still dark; no sign of Reuben, Adam or the others. He turned back to the kennel and found Sara standing in the doorway, her head cocked to one side and her tail wagging eagerly. In practiced fashion, Jesse dressed Sara for work – SAR vest and dog-pack, short lead and leather booties for her feet. Jesse shouldered his own SAR backpack with snowshoes and poles strapped to the outside and gave Sara the go sign. Together they headed off into the night.

When Reuben and Adam arrived at the kennel they took only a moment to realize that Jesse and Sara were gone. After telling Clement about Jesse, they equipped their dogs and set off for the Sagatuck trailhead, hoping to overtake Jesse on the way. At the trailhead, they found the minivan buried in snow but no sign of Jesse or anyone else.

Reuben popped the lock on the van's rear gate and quickly found an adult's sweatshirt and a doll wrapped in a pink blanket on the back seat. He packed the doll blanket in a plastic bag and put it in his inside pocket. Then he and Adam strapped on their snowshoes, held the sweatshirt to the dog's noses and gave them the command: find more. In a moment they were headed up the mountain.

They climbed steadily in single file for nearly an hour. The deep snow slowed their progress. Reuben and Adam took turns on the lead breaking the trail and letting the dogs walk between them. The dogs usually led the way, but in difficult conditions they had learned to scent even while following. It was a drill they practiced each winter to be ready for a search like this one. So far, despite repeated attempts to pick up the scent, the dogs had not indicated. They stopped for rest breaks at thirty minute intervals, staying hydrated, giving the dogs a chance to refresh the scent and calling out for the missing family members. Reuben also called out for Jesse, surprised they had not picked up his trail yet.

As they came to a clearing where the trail leveled out, Skipjack stopped, his nose high in the air; Stonewall indicated at the almost the same instant. The dogs both waited calmly until they were released from their leads and given the command to go. Bounding through the deep snow they headed away from the trail at a sharp angle, down the slope toward a rock face. Reuben and Adam followed as quick as they could, but losing ground at each step. The dogs left an easy trail to follow as they plunged through the snow, zig-zagging around downed trees and ducking under snow covered branches drooping low. At the base of the rock face, Reuben saw a man, sitting up, wrapped in a silver foil rescue blanket. As they came closer they realized he was not alone – a woman was huddled under the blanket with him.

"Mr. McKinley? Roger McKinley?" Reuben called out and the man slowly lifted his arm and waved.

As they approached the couple, Reuben spotted another set of tracks in the snow, approaching from the opposite side. The tracks were clearly those of a hiker on snowshoes and a dog.

"We're OK, but we can't find Lulu! She's only seven – you've got to find her!" McKinley was distraught. "I told the boy who came with you and he went back up that way looking for her. I can't walk – please, you've got to find her!"

Over the next few minutes, Reuben managed to piece together the McKinley's story. Caught in the storm they had tried to follow the trail back to their car. When the sun went down, they took shelter in a shallow cave. Roger was an Eagle scout who had been through winter wilderness training, and he did all the right things. He piled snow in front of the opening for insulation from the falling temperatures. His daypack had birch bark strips and matches to light a fire, space blankets to conserve body heat and a variety of high-calorie snack foods. They passed the night safely and at first light got back to the trail.

"Somewhere I lost track of the trail markers. In the snow, everything looks the same. Suddenly, the trail gave way under our feet and we bounced along in a mini-avalanche ending up here. I banged-up my head pretty good on those rocks and I think I broke my ankle. Lulu was walking in between us, but somehow she did not end up down here. I tried to get up but…"

"We'll find her. How long has it been since Jesse – the boy – was here?" Reuben asked.

"He left maybe 20 minutes ago. He's so young…"

"Yes, but he is very good."

Reuben tried the radio but as he expected, he had no service. "We need to leave you here while we look for Lulu. Don't worry, we will get you out of here."

Adam pulled the doll blanket from his pack and rubbed it to the dog's noses. Almost immediately they indicated toward the crest of the hill above them. The climb was difficult for the first hundred yards. The snow gave way repeatedly as they struggled up the mountainside.

On the crest of the hill, Reuben thought he saw something moving in the distance and he called out, "Lulu! Lulu!"

The figure in the distance stopped and waved, shouting something that Reuben could not hear. The dogs bounded off toward the sound. Reuben heard a bark in the distance and in a moment saw three dogs instead of two. He heard the voice again and this time it called his name.

"Reuben! I've got her!"

Moments later Reuben and Adam reached the spot where Jesse huddled over a small form wrapped in his SAR parka. Lulu peeked out of the coat her eyes intently locked on Jesse, not making a sound. Sara nuzzled the little girl's cheek and she smiled slightly even as she tightened her grip on Jesse's hand. Jesse was shivering in his shirtsleeves, but his face positively beamed.

The trek down the mountain was difficult but no one seemed to mind. Jesse carried Lulu, on his back, piggyback style. The girl had still not spoken and her arms wrapped so tightly around Jesse's neck that he could not get a full breath. Reuben and Adam dragged Roger on an improvised toboggan with Maureen's help. They stopped on a high ridge that stood open to the west and Reuben finally made radio contact.

An hour later, they reached the trail head and found rescue squad volunteers waiting for them along with a stringer who covered local news for the Glens Falls Courier. The story he filed proved to be largely forgettable but his claim to fame from that day forward was "the photo". He snapped dozens of pictures with his new point-and-shoot digital camera but only one mattered.

The picture of Lulu snuggled close against Jesse's back, looking every bit the lost girl that she had been only a couple of hours ago. The image melted the heart of anyone who saw it – and millions of people saw it. It appeared on the front page of the Courier, above the fold, the very next day, but it went viral from the paper's on-line edition. Every national network news program picked it up over the next thirty-six hours and no one was the least surprised when it won award after award. By the time the Pulitzer arrived – the first ever for an Adirondack newspaper – it seemed an afterthought.

Jesse's instant notoriety in the outside world carried little water within the Priory. He still had to answer for his behavior and the risk he took. Brother Clement's discipline was swift and appropriate although meted out with obvious love and pride for the remarkable young man Jesse had become.

Down from the Mountain

Somewhere, out there, are

new mountains you should climb

And dreams to dream

Enough to last a whole lifetime...

Chapter Seven

Devoe College was not at all what Jesse had expected. Of course, truthfully, he did not know what to expect. He had never lived anywhere outside of the Priory, never spent any significant amount of time beyond the Adirondack Mountains, never had any close friends his own age and never found much to interest him in classrooms or textbooks. Now, only halfway through the first semester of his freshman year, he wondered what the big deal was about college.

Brother Clement had been insistent; Jesse had to go to college. No, he could not just remain in the Priory and work with the dogs. No, they would not make an exception and receive him as a full member of the Priory community; he must wait until at least his twenty-fifth birthday like everyone else. Education is important. Life is important. Learning about yourself is important.

"Jesse, you need to go out and see some of the world," Brother Clement had said. "Learn new things, meet new people – people your own age, people who have other interests besides dogs. Making a commitment to live as a member of the Priory community is a big decision and it must be made knowingly. Knowing, not only what you are choosing, but knowing what you are giving up. The world out there is an amazing place. Some of it is heartbreakingly beautiful and some of it is just heartbreaking. You can't decide to give it up, to live your life within the community and limits of the Priory without knowing exactly what you are doing. You will always be part of our family, part of what makes us a family, and this will always be your home. But everyone needs to leave home at some point and this is your time."

"But, college?" Jesse had argued. "Why college? I don't need to go to college. I know what I'm going to do with my life. You said so, yourself – I have a gift for training. I love working with dogs and I am good at it. I don't need a college education to be a trainer; Brother Reuben says I am already better than most trainers and what I need to learn to get better they don't teach in college."

Brother Clement was unmoved. "Jesse, college is not about learning how to do something. College is about learning who you are, who you can be. It's about growing and becoming and discovering things about yourself, about others, about the world; things that you never imagined. It may not teach you to be a better trainer but it will make you a better person and that will make you a better trainer."

During his senior year of high school Jesse had hoped against hope that Brother Clement would change his mind, or forget or grant him a reprieve. He wanted no part of living anywhere other than the Priory and he could not imagine living without the dogs. Sara was in her prime years for search and rescue and Brother Reuben had her on a regular breeding schedule. She may have been the runt of her litter, but her breeding had produced spectacular results. Sister Serena's bloodline lived on in Sara's pups and Jesse had weaned each one of them and taken a major role in their training. Each time she came up on the breeding schedule Reuben had four times as many requests as he had puppies. If he was away at college, who would be there with Sara and her puppies?

The solution materialized unexpectedly although Brother Reuben saw it clearly as an answer to his prayers. Roger Carlson was a regular visitor to the Priory and a well-regarded breeder and SAR handler from Kittery, Maine. He was also a Trustee and third generation graduate of Devoe College. His son, EJ, would soon be the family's fourth generation Devoe alumnus. Carlson had followed Jesse's development as a trainer and currently had two of Sara's offspring on his SAR team.

On one of Carlson's visits to the Priory he and Brother Clement concocted a college plan for Jesse's consideration. One that seemed to satisfy Jesse's concerns and Clement's wishes.

At first Jesse was dubious, "So I could go to college but still work with Sara and her puppies?"

"On college breaks and some weekends," Clement answered. "But college would still be your number one priority."

"Devoe College is a good school, Jesse," Carlson offered, "and it is only a couple of hours from my kennel. You will live at my home and work for me – on a schedule we can all agree to – when you are not at school. I'm confident I can arrange an academic scholarship for you to cover tuition and the cost of the dormitory. You will work to cover your books and other living expenses. You get your education and I get a talented trainer. Sara can come, too, when Brother Reuben does not need her for breeding, and I have two pups from her last litter so you can complete their training."

It took some time, but eventually everything worked out the way Carlson said. All things considered, if Jesse had to go to college, this arrangement was as good as he could hope for. Jesse and Sara arrived in Kittery at the beginning of August, giving them a month to settle in before classes began. Mr. Carlson was a good man and his kennel was top-notch. He no longer worked SAR missions himself but he was something of a godfather for the biggest and best SAR team in Maine, maybe in all of New England. At any one time, the team had fifteen to twenty dogs and their handlers training and working together. They were the "go-to" team for any major search in New England and senior members of the team often deployed across the country.

At first, the team members were understandably skeptical about Jesse. At eighteen, he was the youngest handler in the group and half the age of the youngest trainer. But the team members were dog people, and Jesse's skills with the dogs were obvious and undeniable. By the time classes began, Jesse was accepted as an integral part of the team and acknowledged as the lead trainer for new dogs and handlers.

Freshmen at Devoe had their own floor in the dormitory and Jesse adjusted easily to dorm life. Two students were assigned to each room but Jesse's roommate spent nearly all his time at the other end of the floor in his girlfriend's room. Gregor kept his clothes and some personal belongings in the room, so when his parents visited they could see the room they were paying for, but otherwise Jesse had the room to himself. EJ Carlson lived on the first floor and warranted a private room as a senior and an athlete. Actually EJ qualified as something of an anomaly having lived in the dorm all four of his years at Devoe. Most students departed for the freedom of off-campus housing after fulfilling the mandatory freshman year in the dorm. Only four seniors, including EJ, lived in the dormitory. The other three were Resident Advisors earning their room and board by trying to keep the peace and deal with squabbles of dorm life. EJ wanted no part of being an R.A., although he knew more about life at Devoe than just about anyone. He knew everyone on campus, or so it seemed, but he mostly kept to himself. He never missed a class and spent more time in the library each week than most students did in a year. When he was not in the library he was in the gym either swimming or working his upper body in the weight room.

At first, Jesse did not know what to make of EJ. Before they moved into the dorm for the semester they had seen little of each other. EJ had spent the summer traveling much of the eastern seaboard competing. At Devoe he did the decathlon, but the summer was given over to road races – 5K, 10K, marathons – EJ did them all with grit and determination. It was not about winning for him. He seldom finished near the leaders, but he was driven to compete, to push himself, chasing personal-best times and proving to anyone who doubted his ability that he was a serious athlete not to be overlooked.

Jesse did not understand all of this and even more mystifying to him was that EJ had no interest whatsoever in dogs. His father's kennel and breeding program were among the best in the country. SAR dogs, service dogs, working dogs of all kinds moved in and out of Carlson's every week; some coming for breeding, some coming to be trained, some coming for their handlers to train with EJ's father. Jesse could not imagine a more interesting place but EJ ignored it all. Jesse intuited some kind of tension between father and son, but neither of them offered any explanation. The two of them led separate lives, physically living in the same house but emotionally miles apart. They showed no animosity toward one another, in fact, they showed little more than indifference. Jesse wondered about Mrs. Carlson; she smiled sweetly in several photographs around the house but neither EJ nor his father ever mentioned her. Jesse decided to leave well-enough alone, after all, who was he to question someone's family life.

On campus Jesse found EJ to be a totally different person. He treated Jesse like a younger brother showing him around, helping him navigate the unnecessarily complicated class scheduling process, even introducing him to upperclassmen who normally treated freshmen with complete disdain. Gradually, the two of them became good friends, often sharing meals in the student center and studying in side-by-side carrels in the library.

Their on-campus friendship began during the first week of classes when seniors challenged the incoming freshmen to a series of supposedly friendly competitions. However, with each passing event the clashes became more heated and more physical. The finale was a wheelchair race around the quad at the center of the campus. Whichever class won the race would be the overall winner since they had split the other four events. EJ captained the senior team and Jesse joined in with the freshman. Before the race, EJ took Jesse aside and gave him a friendly warning: there was no way the seniors were going to lose this race, so be careful.

At the end of first lap, two gangly freshmen from Boston were in the lead, followed closely by a group of seniors led by EJ. Jesse tried to keep up but he lagged far behind. Going into the final turn EJ cut to the inside and with a burst of speed overtook the leaders. One of the Boston boys made the mistake of trying to crowd EJ off the course onto the grass. EJ pushed back hard and the two Boston boys collided, got their wheels entangled and flipped out of their chairs. The entire senior team passed them and crossed the finish line ahead of the first freshman racer. Jesse finished dead last but just in time to see one of the Boston boys charging at EJ, his fists doubled up and shouting a stream of obscenities.

Before anyone else could intervene, Jesse jumped out of his chair and stepped in between EJ and the other student.

"Back-off, guy! It's just a game – nothing to get upset about," Jesse said.

"Let him go, Jesse," EJ said. "He's got nothing to say to me."

The Boston boy shoved Jesse to the ground and yelled at EJ, "Get up! Get out of that chair and I'll show you what I got!"

"Sorry," EJ said, "I get out of this chair for no man – and certainly not for a hothead from Southie."

The boy took another step toward EJ and Jessie grabbed him from behind. "Knock it off! Don't you get it? He CAN'T get out of the chair! He's paralyzed!"

The boy looked at EJ and then looked at the others who had gathered around them and he knew Jesse was telling the truth. Jesse felt the fight drain right out of him and he let him go. The boy turned and walked away.

"You change your mind, Southie, I'll be right here," EJ called after him. Then he turned to Jesse and said, "I don't need you to fight my battles for me. I could take you and him at the same time and not even break a sweat. I don't need you or anybody else to protect me – got it?"

"Protect you? I wasn't protecting you – I was protecting him! I knew you were going to take him apart and I was just trying to keep him in one piece. As much as you work out, and with all your Paralympic competitions, you might have killed him. Your legs might not work but from the waist up you are like a rock." Jesse gave a sly smile, "Besides, I'm a pacifist – I can't stand the thought of violence."

EJ laughed and grabbed Jesse by the wrist giving him three quick jabs in the upper arm. From that day Jesse had a true friend in EJ.

Jesse spent nearly every weekend working Sara and training Carlson's dogs. EJ seldom went home on weekends. He often had Paralympic competitions and on those weekends he had free Jesse noticed he would find other excuses to stay on campus; sometimes even making up reasons to explain to his father why he was not coming home. Mr. Carlson tried not to show it but Jesse knew he was disappointed. He often worked EJ into his conversations with Jesse.

"So, Jesse, did you see EJ this week?" Carlson would ask and Jesse would try to think of something interesting to say about the generally dull routine of campus life. Often the best he could do was to relate some conversation he had with EJ over lunch or to remark on EJ's latest Paralympic victory. He was sure that Mr. Carlson knew all about EJ's competitions, but he always seemed to hear Jesse's description as something new to him.

When EJ did not come home over the long Columbus Day weekend Carlson seemed especially upset.

"Did he say anything to you?" Carlson asked. "I was sure he planned to come home. I got tickets for the Patriots game on Sunday..."

Jesse just shook his head and tried to avoid Carlson's eye. In fact, EJ had told him he planned to hang around the dorm and catch up on his sleep. He had never intended to travel home.

Several of the handlers on Carlson's SAR team were around all weekend. Usually they trained on Saturday and left Sunday open, but this weekend two or three of them were around constantly. Each time someone would pack up to go, someone else arrived and Jesse noticed whispered conversations accompanied by furtive glances in Carlson's direction.

Late Sunday afternoon, Jesse walked into the kennel where three handlers were huddled. As soon as Jesse walked in they stopped talking and awkwardly pretended to be stocking first aid kits.

"OK, what is going on?" Jesse said with an obvious frustration in his voice. "All weekend you guys have been acting like you are planning a coup d'état. Groups gathered in corners, private conversations that end abruptly when I come into the room, guilty looks. What's up? Did I do something wrong?"

The three looked at each other then back to Jesse. Finally, one of them spoke, "No, Jesse, it's not you; it's Carlson. This is 'the weekend'; the accident was nine years ago today. He pretends that it doesn't bother him anymore but we know better. Anyway, every year we schedule shifts to make sure he is not alone. We pretend we have things to work on through the weekend and he pretends not to know what we are up to. No one ever mentions the accident but everybody knows that is why we are here."

Jesse had no idea what they were talking about but instinctively he knew better than to ask. It reminded him of times at the Priory when the others were trying to protect him from hearing bad news or problems with one of the dogs. He knew they were acting out of kindness so who was he to question their tactics.

Later that night, Jesse was sitting on the porch trying to read Tolstoy for his literature class. Carlson lurched through the door rattling the ice cubes in his glass and sloshing his drink over his hand. Jesse recognized the smell of bourbon from the bottle Brother Clement kept in his office. Carlson wiped the back of his hand on the sleeve of his shirt and then noticed Jesse looking at him.

"Jesse – I didn't know you were out here. In fact, I guess I forgot you were even here. Did you find something for dinner? I didn't feel like eating tonight..."

"No problem, Mr. Carlson," Jesse replied. "Are you hungry now? I left some cold cuts on the counter."

Carlson just looked at his glass, swirling the amber liquid around and around as if he was deep in thought.

"Did the others tell you?"

"Tell me what, Mr. Carlson?"

"Don't be coy, Jesse; it doesn't suit you. Did they tell you why they were hanging around all weekend, pretending they had things to do? Did they tell you about the accident?"

His voice was thick and heavy; Jesse wondered if it was the bourbon he was drinking or the reason behind the bourbon.

"No, sir, they didn't tell me anything."

"It's sad, really. They feel so sorry for me. Am I that pitiful, Jesse? Am I so pitiful that grown men and women have to skulk around in corners whispering about me, afraid that I might 'do something'?" Carlson took a long drink draining his glass.

"Mr. Carlson –" Jesse began.

"Shhh, there's no need to answer. That was a rhetorical question, Jesse. You know what that is, Jesse – a rhetorical question? It's a question that everyone knows the answer to but no one has courage enough to say it out loud."

Carlson slurped on his empty glass.

"Jesse, inside on the kitchen counter, you will find a half-empty bottle of bourbon. Get it for me, would you?" Jesse started to object but Carlson waived him off. "Just get it, OK? I know what I'm doing."

Jesse got the bottle and brought it to Carlson who had slumped down in one of the Adirondack chairs on the porch. Carlson clutched the bottle to his chest and sat there silently with his eyes closed seemingly lost in thought. When he began speaking his voice was so low that Jesse had to strain to hear.

"Maureen and I were married sixteen years. We met in college when we were just about your age. I thought I knew all about love. I had been in love with other girls, but when Mo came along I realized that whatever I had felt before, it wasn't love. This was different; this was love, real love; love that sits like a weight on your chest until you know you will never draw another breath unless you have the one you love by your side. I was terrified but I knew right then there would never be anyone else for me.

We got married right after graduation – my graduation – Mo still had another year to go and then her student teaching. Her parents wanted us to wait; they were sure she would never finish school if we got married. We told them we were getting married now, even if we had to elope. They gave in but I don't think they ever forgave me. It took a couple of years longer than it should have but Mo finished her degree. She did her student teaching and the week after Mo received her certification she gave birth to EJ and we were complete. That's what Mo said – we were complete: an EMT and a teacher with a family of our own. It didn't matter what anyone else thought or said this was our life. I can't help but wonder what she would say now."

Carlson refilled his glass and drank deep. Jesse frantically tried to think of something to say but came up empty. Brother Clement used to say the best you can do for someone is to be present to them; to let them talk or cry or sit in silence knowing that they are not alone. Being present without doing or saying something is not easy.

Brother Clement emphasized, "You need to really be there; you cannot fake it, you can't pretend to be present while doing other things in your mind. You may feel powerless, unable to stem the person's suffering. But your presence is a gift of immeasurable value. Give it gracefully."

Carlson's voice brought Jesse back to the moment.

"Nine years ago, on Columbus Day weekend, we were driving home from a soccer tournament in New Hampshire. It was EJ's first year on the traveling team and Mo and I rarely missed a game. Usually EJ traveled with the team, but this time we took him home with us so we could stop at our favorite diner for dinner together."

Carlson's voice dropped to little more than a whisper. His tears flowed freely, dripping from his chin into his bourbon. "The truck came out of nowhere and rammed us broadside, caving in the passenger-side door. They said Maureen died instantly. EJ and I were pinned in the car until the rescue squad cut us out with the Jaws of Life. By some cruel twist of fate, I not only lived but made a full recovery. EJ spent weeks in the hospital and then months in physical therapy learning how to live as a paraplegic. Why him and not me? Why did Mo have to die? I would trade places with either of them in a heartbeat.

Jesse, you know about these things; you grew up at the Priory. Does God have some kind of sick sense of humor? What kind of selfish God takes a beautiful vibrant woman away from her family in the prime of her life? What kind of God lets me walk away but leaves an innocent twelve-year-old paralyzed from the waist down? What did I do to deserve this kind of hell on earth?"

Jesse did not know what to say or even if he should say anything at all. Maybe this was another of Carlson's rhetorical questions. To his own surprise, Jesse heard himself start to speak.

"Mr. Carlson, I don't have the answers you want, but I think you are asking the wrong questions. God –"

"The wrong questions!" Carlson growled at Jesse. "Who do you think you are? You can't possibly know the pain... I lost everything! My whole life was destroyed that night. Where was your God then? Tell me – I really want to know."

"I don't know your pain, Mr. Carlson, but I do know something about being lost and something about God. You want to know where God was on that night? God was in the same place God always is, right there with you, with your wife, with EJ. God wasn't driving that truck. God didn't take your wife or paralyze EJ. God creates life; God doesn't take it away; not the God I believe in.

God gives us life. God shows us the way through this difficult world. When we laugh God laughs with us. When we suffer God knows our pain. One day, in another place, God will make it all better, but right here, right now, life is up to us. But God never leaves us alone; God is always there.

I was abandoned on the steps of a mountain priory only hours after I was born. I don't know why or even who left me there. Did my mother ever look at me, did she ever hold me? Is she alive? If she is alive, does she ever think about me, about what happened? Does she ever wonder how I grew up, who I am today? I asked Brother Clement about her, how she could leave me there. You know what he said? He said a parent's love is the closest thing we have in this world to God's love. He said that if it was my mother who left me at the Priory it was proof that she loved me. She sacrificed everything to give me a life and it was my duty to make the best of the life she gave me. Over the years, I heard him say the same thing about God, how God gave us life and it was our duty to make the best of the life God gave us. Even in the worst of times, life bears a gift from God if only we can find it."

Carlson looked at him intently. "A gift? What gift could there possibly be in an accident that destroyed my life?"

"EJ for one," Jesse said gently. "Your wife lost her life in the accident but your son is very much alive and he is like no one I have ever known."

"How dare you!" Carlson wailed and smashed his empty glass against the porch rail.

Jesse slumped back into his chair and waited, unsure and a little afraid of what might happen next. But Carlson slouched into his own chair, as if all the pain and rage and self-loathing had gushed out of him and left him spent. The two of them sat silently lost in the darkness of the October night.

Chapter Eight

  Two weeks later EJ rolled into Jesse's dorm room just before midnight. Jesse sat hunched over his computer trying to will the final pages of a paper on colonialism in Central America to somehow appear on the screen.

  "What's up?" Jesse said, grateful for the interruption.

  EJ handed him his cell phone, "My father wants to talk with you. He's been trying to call your phone but couldn't get through."

  Jesse had not spoken to Mr. Carlson since their confrontation on the porch. He had stayed on campus last weekend, studying for mid-terms but also hoping to avoid another uncomfortable conversation.

  "Mr. Carlson – sorry, I need to charge the battery on my phone."

  "Jesse, we have a call in Boston. A building collapsed and several people are missing. We need the whole team – can you come? EJ said he would drive you to the Natick rest area on the Mass Pike and we can pick you up there."

Jesse took less than twenty minutes to post messages for his professors and double check his go-bag. Being prepared to respond on short notice came with the SAR territory. Even though EJ was not part of the team, this late night quick response was nothing new for him. He was behind the wheel ready to go by the time Jesse got to the parking lot. They met up with the rest of the team less than an hour later.

Goose Hill rose above the northern suburbs of Boston just high enough to catch the breeze drifting off the Bay. At one time, up and coming merchants and businessmen built comfortable homes on the hill, their relative position a measure of the owners' wealth and success. The higher up on the hill you climbed the more impressive the homes. All the homes on the hill shared one feature: a clear view looking down on the tenements and multi-family homes of the working class neighborhood below. Over time, the houses on the hill aged in a dignified way but the neighborhood below did not fare as well.

The three-story building that collapsed on this autumn night sat at the base of Goose Hill. Built as tenement housing at the turn of the twentieth century, it recently had been converted into housing for developmentally disabled persons. Prior to the collapse it had been home to sixteen residents, two live-in house parents and a small staff working rotating shifts.

Jesse and the others walked into a chaotic scene. What remained standing of Goose Hill Home sat uneasily on a crumbled foundation while the rest spilled over onto the sidewalk and into the street. The air was thick with a mixture of dust and smoke although Jesse did not see any evidence of fire. Truthfully, he could not see much of anything amid the flashing lights of a whole fleet of fire engines, ambulances and police cars that blinded him and seemed only to add to the confusion surrounding the scene.

Carlson acted as their liaison officer gathering the latest information while Jesse and the other handlers readied the dogs. Jesse noticed that several of the dogs appeared disoriented by the flashing lights and the noise of dozens of idling engines. He made a mental note to incorporate more urban rescue scenarios into their training.

Carlson reported, "The latest sitrep has two fatalities, seven injured have been transported to local hospitals and four residents are unaccounted for. A ten-foot perimeter must be maintained around the site; the building is still settling and very unstable. The house parents think that some of the residents might have become frightened and wandered off. This is a tough neighborhood and residents have been harassed in the past, even assaulted. For our own safety and for local knowledge each team will have a police officer assigned to escort them."

The team's protocol called for rotating forty-five minute shifts to keep the dogs fresh. With six dogs and handlers they would be able to maintain peak performance for three to four hours in these conditions. After that, sensory fatigue would begin to degrade their effectiveness. Of course, the handlers were already fatigued from lack of sleep and were counting on adrenaline to keep them going.

Jesse and Sara took one of the first rotations and got lucky right away finding a forty-seven-year-old woman with Down's syndrome trapped in an alleyway by falling debris. A team of firefighters carried her out. She had a sprained ankle and some scrapes and bruises but no serious injuries. Two hours later another team found two of the missing residents hiding in an abandoned building a block away. They were uninjured but fearful that they would be blamed for the collapse because they had been smoking in the kitchen and they knew that was not allowed.

The teams kept working through the night but as dawn slowly appeared one resident had still not been found. A cadaver dog had been called by the fire department to join the search but had not uncovered anything. About six in the morning, Marie, one of the house parents, came forward with a photograph of the missing resident. In the picture, Jimmy Clanton was holding a kitten and smiling a smile so big that it distorted his whole face. With his red hair, short stature and Kelly green sweatshirt, Jesse thought he looked something like a leprechaun.

"Did you get this picture from his room?" Jesse asked.

Marie nodded. "His room is about the only one left standing."

"Can you bring me something for Sara to scent from – a shoe, a piece of clothing, anything Jimmy wore recently?"

Marie and a firefighter went back to the building and returned a few minutes later with one well-worn slipper.

Jesse knelt down in front of Sara; he could tell she was tired, but her eyes were still alert. He gave her a good whiff of the slipper and then said, "Find more, Sara. Find more!"

All night, Jesse had kept Sara on the lead while she worked. The unfamiliar setting, the darkness, the flashing lights made him uneasy. Now, in the first light of day, he unclipped the lead and nodded at her.

Sara immediately set off down the hill away from the collapsed building. She moved steadily zig-zagging across the street with Jesse close behind and Officer Duncan doing his best to keep the street clear. At the bottom of the hill, she stopped and looked up a side street. Sara started up the side street then stopped again and came back to the intersection. Then she turned and looked at Jesse with that look he had seen so many times – she had something! When Jesse nodded again, Sara started forward, only this time moving much faster. Jesse and Officer Duncan had to jog just to keep her in sight. Three blocks later Sara stopped and sat down facing a corner building.

The building was dark but the neon sign over the door was still lit. The Shamrock appeared to be a neighborhood tavern. Jesse reached in his pocket for the picture of Jimmy and confirmed what he thought he remembered: Jimmy's sweatshirt had a shamrock on the front – one that looked just like the shamrock on the tavern sign. He showed the photograph to the policeman.

"Well, I'll be..." Duncan said.

Duncan tried the front door but it was locked. He walked around to the alley behind the bar and called out, "Jimmy? Jimmy Clanton? Are you in there?"

No reply, but Jesse noticed Sara's ears prick forward. "Shhh – listen closely," he said.

Silence. Then they both heard it at the same time – a cat, most likely a kitten, mewing.

Duncan pulled out his flashlight and entered the alley. Only moments later he came out again, his arm draped around the shoulders of Jimmy Clanton who was still cradling his kitten.

"Jimmy," Duncan said, "this is my friend Jesse and his dog..."

"Sara," Jesse chimed in. "Good to meet you, Jimmy. Are you alright?"

Jimmy nodded looking at Sara with that same smile that Jesse remembered from the photo.

"You like animals, don't you Jimmy?" Jesse said. "Sara loves to have her ears scratched. Would you like to pet her?"

Jimmy knelt down and Sara licked Jimmy's face while he scratched her behind the ears.

"Let's go home, Jimmy," Duncan said.

Jimmy shook his head violently from side to side and he tried to pull away from Duncan. In a split second his expression changed from pure happiness to pure terror.

"It's OK, Jimmy," Jesse said quietly. "Marie and the others are worried about you and they are waiting for you to come back. Sara is going to come too, so we can all go together. Is that OK?"

Jimmy looked from Jesse to Sara to Officer Duncan and back to Sara again before nodding his head. Sara nuzzled his hand and Jimmy rubbed her head again as the smile came back to his face.

Back at the turnpike rendezvous site, the team's customary celebration of coffee, donuts and kibble also passed for breakfast. Dogs napped and their handlers slumped in their seats, all of them exhausted from the intensity of the search and the lost night of sleep. On the road home Carlson drove the team van with Jesse riding shotgun and the others piled haphazardly in the rear seats.

"You did good work tonight, Jesse," Carlson said.

"The team worked well together, but we need to drill more in urban settings," Jesse replied.

"You're right, urban SAR is a whole different animal. A couple of the dogs lost focus with the constant distractions and the myriad scents. Not Sara, though; she stayed on point through the whole search. You and she are an exceptional team – I wish I could clone the two of you and make about a hundred copies."

"Sara is good," Jesse answered, "but I think what makes the team work is the diversity. Each dog, each handler, has their own strengths and weaknesses. Together we amplify the strengths and compensate for one another's weaknesses so the job gets done."

"And that attitude is why the others accept you as the team leader, even though you are the youngest of the group. You're right, we do make each other better and as a team we can do things we could never do alone. But the team may be holding you back. You and Sara impressed some people tonight. The battalion chief asked about you; he said he had never seen any team work so well and so effortlessly.

My point is, Jesse, people are going to notice you and opportunities are going to come your way. You need to think about what you want to do so that when the offers come you pick the right ones. I know you have three more years of college in front of you, and I hope you do finish, but it's not too early to start thinking about what happens next. Most people in SAR have to support themselves with other occupations. A few eke out a living as breeders or trainers, but you are clearly not like most people. You can be a rock star in the SAR world – training, consulting, being the go-to guy for the BIG jobs all over the world. Mark my words, Jesse, you can have it all.

Now, you better try to get some sleep. EJ will probably want to head back to campus as soon as we get home."

Jesse slept fitfully, plunging into deep sleep only to wake again each time the van turned onto a different road. Thankfully, EJ took one look at him and decided there was no hurry to return to campus. Jesse fell into bed and slept the sleep of the dead.

Chapter Nine

Christmas break could not come soon enough for Jesse. Final exams and papers had left him frazzled after pulling several "all-nighters" and spending every waking minute either in class or in the library. When he dropped off his last paper on the Friday before Christmas he wanted to celebrate but barely had enough energy to make it back to his dorm room and collapse on the bed.

Ten minutes later, EJ was pounding on the door. "Jesse! I know you're in there – open up! Its time!"

"Go away!" Jesse hollered although his voice was muffled by the pillow that covered his head.

"Come on, Jesse, it's a Devoe tradition. You're gonna love it!"

Before Jesse could answer, he felt himself being dragged out of bed by the ankles until he landed hard on the floor. Kicking free he rolled over and saw EJ sitting there with a maniacal grin on his face as he dangled a key over Jesse's head.

"You gave me a key for emergencies, remember Dude? Well, this is an emergency! It is the beginning of Christmas break and you know what that means – the Devoe Downhill! Let's go freshman, the snow gods await and only a virgin like you will sate their fiendish appetites!"

French Peak hardly lived up to its name. Anywhere else, it would be described as a hill and not a very big one at that, but among the gently rolling slopes of Massachusetts French Peak managed to pass for a mountain, if only in miniature. However, among Devoe students, French Peak stood head and shoulders above its peers for two reasons. First, the ski center included an outrageous tubing hill complete with rope tows, moguls and three ramps big enough to offer the adventurous tuber serious "air-time". French's second claim to fame rested in its notorious and long standing laissez faire attitude about under-age drinking. The laws were strictly enforced in the stylish-for-the-fifties après-ski lounge but French Peak staff turned an intentional blind eye to beverages consumed elsewhere on the grounds.

When EJ and Jesse arrived the bash was well-underway. French Peak regulars knew enough to avoid the slopes on Devoe Downhill day, so the resort belonged almost exclusively to the students. Some skied, some tobogganed, but most clustered around the tubing hill which was lined with cases of beer chilling in the snow banks that defined the slope. EJ and Jesse joined the throng just as the "VIR-GIN, VIR-GIN" chant grew from a scattered cheer to a roar that echoed off the nearby hills.

EJ pointed to the top of the hill, "Well, well, it's your two buddies from Southie."

"They're hardly my buddies. So how does this work, again?" Jesse replied.

"It seems easy enough, until you try it. All you have to do is make it to the bottom of the hill holding an empty can of beer without falling off the tube."

"Why an empty can of beer?"

"Well, the can isn't empty when you start – that's the fun. The object is to finish the whole can as you slide, without spilling any or falling off the tube. No one gets it done on the first try so they have to go again and again and again – you get the picture. After a couple of failed attempts, it really gets interesting."

"No one gets it on the first try?" Jesse questioned.

"Nope. Guaranteed. Watch."

Jesse watched the two freshmen straddle their tubes. Each of them holding a beer high with one hand they pumped their free fist into the air with each VIR-GIN chant. Then with a push from a pair of bystanders they were off, sliding down the hill while guzzling their beer. The first one flipped out of the tube in the first set of moguls, but his friend sailed through, although turned completely backwards. It looked like he might be the first one to reach bottom unscathed. Sucking down the last of his beer, he never saw the senior with the long handled broom lurking by the ramp. One well-placed nudge did the deed, steering the tube onto the ramp where in a split second the boy separated from his tube in mid-air. The tube bounced away harmlessly when it hit the ground; the boy landed with a bone-jarring thud on the crusty snow as his empty beer can skidded on down the hill.

EJ laughed, "Like I said, guaranteed!"

Jesse laughed too, in spite of himself, until he saw EJ looking at him with what could only be described as sinister delight.

"Vir-gin," EJ said pointing at Jesse. "Vir-gin, Vir-gin, VIR-GIN!"

Other students around them took up the cry and soon Jesse found himself being dragged to the top of the hill. He thought about resisting, but then decided to go with the flow. He lost his first beer in the moguls, his second slipped from his grasp as he tried to avoid the ramp. The third beer tasted pretty good going down but not so good coming up after he crashed only 10 yards from the finish.

EJ helped him get cleaned up but chided him mercilessly, "Puking on the third run – a new world record but not one anyone would be proud of."

"Somehow, I don't think this is what Brother Clement had in mind when he told me to leave the Priory and experience life in the real world."

"I don't know, it looks pretty real to me," EJ said with a smirk. "You know life in the real world is not always very pretty. Life in the Priory must be like living in a time warp or something, you know, out of sync, cut off from what's going on. Aren't you glad to be out of there, even a little bit?"

"You make it sound like some medieval monastery. It wasn't like that at all. Did you ever come to visit when your father came with the dogs? I don't remember you being there..."

"No – I never went with him. You know how he is with his dogs; they get his complete attention. I would have been in the way."

"Someday, you have to come and visit. I really think you would like it there. The people in the community are not like people anywhere else; I know they would like you."

"You're going back for Christmas break, right?" EJ asked.

Jesse nodded, "I leave tomorrow morning. You're not thinking about coming with me for Christmas?"

EJ shrugged his shoulders, "I don't know, maybe."

"What about your father – you wouldn't take off and leave him alone for the holidays," Jesse paused. "EJ, maybe it's none of my business but what's going on with you and your father? It's like you've been avoiding him all semester."

"I haven't been avoiding him; we've just been going our own ways. Anyway, I think he likes it better that way. He's got his dogs and now he's got you. You're like the son he never had – what does he need me for?"

"Wait a minute, EJ – that's not fair to him or to me. Your father talks about you all the time. When I get to the house the first thing he does is ask about you. 'Is EJ coming home? Is he alright? Did he say anything about when he will come?' He loves you, EJ."

"That's not love; it's guilt. He feels responsible for me being in this chair, for me not being the son he always wanted. When I'm around I just remind him of his sins..."

"Cut the crap, EJ! If you want to feel sorry for yourself, that's up to you, but don't lay it on him. He's just trying to be a good father."

"What do you know about it? You don't know him or me, and you certainly don't know anything about father-son relationships." EJ winced and looked away but his words hung in the air for long time.

"I'm sorry, I –"

"No," Jesse cut him off, "You said it now own it! Maybe I don't know about fathers and sons; I never knew my own father or my mother either. At least, I never knew my biological father, but I know what it looks like and feels like when people love you like a son. If you are too stupid or too shut-down to see that in your father, then I feel sorry for you. The only thing I can think of that would be worse than not having a father is having one and being oblivious to how much he loves you."

They made the trip back to campus without speaking. In the morning, Jesse finished packing and was putting on his coat when EJ knocked on his door.

"I thought you might need a ride to the bus station."

"I can walk," Jesse answered.

"Look, man, I'm trying to say I'm sorry. Sometimes I go off the deep end and I need a good friend to haul me back in. Besides, it's almost Christmas and you can't stay mad at someone for Christmas – it's a rule. It's in the Bible – check it out!"

Jesse tried not to smile but finally gave in, "You are pathetic, you know that? Have you ever read the Bible – any of it? It doesn't say anything like that, but it does say to forgive fools, especially those who show up at your door offering a ride to the bus station."

EJ picked up Jesse's duffel bag, neatly turned his wheelchair around and rolled out the door with Jesse close behind.

When they arrived at the bus station, they were both surprised to find Mr. Carlson waiting for them. Sara was with him, fully decked out in her SAR gear.

"Uh-oh, I don't like the looks of this," Jesse said. "Sara looks ready to work - do we have a job to do?"

Carlson smiled, "Actually, no, but I checked with the bus company and they said service dogs were allowed to travel on board if they were clearly identified – even SAR dogs. I thought Sara might like to spend Christmas with you at the Priory..."

"Thanks, Mr. Carlson," Jesse replied, "I was wondering how I would explain to everyone that she wasn't with me. I hope you and EJ have a good Christmas – we will be thinking of you."

Sara actually seemed to enjoy the nearly five-hour bus ride. Most of the way she sat alertly, her nose twitching as she sampled the scents of all the passengers. Jesse, on the other hand, slept most of the way to Albany, where they changed to another bus to Glens Falls. Brother Reuben was waiting for them when they arrived.

"Jesse, it's good to see you! And you brought Sara, too! You can't imagine how much I've missed you – how much we've all missed you," Reuben said as he embraced Jesse.

"We missed all of you, too," Jesse replied. "Let's go – I can't wait to see everybody!"

The hour-long drive to the Priory passed quickly as Reuben asked Jesse question after question about his first semester at college, about working with Carlson and his team and about his SAR missions with Sara.

"I heard about the building collapse in Boston. You and Sara are getting quite a reputation."

"She is amazing," Jesse answered. "Some of the dogs really struggled in an urban setting, but not Sara. When I let her go off-lead it was just another mission for her."

"I am so proud of her, and of you. I know Brother Adam and Sister Hannah are your official parents, but I couldn't be more proud of you if you were my own son. Watching you grow-up and become this gifted young man – it's been just about the best part of my life."

Reuben's voice cracked a bit and he stopped talking.

Jesse spoke, softly at first, "EJ Carlson and I had an argument about fathers and families. He said I didn't know what I was talking about since I never knew my father or even my mother."

"What a hurtful thing to say! I can't believe – "

"No," Jesse interrupted, "he's right, in a way. I can't tell him how to work out his problems with his father. I don't understand how fathers and sons get along. But like I told him, I may not know about fathers and mothers and sons but I learned so much about family from you and all the others at the Priory. In some ways, I have it better than if I knew my own parents. I have a whole community of people who are like an extended family. What more could I want?"

"Do you ever wonder about your mother and your father?" Reuben asked.

"Sure, I think about them sometimes. I wonder who they were and what happened – why they left me at the Priory. I wonder what it would have been like to grow up with a normal family." Jesse noticed Reuben cringe a bit and quickly added, "But then I think about how lucky I was to end up with all of you at the Priory. Somehow, it seems like I was meant to be there with you and with the dogs. After all, I am 'Jesse the dog-boy' so how would that have been possible without living at the Priory?"

Reuben shook his head, "I don't know, but I hope you understand when I say that I thank God every day for bringing you and me to live at the Priory. I can't imagine my life anywhere else."

"Reuben, were you at the Priory when I came?"

"No. You were a baby when I arrived."

"Why did you come? I don't remember..."

Reuben did not answer right away, as if he was thinking about what to say. "I had visited the Priory many times. I was not a religious person, but the dogs fascinated me and I gradually got to know Marcel and the others. I had hopes of becoming a veterinarian, but then my life took a wrong turn and everything I hoped for kind of fell apart."

Reuben seemed lost in thought for a while. Then he continued, "I was in love with an amazing young woman. We wanted to get married but her uncle, who was raising her, hated me. Actually, I think he would have hated anyone who wanted to take away his niece. I never could understand him. He was so possessive of her, but he treated her terribly. He would never let her go anywhere and although she would never admit it, I was sure that he beat her. We had to sneak around to see one another.

We made plans to run away together but somehow he must have found out. When the day came for us to leave I went to her house and they were gone – vanished. They took off in the middle of the night and I was never able to find out where they went. I followed every lead I could think of; I even went to the police but they wouldn't do anything since there was no evidence of any crime being committed. After a couple of months, I gave up.

I was devastated; I couldn't imagine life without her. I even thought about taking my own life. One day I was out walking in the mountains and found myself standing outside the Priory. I heard the most beautiful music, people singing like angels or so it seemed to me. I followed the sound to the chapel and went inside. There were all these people circled around a little baby being baptized. You were not happy about the water being poured on your head, but the more you cried the sweeter they sang to you.

I sat down in the back pew and before I knew what was happening I began to weep. I tried to wipe away the tears but they would not stop coming. The next thing I knew I felt Brother Clement's arm around my shoulders and I had this strange feeling that everything was going to be alright. It was as if I had come home. I've been here ever since."

The rest of the trip passed in silence except for Sara's gentle snoring in the back seat. They arrived at the Priory just as the first star appeared in the evening sky.

The Priory community welcomed Jesse home like a conquering hero. Everyone came out to greet him, to marvel at how much he had grown in four months, to tease him about how he had matured from a dog-boy into a college-man, and in every way possible to remind him and to remind themselves that they are and will always be family. By the time Jesse slumped into bed that night he had no doubt he was home again.

The next day, things settled into a more normal routine except for Brother Seth making Jesse's favorite blueberry pancakes with real maple syrup for breakfast – a treat reserved only for special occasions. After breakfast, Jesse quickly assumed his usual place in the daily order of things, working with Marcel and Reuben in the kennels, getting up to speed on the dogs training needs and helping prepare the chapel for Christmas Eve services.

The early service on Christmas Eve had always been Jesse's favorite. People traveled from as far away as Plattsburgh and Malone to see the living nativity and attend the family-oriented recitation of the Christmas story. Neighboring farmers supplied much of the livestock needed for the living nativity: a donkey and two cows came from the Tucker's just down the road and Wilfredo Baez brought a few of his sheep from Gilead. Other animals, traditional and not so traditional, would often appear with their owners and in some years, Marcel had been known to fill in for any missing livestock by dressing-up some of the more patient dogs. The Priory's living nativity was a true reflection of the Priory itself: all were welcome and sure to be included whether they seemed out of place or not. Of course, the young children loved the animals and they always enjoyed Brother Clement's reading of the Christmas story from the Gospel according to Luke.

This year, however, Jesse found the midnight communion service to be the one that truly captured Christmas for him. The late-night service included a few families from outside but most of those attending were members of the Priory community and their visiting friends and relatives. The chapel took on an ethereal quality bathed in soft light and music that seemed other-worldly, as though echoing the song of the angels at the first Christmas. The service ended with the singing of Silent Night as the light of Christmas passed from candle to candle among the congregation until the pale glow of flickering flames filled the entire chapel. When the service ended people lingered whispering words of blessing to one another or sitting in silence hoping to prolong the numinous moment.

Jesse carried his candle out into the still night. Thousands of stars floated in the night sky as if each one was a candle held in the hands of a heavenly angel. He walked out by the kennels that stood dark and quiet, simply silhouettes against the snow. He leaned silently against the doorjamb and breathed in the familiar scent of dogs and puppies. A smile came to him and he shook his head and whispered to himself "dog-boy". Sara came out of the shadows, her tail slowly wagging side-to-side. Jesse knelt down and scratched her behind the ears while she nuzzled against his leg.

"Merry Christmas, girl," he said softly.

Christmas morning in the Priory began with early morning worship in the chapel but after that it was like Christmas morning in most homes. Families gathered, opened presents, laughed and hugged and simply enjoyed being together. Jesse had always made the rounds on Christmas morning spending time with all the members of his extended family. It had started when he was the only young child in the community and had continued not simply out of habit but because Jesse had become a part of all the families.

By late morning, Jesse had finally made his way to Brother Clement's residence where he found Clement and Sister Miriam waiting for him. Over the years, he had come to think of Miriam as most children thought of their grandmothers and Miriam had relished the role. Her own family thought she had lost her mind when she announced she was moving to the Priory, but she never had a moment of regret. From the first time she had come, intending to take Jesse into foster care she had been drawn to the people here and to the life they lived together. She would never give Brother Clement the satisfaction of admitting it but she knew from that first meeting that the Priory would be the perfect place for an abandoned child to grow up. Now when she looked at Jesse she saw the best evidence of the worth of her work; her lifetime spent working to help children. In fact, she could seldom look at Jesse without getting misty eyed.

"Jesse, there is this one Christmas present under the tree that seems to have your name on it," Miriam said with a smile.

Jesse pulled a large box from under the tree. It was almost too big to pick up, but he noticed it was very lightweight. He ripped open the paper and opened the box only to find another box inside. He opened the second box and discovered a third box nested within.

"OK," he said with a smirk. "Just what I always wanted: a cardboard box!"

"Don't give up yet," Clement said. "Good things come to those who wait."

Jesse opened the third box and found yet another box inside. He opened the fourth, and then a fifth and a sixth box each neatly nested inside the other. Finally, he came to a tiny box just large enough to hold in the palm of his hand.

"Good things come in small packages," Miriam offered.

Jesse carefully untied the ribbon on the small package and removed the top. Inside, cushioned between two layers of cotton he found a pair of keys. His eyebrows raised expectantly and his mouth dropped open.

Clement spoke in his best fatherly voice, "Now, Jesse, don't get too excited. It's ten years old and has nearly a hundred thousand miles on it but the body is sound and Brother Zach says that mechanically it should be good for another hundred thousand miles. He says Jeeps will last forever if you take care of them."

Jesse only heard about half of what Clement said. He could not believe it – his own car! No more buses or waiting for EJ to take him somewhere! He ran over to Miriam and Clement and hugged them both at the same time.

"Thank you! Thank you! Thank you!" he stammered. "I never expected this!"

"You're welcome, Jesse" Clement said. "Let's go outside and take a look at her."

A moss green Jeep Cherokee sat in the driveway, next to the main building. Jesse had seen it there but assumed it belonged to one of the visitors at the Priory for the holiday.

"I know it's not very sporty," Miriam said, "but we thought it would be practical for you. It has four-wheel drive for the bad weather and plenty of room in back for dogs and their gear."

"It's perfect!" Jesse said. "I can't believe it's mine!"

Clement said, "It's all yours but right now it's registered in the name of the Priory and covered by the Priory insurance. You will have to earn gas money and pay for any repairs it might need, although Brother Zach will be happy to maintain it for you whenever you are here."

A week later, Jesse's new Jeep sat outside Clement's residence packed and ready for the return trip to college. Inside, Jesse, Miriam, Reuben and Clement lingered over a goodbye lunch.

"So, Jesse," Miriam said, "are you looking forward to the new semester?"

"I suppose so, but sometimes I wonder what I am doing there. I mean, why do I need to study European literature and macroeconomics? As a dog trainer and handler I'll never use them; truthfully, I can't think why anyone would ever use them, except to force someone else to learn about them. I know you want me to get my degree but sometimes I feel like I am wasting time. I could be learning a lot more working here with Brother Reuben."

"Education can seem that way, at times," Clement said, "but it is more important than you might understand right now. College is not so much about learning things that you will use in the work you do after you graduate, its more about who you are becoming as a person. Learning, stretching your mind, discovering new and different ways to think about the world, and perhaps most important of all learning to think critically – that is what college should teach you.

If you were only out to learn a trade or how to do a particular job another approach might make more sense but if you want to live a full life and live into your potential, then you need a broad education. I know this sounds old-fashioned in today's nanosecond world that worships technology and entrepreneurial innovation but everything starts somewhere, every new thing builds on what came before. No one starts with a blank slate so learning, even about things that seem disconnected or irrelevant at the moment, can prove to be indispensable. If nothing else, you can carry on an intelligent conversation with someone else – even someone who comes from a different point of view."

"I understand what you are saying, Brother Clement," Jesse replied, "but what you are talking about doesn't sound anything like what I am learning in class."

"Well, it's only been one semester, Jesse," Miriam said. "Don't give up yet."

Reuben chimed in, "Maybe this semester will be better."

"Jesse," Clement said, "stick with it. You have so much potential. I know you are a gifted trainer and handler but I also think that God created you for so much more than that."

"Like what?" Jesse asked.

"I don't know," Clement answered. "That is the joy of living. Some things are easy for us to understand but others are only revealed over time and with hard work. We can't see or even begin to imagine all the possibilities God has created for us. I just hope I am around for a very long time because I really want to see what else God has in store for you."

Chapter Ten

Miranda Curtis went missing on Valentine's Day. Her boyfriend had made dinner reservations for them at the same restaurant where they had their first date, eight months before. She was supposed to meet him there after work but she never arrived. Television news covered her disappearance on every newscast for days until her face became as well-known as any TV or movie star. Twenty-two years old, long brown hair with a slightly gap-toothed smile that made people smile back, until they remembered she was missing.

One week after Miranda vanished, Jesse and the team were activated and told to rendezvous at the fire house in Calvin, New Hampshire about forty miles from the village on Lake Winnipesaukee where Miranda had disappeared. The State Police were still running the investigation but expecting the FBI would take over soon.

Carlson briefed the team. "The Staties have a person of interest in custody, but he is not being very forthcoming. They had evidence from the beginning that this was an abduction; which is why we were not called in before. They think this guy took her and that she may still be alive, held somewhere between here and Amesbury, about 20 miles to the southeast. Their suspect was spotted in both towns in recent weeks. The problem is that there are hundreds of secluded hunting cabins in these mountains where she might be stashed away.

Even though this is a criminal case, we should treat it like any other missing person search. As always, time is a concern. The longer she is out there the more danger she is in. To make matters worse, if we don't turn up something soon, the Staties will have to cut this guy loose and then who knows what will happen.

I've set up a two-part grid. Jesse will lead the team working from here and Ronnie's team will head down to Amesbury and work a grid coming back toward us. Hopefully we will find her before the teams meet in the middle. We will work extended shifts; we go as long as the dogs can go. I want radio check-ins every fifteen minutes; communications may be tricky with the geography but let's do our best."

By the time the team had been briefed, geared up and had finalized their grid assignments, the parking lot outside the firehouse had become a media frenzy. Television crews from as far away as Boston and Hartford swarmed around the handlers and their dogs shouting questions. The team members kept their heads down as they moved purposefully toward the State Police vans that would transport them to the search area. As they went, other troopers restrained the press from following after them.

Jesse's team of four handlers and their dogs fanned out and began working their grid. They had only about four hours of daylight so they had to work quickly but without sacrificing thoroughness. The dogs handled the mountainous terrain better than their handlers. The mild winter was the only thing working in their favor, as the snow cover at this elevation was only ankle deep. Still the search progressed slowly. By nightfall, they had searched dozens of primitive hunting camps but had covered only a small portion of the search area.

At the morning briefing, Carlson had some new information from the State Police. "Their suspect has been talking and it sounds like the Amesbury side of the search might be more productive. The Staties want us to saturate the search on that side."

Jesse said, "You don't sound convinced."

"I might be wrong, but it sounds to me like this guy is trying to throw us off the trail. I used to hunt these mountains with my Grandfather and what he is telling them just doesn't ring true. I talked to some of the local guys and they have their doubts, as well. They have had this guy in custody for three days now, so if she is out there, time is running out. Whatever we do, it better be the right decision, for her sake."

Jesse thought for a moment, then said, "Two more SAR teams arrived last night. Why not send them over to Amesbury with Gary and Peter from my team. That will keep the State Police happy. If you can get one of the locals to drive us, Anne Marie and I can keep searching from this side just in case your hunch is right. We'll have to narrow the grid but maybe the locals can point us in the right direction."

Jesse's plan quickly took shape and shortly after sun-up they were back on the grid. The morning passed without success on either side of the search. By mid-day Sara still seemed fresh but Anne Marie's dog, Buster, was distracted by every sound and movement in the woods. They stopped for a meal break and to re-examine the search grid.

Looking at the map, Anne Marie said, "There's just too much land. We could be out here forever and we don't even know that she's here. Maybe they got the wrong guy; or maybe he's the right guy but he ditched her long before he showed up here."

"Or, maybe she is here and you and I are going to find her," Jesse said. "Let's leave the police work to the pros and stay focused on what we can do. The guy that drove us up here, what was his name?"

"Tanner."

"Yeah, Tanner. He said something about this quadrant right below the old fire tower. He said he had been deer hunting here last fall and he noticed that one of the cabins looked like it had been used recently even though it had been abandoned for years. Remember?"

"Yeah, but that was months ago, long before Miranda went missing," Anne Marie said.

"I know," Jesse answered, "but what if the guy was doing some prep work? Or, what if Miranda isn't his first?"

"Now you're spooking me, Jesse. It's bad enough you and I are out here without any backup. I mean the others all have troopers or deputies or somebody with them. What if we find her and this guy has an accomplice? I don't even want to think about this guy being some kind of serial killer or something."

"Whoa – slow down. I didn't mean to go that far, but I think we ought to check out that cabin, if we can find it."

Jesse smiled but he could tell Anne Marie wasn't buying it. "Let's go," he said quickly.

An hour later, Sara stopped dead in her tracks, her nose in the air and her mouth slightly open. Jesse knew she had picked up a scent. Normally he would have taken her off lead, but given the uncertainty of what they might be walking into he decided to proceed cautiously. He signaled to Anne Marie to come closer; on their way over Buster indicated, too. Both dogs had hit on a scent.

Anne Marie took out her radio, "Team 1A to base, do you copy, over."

Silence.

"Team 1A to base, do you copy, over," she repeated.

No response.

Jesse said, "Let's move on up the mountain. Maybe we'll be able to get through."

"But that's the way the dogs are indicating. Whatever they have found is up that way."

"Right. But we don't know what they have hit on. Let's move slowly and quietly, on lead. We can try the radio again when we gain some altitude."

Before Anne Marie could argue, Jesse set off up the slope with Sara leading the way. Anne Marie hesitated but eventually followed lagging a short way behind. Sara led them on a typical zig-zag pattern but steadily moving upward. Downed trees and slick rock surfaces made for slow going. After about twenty minutes, Jesse spotted a cabin about a hundred yards in front of them barely visible through the dense forest. If the trees still had their leaves he never would have seen it. He pulled firmly on Sara's lead and signaled Anne Marie to stop.

"Anne Marie, duck behind that boulder and try the radio again."

A few moments later she came back into sight shaking her head. Still no contact.

"You stay here with Buster. Sara and I will move in closer and see what we can see. Get out your walkie-talkie and let's be sure we have local communications."

The walkie-talkies checked out. Jesse and Sara moved slowly toward the cabin coming to a stop when they were about half-way there. Jessed scanned the woods on all sides and then took out his walkie-talkie.

"Anne Marie?"

"Yes, Jesse."

"Someone's been here recently. I can see tracks in the snow around the front of the cabin. They lead away uphill. I will approach from the side and see what else I can find. If something happens to us, you and Buster need to get out of here; head downhill until you can make radio contact. Do you understand?"

"Jesse, I don't – "

"Anne Marie, please – just do it."

Jesse approached the side wall of the cabin in complete silence. Footprints scuffed up the snow all around the outside.

Jesse could not be sure but it seemed the prints were all made by the same pair of boots. When he reached the wall of the building he could hear what sounded like muffled crying coming from inside, but he heard nothing else: no voices, no footsteps, nothing.

The window was about shoulder height so he tried to peek inside. A ragged green curtain covered the window, but it was threadbare in spots; enough to make it possible to see through. Jesse saw only one person inside: a woman bound and gagged lying on a mattress on the floor.

Jesse pulled the hatchet from his daypack; it had a blade on one side and an oversized hammer-head on the other. It was the best he could do. He looped Sara's lead around a small pine tree and approached the front door. He breathed a sigh of relief when he found it padlocked on the outside. He scanned the surrounding woods, one more time, but saw nothing. Two solid blows from the hatchet separated the hasp from the worn wooden doorframe and the door flew open. Jesse took a step back, just in case, but the only sound was a muffled scream from the woman. He stepped inside and found Miranda Curtis terrified, battered, but alive.

He quickly went to her side, "Shh, it's okay, I'm here to help you. Please listen carefully: was it one man who did this to you?"

She nodded.

"You are sure he was alone?"

She nodded again, harder this time.

Jesse spoke into his walkie-talkie, "Anne Marie – I've got her. I've got Miranda – she's alive! I think it is safe – but you need to make radio contact now and give them our GPS position. I don't want to contaminate this crime scene before the Staties get here. Do whatever you have to do but get through to base now!"

An hour later, the cabin was swarming with police and four paramedics were caring for Miranda. Jesse and Anne Marie stood off to the side watching it all, relieved to have found the woman alive and without having to confront the demented man or men who had done this to her. After giving their preliminary statements to the officer in charge Jesse, Anne Marie and their dogs began the long slow walk out of the woods.

Late in the afternoon, timed to make the evening news, the State Police held a press conference at the firehouse "command center". The Major in charge sat behind a table with a dozen microphones lined up in front of him. Miranda Curtis sat next to him, wrapped in a blanket and looking understandably distraught. The female paramedic at her side rested her arm around Miranda's shoulders protectively.

The Major searched out the camera from the Boston NBC affiliate, looked commandingly into the lens and said, "I am Major Donald Ferris of the New Hampshire State Police and I have two announcements to make. First, after one of the most intense searches in New Hampshire history, Miranda Curtis was rescued this afternoon from a remote hunting cabin here in the White Mountains about forty miles from Lake Winnipesaukee where she was abducted nine days ago. Miss Curtis has been through a difficult ordeal but she is alive and well enough to assist us in our continuing investigation. Although she is here with us, she does not feel up to speaking to the media at this time."

Jesse stood off to the side watching and listening as the Major described, in great detail, the police work that led to Miranda's rescue.

"Listen to him!" Anne Marie whispered. "You would think that the Staties analyzed the clues and marched right into the woods and rescued her themselves! Not a word about you or me or the dogs; certainly no mention that they wanted us searching a totally different area. Turn on the TV cameras, and they are all the same."

Jesse smiled at her, "Lucky we don't do this to become rich and famous. Besides, they did good work to narrow down the search area and then – "

"And then call us in," Anne Marie finished.

"Yeah, well, she's alive and they seem pretty sure they've got the bad guy so that's all that matters," Jesse said. "Let's go. We're not needed here and Carlson and the team are waiting for us. It's a long ride home."

As they walked away, Major Ferris continued speaking, "My second announcement is that we have a suspect in custody who we believe is responsible for Miss Curtis's abduction. Malcom Yeats, fifty-six years old, of Cabot Mountain, New York…"

Jesse stopped and turned toward the press conference.

"What's the matter, Jesse?" Anne Marie said, and when he didn't answer, she said again, "Jesse?"

"Nothing. Just that Cabot Mountain is a stone's throw from the Priory where I grew up. Huh, what are the odds…"

Before Jesse could say anymore, a commotion at the press conference distracted him. Miranda Curtis had jumped to her feet, dropped her blanket and began pushing her way through the reporters half-running toward the spot where Jesse and Anne Marie stood. When she reached them, she threw her arms around Jesse's neck and pressed against him, her entire body convulsing with powerful sobs.

"You saved me. You saved me. You saved me." She repeated the words over and over again, barely above a whisper.

Jesse dropped his go-bag and wrapped one arm around her to comfort her as Sara sat patiently by his side. By this time, every camera at the press conference was trained on them, the clicking and whirr of shutters the only sounds heard in the silent vacuum that surrounded the distraught woman and her rescuer.

The evening news and nearly every newspaper in the Northeast led with the story of the rescue and the visual they chose was a close-up of Miranda clinging to Jesse. Although, Jesse declined to be interviewed, he appeared in every photo and news video.

The case continued to make news over the next several weeks. First came the announcement that DNA evidence found in the cabin had linked Yeats to two unsolved disappearances of young women. Yeats continued to proclaim his innocence but when cadaver dogs found the remains of the missing women buried only a half-mile from the cabin he seemed to accept his fate. It would take several more months, but eventually Yeats was charged with multiple counts of abduction and murder. With each break in the case, the pictures of Miranda and Jesse flooded the news outlets again. Something in that image brought comfort to both reporters and the public; like a healing balm salves an open wound.

Chapter Eleven

The Spring semester passed in a blur for both Jesse and EJ. Jesse immersed himself in his classes hoping to find some traction for his fledgling college career, but he knew he was only going through the motions. EJ, on the other hand, was like a thoroughbred racing down the home-stretch. The finish line was in sight and he would not be denied. He designed an elaborate flow-chart to track his progress toward graduation. One by one he checked off every project and paper, every final requirement and form, every senior celebration and ceremony. Jesse ragged on him mercilessly for his "nerdly" fixation but EJ good-naturedly dismissed his taunts as freshman jealousy.

"You may get here someday," EJ would say, "but you will always know I got here first. So, deal with it."

In mid-May, EJ took down the completed flow chart from the wall, rolled it up like a diploma, tied it with a red ribbon and presented it to Jesse. "Just in case you never get the real thing. Enjoy the moment!"

Jesse laughed at EJ's jab, but secretly wondered if he might be right. College still felt like foreign ground.

Every detail of graduation day at Devoe College dripped with pomp, circumstance and symbolic significance rooted in traditions amassed over its 220-year history. The procession of graduates began in Weatherly Hall, the lone structure still standing from the founding of the school. Now reserved for ceremonial occasions, it stood at the intellectual and physical heart of the campus. An aerial photograph of the campus hung in the entry way, clearly showed how the rest of the campus radiated outward, in concentric circles, with Weatherly at the epicenter. The graduation procession followed a similar pattern. At Weatherly the provost and senior faculty, in full academic regalia, stepped off as the campanile chimed the hour. Normally, the bells tolled only the number of the hour, but on graduation day following the hourly chimes the bells intoned the Devoe Alma Mater in a martial rhythm timed perfectly to a purposeful pace for walking – not quite a march but as close as a New England bastion of higher education dared to come. In time with the bells, the procession moved counter-clockwise from Weatherly Hall to each of the seven academic buildings surrounding it. At each building the procession grew as the graduates and junior faculty joined-in, grouped by the schools awarding their degrees, their academic stoles color-coded to reflect each course of study. By the time the procession reached Hahner Hall, where EJ waited with 127 fellow Information Technology graduates, it had swelled to nearly one thousand students and faculty. At some schools, graduation had become a formality that many students chose to forgo – but not at Devoe. From freshman orientation through the final senior banquet the expectation came through, loud and clear, that all Devoe students participate in graduation.

  EJ led his group of fellow IT grads joining the procession, not because of academic standing but to ensure his place with other graduates in wheelchairs. Academically, EJ was something of a disappointment to Devoe, one of those students brilliant in his field but with little interest in other academic requirements. In his freshman year, he quickly gravitated to Hahner Hall and its cutting-edge technology. The enthusiasm he showed for computers and algorithms was matched only by his disdain for the general education requirements of a good liberal arts education. He attended his required math class three times – on the first day of classes to receive the syllabus, on the day he aced the mid-term exam and once more to steamroll his way through the final exam. His professor threatened to deny him the A that he earned with perfect scores on both exams, but the department head reluctantly intervened. EJ showed even less interest in literature and social sciences requirements, but quickly emerged as a rising star in his major field. He would graduate with an overall grade point average far below his potential but with top honors among Devoe's IT graduates.

    Jesse joined the other students and family members lining the procession route as the graduates passed by. Tradition dictated that the graduates and faculty be the first to enter Woodley Amphitheater. They would take their places but remain standing to applaud the entry of the family and friends who followed. The symbolism made a powerful statement about how Devoe viewed its relationship with families and alumni. Devoe annually led all private schools in New England in the number of legacy students, those second or third or even seventh generation scholars enrolled at Devoe.

    The commencement ceremony followed its carefully crafted script right down to the synchronized launch of the graduates' mortar-boards at the conclusion. The rest of the day was only slightly-less choreographed. Luncheons and receptions dotted the campus as students and family members lingered in the celebratory glow.

    Jesse and the Carlson family contingent joined EJ at Hahner Hall for refreshments and a tour of the computer labs. EJ's senior thesis was among the graduate projects on display. Jesse tried to understand the premise but no matter how many times EJ had explained it to him, he still felt EJ must be speaking some other-worldly language. In truth, Jesse was still not convinced that he belonged in college; not just Devoe College – but any college. He had struggled through classes earning passing grades, but not finding anything that excited him the way IT excited EJ. If not for his SAR work with Mr. Carlson's team, the year would have been a total loss. He had begged Brother Clement to let him spend the summer at the Priory but Clement insisted he remain with the Carlson's. How could he learn about life in the outside world if he constantly returned to the Priory at every opportunity? Jesse understood the logic but it seemed flawed. EJ had found his calling at Devoe, but Jesse foresaw his destiny long before leaving for college. Still he respected Brother Clement and was determined to do whatever it took to earn his permanent place in the Priory community.

Summer passed quickly. The team added two new members in July and Jesse took responsibility for their training. They learned quickly with Jesse's patient but thorough approach. In addition to training, the team completed seventeen actual search and rescue missions –everything from a lost child in the Cape Cod dunes to rescuing survivors of a light plane crash near the summit of Mount Washington in New Hampshire. The team's reputation put it at the top of the list for most emergency squads and law enforcement units in the region. That summer only enhanced their status as time after time they successfully completed their missions, due in large part to Jesse and Sara. Mr. Carlson retained the title of team leader but, in the field, everyone looked to Jesse and followed his lead. Jesse respectfully deferred to Carlson often but when the job was on the line everyone, including Carlson, turned to Jesse.

In mid-August EJ, acting very mysteriously, invited his father and Jesse to dinner at Rino's, their favorite Italian restaurant in Boston. Clearly, something was up, but EJ refused to talk about it even on the ninety-minute car ride to the restaurant.

When they arrived they found a corner table reserved for them and a bottle of fine Asti Spumante on ice. Rino's was Italian through and through, there was no champagne on the wine list. After they ordered and before the antipasti arrived, EJ lifted his glass and proposed a toast.

"To you, Dad! I know I have not always lived up to your hopes for me but thanks to you I have the gift of living my life, my way. Not everyone can say that and I am grateful for all you have done to make my life possible. I could not have done it without your unwavering, if uncertain at times, support. But here I am: a college graduate and as of September first I will be gainfully employed. You are looking at the newest employee of the Federal Bureau of Investigation, New England Division!"

Carlson could not hide his surprise, "The FBI? I don't understand — I thought they had a minimum age requirement. How?"

"You're right," EJ replied, "they do have a minimum age of twenty-five to be an agent, but they hire specialists based on other criteria. They finally realized that to keep up with hackers, terrorists and other technology savvy malcontents they need younger, more agile minds; minds more likely to think like the bad guys. In other words, they need people like me! Of course it is possible that they hired me to be sure I would not fall in with the wrong crowd and end up on the other side."

EJ smiled a sly grin and took a long slurp of his wine. Carlson and Jesse looked at each other, suppressed a smile and quaffed their own drinks. Over antipasti and their entrees, Carlson and Jesse took turns quizzing EJ about his new career, how it came to be and what might happen next.

When the cannoli arrived the conversation lagged for a few moments and Jesse found his mind wandering to his own future. Next year at Devoe would not be the same without EJ and after such an amazing summer with the SAR team going back to academia held little attraction.

Carlson noticed Jesse's distant look and asked, "What's up, Jesse? Are you OK?"

Jesse nodded, "I'm fine. I'm just trying to imagine EJ in dark glasses wearing a suit and tie."

This was EJ's night – not the time for Jesse to voice his own uncertainty.

"Hey, I'll make those Ray-Bans look cool, again! But no suit and tie for me; I'm thinking jeans and maybe a Hawaiian shirt..."

Jesse laughed, "Right – that will scare the bad guys. Nothing like a computer nerd with no fashion sense to make you worry!"

EJ and Jesse left Carlson's on the same day: EJ for basic FBI training and Jesse to go back to college. As Jesse feared, Devoe without EJ was deadly dull. Jesse missed EJ's brotherly harassment and realized that much of EJ's act had actually been pushing him to be more than the "dog-boy" he had always been. Without EJ there to cajole and shepherd him Jesse quickly slid onto the shadowy fringe of college life. First to go were the social events that EJ had dragged him to; Jesse had never liked what EJ called the "beer and bimbos scene". Beer did not hold the magical power for Jesse that it seemed to hold for most college students and he resented the way women were treated at the frat parties EJ seemed to love. The coeds who attended deserved to be treated better and the townie girls would never have come if they knew how the guys talked about them when they were not around. Jesse was no prude, but he knew what was right and this was not right. Often when he went along with EJ to a party, he ended up being the one to drive home the local girls too drunk for their own good, and although he had regular opportunities – even invitations – to take advantage of their situations, he never did.

EJ insisted Jesse's warped view of the world simply reflected a lingering effect of his years at the Priory, "You will outgrow it, one day," EJ said. "You will wake up and see life as it is and then you will kick yourself, repeatedly, for the years and the opportunities you have wasted with your 'good-guy' routine."

His social life was not the only thing that suffered in EJ's absence. Jesse soon began cutting classes and sloughing off assignments. EJ had pushed him relentlessly to keep up his academics. The irony was that EJ was one of those students given latitude by their professors to work at their own pace and schedule so EJ seldom had a regular class routine himself, but he gave Jesse no such freedom. He always seemed to know where Jesse was and where he was supposed to be and somehow he always knew when a paper or research assignment was coming due. Now, without EJ as his taskmaster everything began to slip. By midterms, Jesse knew his semester was in serious jeopardy; the email scheduling an appointment with his advisor confirmed his fears.

Dr. Shumway did not particularly enjoy advising first and second year students. He found most of them to be incredibly shallow; often interested only in exploiting their new-found freedom living away from home. Others clearly were deluded by images of themselves as yet-undiscovered geniuses of Devoe certain to turn the world on its ear once they emerged from the shadows imposed by the college's arcane insistence on two years of a broad based liberal arts curriculum.

Jesse was different, however. Shumway recognized his maturity far exceeded his years and while he certainly had undiscovered and undeveloped potential, Jesse seemed completely unaware of it. He remained humble, self-effacing and almost naïve in his self-perception. The only exception Shumway had found surrounded his search and rescue work. In that one arena, Jesse's self-confidence was unshakeable. He spoke of his SAR work matter-of-factly, without a trace of bravado, but with an obvious confidence developed over years of experience and accomplishment. Shumway had never encountered anyone as young as Jesse with such rock-solid expertise. If only Jesse could achieve a similar level of accomplishment in the classroom.

"Jesse, I'm sure you know why I scheduled this appointment," Shumway said after the obligatory pleasantries. "I had hoped that after squeaking by in your freshman year that you would hit your stride this semester, but if anything your academics have slipped further. You are not flunking out, yet, but if something doesn't change soon, this semester may be a lost cause."

Jesse shifted in his chair, "Yes, sir. I am trying to do better."

Shumway thought Jesse's words said the right thing but his body language betrayed him; he looked more defeated than ever. In spite of himself, he cared about this young man, but he was at a loss as to what to do with him.

"Jesse, I've noticed that you seem to do better on papers and research assignments but those grades get pulled down by your exam scores. Why do you think that is?"

"I really am trying, Dr. Shumway. I study hours and hours for those exams but when I look at the test questions, they always seem to ask about the things I didn't study or the things I studied but didn't understand."

"But you do so much better on research projects. I've read some of your papers; they are good – not great, but good – and thorough."

"I like the research – it's like solving a puzzle. Thinking about the topic, dissecting the question and then searching for possible solutions – I can do that. My writing could be better, but the problem-solving, the research, I can do."

Shumway smiled, "Jesse that is the first time I have heard you sound the least bit enthused about your studies. Of course, it is the one part of a college education that has something in common with your search and rescue work."

"I hadn't thought about it that way," Jesse answered.

Shumway continued, "Searching out the facts and rescuing the –"

"Maybe we shouldn't go too far with that metaphor, Dr. Shumway," Jesse smiled.

"No, maybe not," Shumway replied. "So what do we do about all of this? Jesse, I want to see you succeed here at Devoe, but I have no idea what more I can do to help you."

"I appreciate your concern, Dr. Shumway, but I don't think it is your problem to fix. If I am going to earn a college degree, then I am going to have to do the work. Whether I make it or not remains to be seen, but either way, I think it's up to me."

Jesse managed to salvage the Fall semester. He pulled his grade point average to just above the cut-line for retaining his scholarship. Over Christmas break at the Priory he did a lot of soul-searching and decided to give college one last try. For the Spring semester he would scale back his SAR work and put his full effort into his classes. Everyone that mattered to him in his life – Brother Clement, Miriam Fossler, Brother Reuben, Mr. Carlson, even EJ – wanted him to graduate. He felt that he owed them, all of them, his best effort.

The Spring semester started poorly and went downhill from there. He failed one midterm exam and barely squeaked by on the others. He begged his professors to let him do papers for extra credit but they refused to make an exception for him.

Jesse cut himself off from everyone on campus, spending hours in the study carrels at the library and barricading himself in his dorm room on the weekends when everyone else partied and socialized. In spite of this, his grades continued in a downward spiral.

As finals approached in May, he knew the situation was hopeless. Even if he aced the final exams, and he had no reason to think he would, his grades would not be good enough to save his scholarship.

Two days before finals week, he stood at Dr. Shumway's door not sure what he was going to say or do.

Dr. Shumway came up behind him and said, "Jesse, did you want to see me?"

"I – uh" Jesse stammered.

"It's OK; come in. Actually, I've been expecting you."

Inside the office, Jesse found his voice, "It's no use, Dr. Shumway. I can't do it. I've tried but I can't do it."

"I know, Jesse. I've heard from most of your professors about how hard you have been working, but your grades are not good enough. Even if you do well on your finals – "

"I know," Jesse said. "It's no use."

"Jesse, I have a suggestion. If you take your finals and end up losing your scholarship it would be very difficult for you to come back and try again in the future. But if you withdraw, now before final exams, I would be willing to put a recommendation in your file that might help if, in the future, you decide to give college another try. I like you Jesse. I don't know if college is for you or not, but I'd like to see you keep the possibility open, just in case."

"What do I have to do, to withdraw?" Jesse asked.

A second question formed in his mind but went unspoken: What do I say to everyone who will be so disappointed in me?

Chapter Twelve

Book of Jesse   May 16, 1994

    I doubt if you will ever really understand how much we miss you. Priory life has an entirely different quality without you here. I realized today that I can't remember the Priory before the day you arrived. I know I loved living here and always felt blessed to share my life with such a caring community, but the day you came life became real. Living with a child, especially one as precocious as you were, has an immediacy that demands life be lived in the moment. The day you left we began drifting, seeking an identity that no longer revolved around watching your amazing life take form.

    Oddly, you are still at the center of most of our community gatherings. Hardly a meal goes by without someone reminiscing about life with Jesse. Any time someone receives news in a letter or a phone call it quickly becomes community property. Your recent notoriety has prompted a number of impromptu displays of newspaper articles, internet printouts and reprinted photographs reminding us that God's gift to us has now become God's gift to people everywhere who are lost, in trouble or in need of help.

We are so proud of you, Jesse. Pride may be a sin, but we rationalize that taking pride in the good life being lived by someone else is a sin easily forgiven. After all, God is good – all the time.

In the quiet of a May evening, Clement sat at his desk thumbing through the pages of Jesse's book. At his right hand sat a stack of newspaper clippings, stories following up on the rescue of Miranda Curtis. Most of Jesse's press clippings were isolated reports of a successful search completed by an unusual young man. However, the Curtis story had been going on for months as the police investigation gradually revealed grisly details about her abductor and his other victims. Invariably, when a photo of Miranda Curtis accompanied the story, the picture chosen was the one of her with her arms wrapped around Jesse's neck as she sobbed into his shoulder. Something about that picture captured the emotions of the moment for the public. A young woman, a victim of unspeakable terror, clinging to the young innocent-looking boy who had saved her somehow redeemed the moment and offered reassurance of the eventual triumph of good over evil. The expression on her face said it all: release, relief, gratitude, a turn away from hopelessness toward the promise of possibility.

Reuben knocked on the doorjamb of the open doorway. "Sorry to interrupt; you seem deep in thought."

Clement smiled, "No, come in Brother Reuben. I was just thinking about our boy, Jesse."

"Funny, that's why I am here. I am heading over to Afton on Thursday to deliver those three guide dog prospects and I was thinking I might detour to see Jesse. I wondered if you would want to come along."

"Thursday?" Clement said pulling out his calendar. "Thursday is good. Thanks for the offer, I would love to go with you. Truthfully, I am a bit worried about Jesse. When we talked last week I could tell something was not right; he seemed distracted and when I asked about school he changed the subject."

Reuben nodded, "I know what you mean. I thought it was me, but lately when I talk with him I get the feeling that school is not going well. I think it's been a tough adjustment for him to be there since EJ Carlson graduated."

"I had a call from his advisor a couple of weeks ago," Clement said. "He couldn't or wouldn't go into details but he made a point of encouraging me to talk to Jesse about his grades. Every time I try to bring it up, though, Jesse doesn't want to talk about it. Maybe if I can talk to him in person, look into his eyes, I can figure out what is going on."

Reuben nodded again, "Well, Thursday may be our chance. Do you think I should tell him we are coming or shall we just drop in?"

"You should tell him you are coming, but don't mention me. If he hears we are both coming, he may assume that something is wrong."

Clement picked up the stack of newspaper clippings, "Have you been following the Miranda Curtis story?"

"It gets stranger and stranger with each article. How many victims are they up to now?"

"He's been charged with four but they make it sound like what they are certain of is only the tip of the iceberg," Clement replied. "This guy, Malcolm Yeats, is from Cabot Mountain. Wasn't that your old stomping grounds?"

"I came from Lambeau Valley, just down the road from Cabot Mountain."

"Close enough; did you ever come in contact with Yeats?"

"I don't think so," Reuben said and then quickly added, "So, Thursday morning is good then – maybe leave here about 7:30?"

Clement looked at Reuben intently, then said, "7:30 it is."

Thursday dawned with a light spring rain, but by the time Reuben and Clement reached the Massachusetts Turnpike the rain had given way to brilliant sunshine. The two men, comfortable in one another's company, kept up a steady stream of conversation to pass the time. They arrived on the Devoe campus in time to take Jesse to a late lunch, as planned.

They found Jesse in his dorm room packing the last of his things in a duffel bag that had seen better days. He looked up and smiled at Reuben when he walked into the room, but his smile faded when Clement followed Reuben in.

"Brother Clement – I didn't know you were coming, too."

Clement smiled at him, "When Reuben told me he was coming over, I invited myself to come along. I hope that's OK with you..."

"Sure. It's good to see you both."

"Getting an early start on packing? I thought finals didn't start until next week," Clement said trying not to sound too parental.

"Uh, yeah, finals are next week," Jesse said and then turned away.

Reuben saw the expression on Jesse's face and knew something was wrong. He mumbled a few words about going to the men's room down the hall and left Clement and Jesse alone, closing the door as he left.

Clement sat on the edge of the desk and waited for Jesse to speak. After a few moments of awkward silence as Jesse sealed up the last box, the boy turned to face Clement.

"Did Dr. Shumway call you?" Jesse asked.

"No. I haven't spoken to him in weeks."

Jesse turned away from Clement, his head down, "I've decided to withdraw from school; I'm not going to finish the semester. I'm sorry, Brother Clement. I know how much you and the others wanted me to go to college but I can't do it. I've tried and tried but I can't do it."

"I don't know what to say, Jesse. I had a feeling you were struggling this year, but I never guessed you would decide to leave school, especially this late in the year."

"It's been coming for a while. My midterm grades were borderline and no matter what I did, I haven't been able to get them up." Jesse's voice was controlled but emotional.

"It seems a shame to give up a whole semester's work. If you took your finals, maybe you could salvage, at least some credits."

"That won't help. Even if I earn some credits I will lose my scholarship and that will be the end of college anyway. Dr. Shumway suggested I withdraw and take a leave of absence. If I come back in the next twelve months, I should be able to hold on to my standing and my scholarship."

Clement nodded his head slowly, "You have thought this through, haven't you?"

"I'm sorry to disappoint you, Brother Clement. I know how important this is to you, but I think this is my only option."

Clement rose and walked over to where Jesse stood by the window. He put his arm around the boy's shoulders and the two of them stood together silently for a long moment.

Clement spoke softly and slowly, "Jesse, I could never be disappointed in you. Whatever you do in life, wherever you go, whatever you decide I will always be as proud of you as the proudest father could ever be of his own son. Maybe if you were my actual son you would know that to be true, but trust me Jesse I could not love you more if you were my own flesh and blood.

College was an important time in my life and I wanted you to have that experience, too. But you are your own person, your own man; maybe college is not right for you, or maybe this is just not the right time for you to be here. I don't know, but I trust that you do."

Reuben tapped lightly at the door.

"Reuben, come on in," Clement called. "Jesse has some news to share."

After Jesse told Reuben about his decision, they went into town for lunch at Jesse's favorite burger joint. The conversation remained light until it was time to go.

Reuben asked, "Jesse, what do you plan to do now? Are you going to stay here or maybe come back to New York?"

Jesse shrugged his shoulders, "I don't know for sure. Right now, I plan to stay here, maybe at Carlson's if it is OK with him. I have a busy schedule with the SAR team over the summer. We drill almost every weekend in June and July and Mr. Carlson has three new dogs that he wants me to help train. I also have four weekend workshops scheduled for teams in Maine and Connecticut, so I can stay busy for the next few months."

"Sounds like a hectic summer," Clement said. "Do you need money, Jesse? I mean without your college stipend. We could – "

"No, thank you Brother Clement. I'll be fine. Mr. Carlson pays me well for training and the workshops offer honorariums. If I can stay at Carlson's and pick up an occasional side job smoothing over problems for other handlers, I'll be fine."

"Just the same, I'd feel better if you would let us help," Clement said. "It won't be much but every little bit…"

Jesse knew better than to argue.

Clement and Reuben were on the way back to the Priory before the Boston rush hour traffic reached the Turnpike. They passed the first hour on the road without speaking, both men seemingly deep in thought. Finally, Clement broke the silence.

"Jesse is something else, isn't he?"

Reuben nodded agreement, "He always impresses me."

Clement said, "He is so mature for his age. I have to think that most college students would have a much harder time wrestling with a decision like this, but not Jesse. He thought it through, assessed his options and made his choice. The only part that seemed to trouble him was how to tell us about it. Sometimes I think he is a little too self-reliant, but I have to admire him."

Reuben nodded but said nothing. The two men travelled on another hour until, this time, Reuben broke the silence.

"Brother Clement, I wasn't completely honest with you the other day."

Clement turned toward him, "When I asked about Malcolm Yeats." It was more a statement than a question.

"You knew," Reuben said without real surprise in his voice.

"Reuben we've known each other a long time. I sensed there was more to the story, but trusted that if it was important you would get around to telling me in due time."

"What I said was partially true. I never did meet Yeats but I knew his niece and she spoke about him some; never anything good."

"When was this?"

"Julie and I went to school together. She was two years younger than me but we dated a couple of times in high school. After graduation I enlisted in the Army and I didn't see her again for several years."

"I didn't know you were a veteran," Clement said.

"I'm not, really. I washed out in boot camp; I blew-out a knee that I had injured rock-climbing as a teenager, and I couldn't complete the physical training. So I ended up back in Lambeau Valley running heavy equipment for my father's construction company. When I came back to town I heard that Julie's parents had divorced and she and her mother were gone."

"But you saw her again…"

"Her mother got sick, breast cancer, and she and Julie came back to Lambeau Valley to live with Julie's grandmother. We met again, one night at the bowling alley, and we picked up where we left-off in high school. She was different; older of course, and sadder than I remembered, but still one of the sweetest people I've ever known. We fell in love, but her mother was dying so we kept it our secret; we didn't tell anyone.

When her mother passed away, Julie's uncle – Yeats – seemed to take over everything. He already had legal responsibility for her grandmother and the family property and he began treating Julie like she was his property too. She was afraid of him. She would never tell me exactly what he did to make her feel that way, but he treated her like a servant. He made her take care of her grandmother's house and his house too; cooking, cleaning, and doing laundry. Everything. We would sneak off whenever we could, but she was always worrying that he would find out about us.

I saved every penny I could get my hands on so we could run away together. It took time, but I finally had about fifteen hundred dollars. I didn't think it was enough, but Julie said we couldn't wait any longer so we decided to make our break. We planned to meet at the Stewart's shop by the highway on a Friday night, but she never showed up. I waited until they closed, but she never came. I tried to call her the next day and then the next, but got no answer. Finally, I made up some excuse to go to her grandmother's house but when I got there they were gone. The front door was unlocked, the house was empty – no furniture, nothing. And there was a for sale sign on the front lawn. When I drove by Yeats' house it was the same story.

I went to the Sheriff's office but there was nothing they could do. For almost a year I searched every lead I could think of; I even pretended I wanted to buy the house hoping the real estate agent might know something. I finally found Julie's grandmother in a nursing home down in Glens Falls, but she had Alzheimer's and wasn't able to tell me anything. I never saw Julie again."

"Was that when you came to the Priory?" Clement asked.

"I had nowhere else to go and no idea what to do with my life. I was heartbroken. I don't know what might have happened if I had not found the Priory."

"Thanks for telling me the whole story. You may never know what happened to Julie but at least you know Yeats will be locked away for good. Who knows – if she is out there somewhere maybe she will feel it's safe to come home once he is put away for good."

"I thought about that, too," Reuben said. "But I have this sickening feeling inside that Julie may have been one of his victims. I guess I will never know..."

Into the World

So I packed all my belongings

And set out on the road

Now I'm bent and nearly broken

From carrying that load

Chapter Thirteen

Jesse's summer passed in a flurry of activity. Hardly a week went by without the SAR team being activated. Jesse led most of the team's responses and, on the couple that he did not lead, he assumed responsibility for the team debrief. When he was not actively working a response, he worked with the new dogs, both training them and evaluating their abilities and temperaments. Some things can be taught but each dog comes with innate abilities and predispositions. If a dog has what it takes, the right training makes all the difference in the world. If a dog doesn't have "the gift" then training alone will not be enough. Carlson had an eye for picking gifted dogs and these three were no exception. Each day with Jesse they showed steady progress. Still it would be months, maybe more than a year, before they would be able to be trusted on an actual search.

The third weekend of August, Jesse finished the final workshop on the summer schedule; this one in Camden, Maine. Like most workshops, the handlers had come with hopes that after spending a weekend with Jesse and Sara some of their star quality would rub-off on them and their dogs. And, like most workshops, they left better for the experience but knowing Jesse and Sara were in a league of their own.

Driving back from Camden, Jesse had almost arrived at Carlson's when his mobile phone rang. Jesse pulled off the road into a convenience store parking lot and checked his voicemail. He had four messages – all from EJ Carlson. He listened to the most recent one.

"Jesse! Where are you, man? Please call me as soon as you get this message; it is urgent."

Jesse dialed the call back number and heard EJ pick up on the first ring.

"Jesse – where have you been? I've been calling for the last three hours!"

"Sorry, EJ, I'm just getting back from a workshop in Camden. I must have been out of range for a while. What's going on? What is so urgent?"

"Jesse, we need your help. I'm in the field working a big case and we are desperate. The case is hush-hush; we have managed to keep it out of the press. I can't talk about it now, but I'll fill you in when you get here. You will come, right?"

"Slow down, EJ. We just finished a long weekend workshop and Sara and I need some rest. I'd like to help, but how can I agree to help without knowing what you want me to do, or even where you want me to go?"

"Jesse, the life of a nine-year old boy is in danger. We need you and Sara to help us find him. I'll fill you in on all the details when you get here, but we are desperate. The boy has serious health problems and if we don't find him in the next thirty-six hours it may be too late."

"I assume 'we' is the FBI?" Jesse said.

"Yes, of course. I told my boss you are the best. Please, Jesse, you have to come."

"OK. It's almost eight o'clock. Tell me where to go and we will drive up first thing in the morning."

"No can do; you can't drive here. How soon can you get to Marbury Air Field?"

"Marbury Air Field? I can be there in twenty minutes, but – "

"No time for buts, Jesse. Get to the airport; a private jet will meet you there within the hour. The control tower will be watching for you. I promise I will explain everything when you get here."

Jesse had not flown before – ever – and he had seen private jets only in the movies. Minutes after arriving at Marbury, he watched a nine-passenger Hawker 850 touch down and taxi to within twenty yards of where he and Sara stood. The plane rolled to a stop and with the engines still idling, the door opened and a thirty-something African-American woman motioned to Jesse to come toward the plane. By the time he and Sara reached her, she had lowered a small set of steps for them to climb up. Moments later they were airborne.

The woman introduced herself as FBI Special Agent Delores Greenway but would not discuss anything about the case with Jesse beyond their destination.

"Nantucket Island, Massachusetts," she said. "About thirty miles off-shore; just a hop-skip and a jump in this sweet little number."

Nantucket Island, Jesse thought; well that explained why EJ said he could not drive there. It also explained how the FBI had managed to keep whatever was going on from becoming a news story. Jesse reclined his seat, Sara curled up on the seat next to him and both of them closed their eyes.

When they landed on the island, Agent Greenway led them to a van parked on the tarmac near the hangar where the plane had come to a stop. On the side of the van an outline of a whale spouted the words "Whaler's Inn" from its blowhole. The driver of the van looked to Jesse more like an FBI agent than a courtesy van driver, but he decided not to ask. The van drove through the darkness until it pulled into a small parking lot wedged between two buildings, neither one of which was identified as the Whaler's Inn. In the ground floor window of the smaller of the two buildings, Jesse spotted the unmistakable profile of EJ Carlson.

"Jesse – thanks for coming," EJ said as they embraced. "Your room is at the top of the stairs. Why don't you get Sara settled and then I will fill you in."

A few minutes later EJ led Jesse down the street to a landmark Nantucket tavern called Brother Love's. They took a corner table in the far back, away from the handful of customers still lingering near the bar. The kitchen was closed but their waitress managed to gather some bar snacks to go with their beers.

EJ leaned toward Jesse and spoke softly. "The boy's name is Andrew – Andy – Griffis. He was kidnapped four days ago from his family's summer home here on Nantucket."

"Andrew Griffis," Jesse said. "Why do I know that name?"

"It's the same as his father. Andrew Griffis, Sr. is the CEO of the Griffis Group, a high-tech company working on cutting edge electronics including some with Defense Department applications in smart-bombs and cruise missiles. That was his corporate jet that brought you here."

Jesse nodded, "I knew that name rang a bell. They were big supporters of Devoe College, right? Scholarships, labs named after them, the whole works?"

"Right," EJ said. "That's how I ended up here, in the field. I'm supposed to be chained to a computer somewhere but when this case broke they saw that I was a Griffis scholar at Devoe and dragged me in. Besides, the kidnapper wanted more than money; he was after classified research. It's not clear what he planned to do with the research but he had an axe to grind about innocent lives lost to smart weapons that really weren't so smart."

Jesse said, "So, how do you know this guy is still on the island? Maybe he and the boy are long gone."

"No, he's still here alright; we know that and we are pretty sure the boy never left the island either."

"How do you know? I mean, how can you be so sure?"

"We know because he's dead," EJ said in a voice barely above a whisper. "We set a trap for him yesterday. Unfortunately, when we cornered him he put a gun to his head and pulled the trigger. The guy was a fanatic – he was on some kind of personal vendetta. We are still putting the pieces together about him, but the most important thing now is to find the boy. We are convinced the guy acted alone so wherever he stashed the kid, chances are he is on his own. The boy has diabetes and without his meds and a normal diet he won't last long."

"So, why me? The locals must have a search and rescue team, and surely the FBI has their own resources."

"They do and they are all here, but they have come up empty so far. I told my boss, if I was lost you were the only one I would want trying to find me. He recognized your name from the Miranda Curtis story and gave me the green light to bring you in.

We want you to do what you do, on your own. I'll give you everything the others have worked up but you can freelance. You will report only to me or Agent Greenway. But it's got to happen fast. The boy has been gone four days and as far as we know he has not had any medication."

"OK. I'll need a map of the island and copies of the search grids they have been using as well as any information you have developed to help narrow the search. I know the island is not very big, but we don't have time to do a thorough systematic search. We have to narrow the field somehow."

EJ nodded, "I began gathering materials as soon as I got permission to contact you. There will be a box in your room when you get back tonight. Agent Greenway and I will be ready when you are tomorrow morning."

Jesse was up before dawn. After a quick shower he plowed through the case materials taping maps and grids to the walls and laying out papers and photographs on every flat surface in the room. Nantucket Island is only forty-five square miles and much of it is uninhabited. Still, searching the entire island would take much too long. So far, the search had concentrated in Siasconset at the eastern tip of the island since that was where the suspect, Scott Haffler, had taken his own life.

Jesse studied the file photos of Haffler. He looked like any other young professional you might meet on the street. Wavy brown hair, glasses and a kind smile. Apparently he was unmarried, not politically active and well educated with graduate degrees in anthropology and American history. He had come to Nantucket four years earlier to do research for his PhD thesis.

Jesse shook his head, "Not your typical kidnapper, Sara. What was he up to, and why is that name familiar? Scott Haffler – I know that name from somewhere…"

With Agent Greenway acting as their designated driver, Jesse, Sara and EJ headed toward Siasconset. Jesse spotted a bakery on the way and made EJ buy every fresh donut in the shop, hoping to break the ice with the search team.

The search command center was operating out of the Siasconset Volunteer Fire Department. Jesse left Sara in the van and strolled nonchalantly over to a group gathered around the search grid on the wall. By the time they were on their second donut, Jesse knew most of what they knew; so far, their search had turned up nothing. They had tried to track Haffler's movements but had found nothing beyond his car and the place where he died. They had also come up empty in searching for the boy. The door-to-door canvass had covered every building in town, with no leads and without any sign of a hit from the dogs. They planned to continue to work the grid, but the prospects were not good.

When they were back in the van Jesse said, "We have to find some way to narrow the search grid. They haven't found anything here yet. I doubt that we'll find the boy in Siasconset."

EJ said, "We went through Haffler's studio apartment but came up empty. Apparently, he lived a Spartan existence. Other than his books and copious rock samples, each meticulously identified and labeled, he had few personal possessions.

"How did Haffler pay the bills?" Jesse asked. "I don't imagine his research brought in much income and living on the island must be expensive."

Agent Greenway answered, "Nantucket is pricey during the tourist season but the rest of the year it's not so bad. Haffler had a small stipend related to his research and that paid the rent in the off-season. In the summer months, like most of the locals, he catered to the tourist trade. He tended bar and waited tables. Last year he tried offering guided tours of the island, but apparently that didn't work out."

"So, he knows the island well," Jesse said. "If this kidnapping was not a spur of the moment act, then he could have used his local knowledge to uncover a secure place that he knew would be hard to find."

Greenway said, "It doesn't look like this was an impulsive act. Haffler seems like the kind who thought everything through. I would guess that he has been planning this for some time and picked his spot carefully."

Jesse turned to EJ, "Why is his name familiar? I know I've heard that name or seen it somewhere recently. Is it familiar to you?"

EJ shook his head, "Not that I can recall. He had no police record and lived a pretty obscure existence. We've been scouring the internet and all of the usual sources but not finding much at all."

"I know I've seen that name," Jesse said. "I can almost picture it in my mind, but I can't place where."

"So, where do we start?" EJ asked.

"If there is nothing in Haffler's file to help narrow the grid, then we have to do some guesswork. Who is our best local contact; someone who knows the island and might be able to give us some insight?"

Greenway answered, "The local PD assigned a retired Chief as the FBI liaison. He is getting up there in years, but he's a lifelong island resident."

"Can we talk to him right now? I want to get Sara on the job as soon as possible," Jesse said.

Claude Walls sat behind the duty desk in the Police Station, "Everyone else is working the case so they asked me to hold down the fort. I figured I may as well do something useful since the FBI don't seem to need no liaising."

EJ and Greenway flinched but refused to take the bait.

Jesse stepped in front of them and extended his hand, "Chief, I'm Jesse Tobias and I need your help."

"Not Chief no more," Walls said shaking his hand.

"My daddy said, 'Once a Chief, always a Chief,'" Jesse replied ignoring the quizzical look EJ shot in his direction.

"Your daddy in law enforcement?" Walls asked.

"Not exactly, but he taught me to respect those who are."

"So what is it you want, young fella?"

"Chief, the search out at Siasconset is not turning up much and I'm thinking maybe they are looking in the wrong place. We don't have time to search the whole island, so I'm hoping someone who really knows the island can help us make an intelligent guess about where else someone might stash a kidnapped boy. I'm hoping you are my man."

Walls looked at Jesse long and hard showing no reaction to his request. Jesse held his gaze determined not to be the first to blink.

Finally, Walls broke the silence, "I tried to tell them Siasconset was a long shot. Just because he agreed to meet them there doesn't mean he had the boy nearby. In fact, I would guess just the opposite; that he would meet them as far away from the boy as possible."

Jesse nodded agreement, "Your instincts make sense to me. Tell me, where would you look? In the past, where have criminals with something to hide – drugs, guns, bodies – where have they ended up?"

"Nantucket doesn't have much of a history with 'drugs, guns and bodies'; more likely stolen property. Most criminals who know the island try to avoid both the high traffic tourist areas and the well-to-do residential neighborhoods; too many prying eyes and security cameras. Guinea Hill often appeals and that's not being racist just because that area has traditionally been a black neighborhood," Walls said with a sideways glance at Greenway. "A few years back, we had a burglary ring – all white guys – that hid their stash in a house up on Angola Street. Turned out the house had a secret cellar from the old days of the Underground Railroad."

Jesse's eyes lit up, "The Underground Railroad – "

EJ jumped in, "Yeah, Jesse – Nantucket was a key stopping off point."

Jesse suddenly remembered where he had seen Haffler's name; he could picture it in his mind's eye.

"That's it!" he said. "That's where I saw Haffler's name! At Brother Love's! On the back of the menu it said something about their building being a part of the Underground Railroad and there was a quote from Scott Haffler!"

Agent Greenway added, "Haffler's PhD dissertation is on the Underground Railroad in the Northeast."

Twenty minutes later, Jesse and Sara were standing at the corner of Angola Street and Mill Street. Jesse took a plastic baggie from his jacket pocket and opened it. Inside was a boy's dirty T-shirt provided by Andy Griffis' father.

Jesse held the shirt near Sara's snout, "Find more, Sara. Find more," he said as he unclipped her lead.

Sara was all business. She stood unmoving with her nose in the air, her nostrils flaring almost imperceptibly. Time seemed to stand still as she scanned the early morning breeze. After what seemed an eternity to Jesse and the others who stood nearby, her ears pricked forward ever so slightly. No one else would have noticed it, but Jesse did. She had picked up a scent.

With Jesse following close behind, Sara began to move up Angola Street slowly but steadily using her familiar zig-zag pattern. She stopped twice to chew on whatever floated on the morning air. Toward the end of the street she stopped in the middle of the road and turned to look at Jesse. It was a look he had seen hundreds of times before in training and on live searches: she had the scent.

Jesse nodded his head in her direction and said confidently, "Go."

Sara bounded off at a trot toward an older gray-shingled two-story house on the North side of the street. Jesse looked over his shoulder and waved to the black SUV parked back at the corner of Mill Street. Then he followed after Sara and catching-up with her when she stopped and sat motionless at the bottom of the steps leading up to the front door of the house.

The SUV pulled up into the driveway and Agent Greenway, EJ, Chief Walls and two FBI agents got out. In a moment they were standing with Jesse on the sidewalk.

Jesse said, "Sara thinks this is the place but the front door is padlocked and there's a foreclosure notice on the door. Now what do we do?"

Greenway said, "It will take a while to get a warrant. We can't go in without permission."

"But if Andy is in there he could be in bad shape," Jesse pleaded.

Chief Walls said, "Give me a minute; I've got this."

He pulled a cell phone from his pocket and dialed a number from memory.

"Barry this is Claude Walls. Your bank has a house on Angola Street. I just wanted you to know that we are going to kick-in the door. We think the missing Griffis boy is inside." Then without waiting for a reply he said, "Thanks for your help."

A moment later they were inside moving single file with the agents holding drawn weapons. The house was empty. They moved slowly through the front rooms toward the kitchen in the rear of the house following Sara until she stopped and sat motionless, again, this time in front of an interior door that apparently led to the cellar.

Greenway motioned to the others pointing out a garbage bag overflowing with take-out containers and empty water bottles.

"We're pretty sure this guy was working alone," she whispered, "but be careful."

With practiced movements, the agents opened the door and shone their flashlights down the stairs toward the basement.

They motioned for Jesse and Sara to wait in the kitchen and then moved down the stairs into the darkness.

Moments later the lights switched on and Agent Greenway called to Jesse to come downstairs. The basement was dark and musty; and it was empty.

"I thought this was it," Greenway said.

"Sara indicated," Jesse replied. "If he's not here now, he was and my guess is not long ago."

Greenway said to the others, "OK, let's search the rest of the house just to be sure and let's go through that garbage bag to see if it tells us anything."

"Chief Walls," Jesse called out. "Would you come down here, please?" When the old man came downstairs Jesse asked him, "You mentioned a burglary ring that used one of the houses on this street. You said, they had found a secret cellar from the days of the Underground Railroad; do you remember how they found that cellar?"

"You're thinking there could be a secret cellar in this house," Walls said. It was more a statement than a question.

Greenway interjected, "That's a nice idea, Jesse, but this house was built long after the Underground Railroad."

Walls answered, "You're right about the house, agent, but houses in this neighborhood were often built reusing old foundations. The hidden cellar they found was like an old-fashioned root cellar extending out from the foundation."

"OK, spread out," Greenway said, "Let's cover every inch of these basement walls."

"Agent Greenway, start over here," Jesse said pointing to a side wall where Sara sat motionless once again, indicating she scented something.

Greenway came over to them, feeling her way along the foundation. When she reached an old fuse box on the wall she opened the cover. Inside the box, in place of fuses, she found a lever. One pull on the lever and a four-foot section of the foundation swung open on a hidden hinge. The opening revealed a shallow, dirt floored chamber ventilated by a small exhaust fan humming quietly and lit by the pale glow of a single dim light bulb. Andy Griffis lay against the wall, unconscious, on a deflated air mattress.

"I've got him!" Greenway called out. "I've got Andy! Get the paramedics, down here NOW!"

Jesse and EJ watched the paramedics load Andy Griffis into the waiting ambulance. The boy was still out of it but he was moving around and trying to speak so they were hopeful about his recovery.

EJ said, "You two are amazing, Jesse. That little boy is alive because of you."

Jesse smiled, "I'll feel better when I know he checks out at the hospital."

Chief Walls strolled over to join them, "Nice work, young fella. I've seen search dogs work before but that one is special."

"You broke the case for us, Chief," Jesse said. "If you didn't point us in the right direction we could still be looking in the wrong places."

"Well, I appreciate that, but everybody knows who the real hero is today. You will always be welcome here on the island." Walls nodded at them and walked away.

EJ looked at Jesse, "OK, just one thing. What was all that stuff before about 'your daddy' and 'once a chief always a chief'?"

Jesse laughed, "Just building a little witness rapport. Isn't that what you law enforcement types call it?"

"So you played the old man?"

"No, I meant what I said. I just didn't have time to explain my lack of family history so I put it in terms I thought he would relate to. And, by the way, that 'old man' really did break open the case for us."

Jesse and EJ were invited to a late lunch with Agent Greenway and EJ's boss, Special Agent in Charge Calvin Granich. After five days of non-stop intensity everyone appreciated a chance to unwind a bit.

After lunch, Granich took Jesse aside, "I really am very grateful, Jesse. When Haffler died I was afraid this case would not have a happy ending. I must admit when I approved EJ's suggestion to have you join the search I was pretty much grasping at straws. He said you were the best, but I have never had much luck with search dogs, so I was dubious. Clearly, EJ knew what he was talking about."

Jesse said, "Thank you, sir, I'm glad we could help. We aren't always successful but if there is any chance at all I would put my money on Sara, every time."

"I hope you can stay around for the press conference at five o'clock. Mr. and Mrs. Griffis, Andy's parents, have asked to meet you."

"We'll be there," Jesse answered.

The Press Conference was lightly attended but the story was picked-up off the wire services by most of the national media. Stock footage shot by one of the Boston stations made the nightly news on all of the major networks. Granich managed to explain away the lack of prior press coverage as a blackout necessary to maintain the integrity of the investigation. The press did not like being shut out of a story, but it was more palatable this time because of the good outcome. If things had gone differently Granich knew there would have been hell to pay.

When the reporters left to meet their evening news deadlines, SAC Granich took Jesse and Sara to meet Mr. and Mrs. Griffis.

After handshakes and hugs, Mr. Griffis said, "I've never felt as helpless as I did over the last five days. I'm used to being in charge and, for the most part, getting what I want. When Andy disappeared suddenly all of that changed; nothing I could say or do, no amount of money or influence I could bring to bear could get my son – our son – back.

Jesse, we owe you more than we can ever repay. There is a reward, $100,000, but that is not nearly enough to thank you for what you have done for us."

Jesse shook his head, "Thank you, Mr. Griffis, but I can't accept the reward. There was a whole team out there looking for Andy. It would not be right for any one of us to be singled out. I appreciate your kindness and I hope you aren't offended, but I just can't take it."

Griffis took him by the elbow and led him away from the others, "Jesse, you are a young man just starting out in life. Let me help you. There must be some things you could use that money for; things that would help you on your way."

"Yes, sir, but that's not the point. It's not about whether or not I could use the money; I'd be lying if I said that kind of money wouldn't change my life. It's just a matter of right and wrong."

"I guess I'm just not used to integrity like that; I don't often find it in the business world," Griffis said shaking his head.

Then handing Jesse his business card he said, "I will find some way to thank you, Jesse, but for the moment let it suffice to say that if you ever need anything – ANYTHING – you call my direct number and you will have what you need no matter what it is. You have my word and my undying gratitude."

Chapter Fourteen

After Labor Day, when the college students went back to school, Jesse concentrated on building his training clientele. Using some of Carlson's breeder contacts he soon found himself busier than he expected. Since most of his work involved trouble-shooting, redoing training done improperly the first time or remedial work with a non-responsive dog, each case was unique. The good news of that fact was that Jesse's interest never lagged; he was always facing a new challenge and devising new solutions to unfamiliar problems. The bad news was that such unpredictable situations presented scheduling difficulties that forced Jesse into awkward and often demanding time constraints. Taking on a new client without knowing what exactly would be required also meant not knowing how long it might take and therefore when he might get to his next client. Still, Jesse was young and gifted and never one to shy away from hard work and long hours.

Carlson worried about him, "Jesse, you're working too hard. At your age you are supposed to be enjoying life, not working all the time. You need to get out more. What happened with that nice girl, what was her name, Lorelei?"

"Lorelle; her name is Lorelle and we still see each other at times, but just as friends."

"What happened? I thought you two were good together."

"So did I," Jesse said, "but she said she always felt like the dogs came first and she didn't like being 'one of the pack'. There will be time for relationships but right now personal things have to wait; at least until I figure out a few things like how I'm going to support myself and a family when the time comes. I love what I am doing but I don't know that I can make a living at it."

Then, in late October, a registered letter arrived by FedEx. The letter, on embossed stationery from Archer Blake Financial Services was brief and businesslike:

We have made repeated efforts to contact you, without success. It is imperative we speak with you, in person, about a pressing financial matter. Please call the number below at your earliest convenience.

Jesse showed the letter to Carlson, "What do you think it might be?"

"I have no idea, Jesse. Did you know they were trying to reach you?"

"I'm not sure," Jesse said. "I remember a couple of voice mails from a financial services company. They sounded like salesmen so I ignored them; I mean, I don't need any financial services – I barely have any finances."

"Well," Carlson said, "there's only one way to find out. Call them and see what they say."

Jesse called the next morning and spoke with a nice, but rather evasive young woman who insisted he needed to make an appointment to see Mr. Archer. She said Jesse could come to their office in Newton Centre or Mr. Archer would come to Jesse's home. Jesse decided against the home visit and made an appointment to see Archer the following week.

Archer Blake occupied an entire floor in a low-rise office building in Newton Centre, not far from downtown Boston. Jesse felt intimidated by the formal surroundings. All he could think of was "old money" as he looked around at the antiques and art work that accented the office furnishings. Even the people who worked there exuded that old "Boston Brahmin" essence: expensive business suits, silk ties for the men and fashionable scarves for the women and not one hair out of place on any of them. Jesse had dressed up more than usual for his appointment, but even the messengers that popped in and out of the reception area were better dressed than him.

To Jesse's surprise, Ronald Archer, turned out to be a regular guy; well-dressed, yes, but friendly and very easy to talk to.

"Jesse, thank you for coming in. I'm sorry it has taken us so long to get together; you are a hard young man to catch up with."

Jesse said, "I'm sorry about that, Mr. Archer, but I really don't need any financial services, so this may all be a waste of your time."

Archer smiled, "Let me explain why I needed to see you and I think you may be pleasantly surprised to discover a need you didn't know you had."

Without waiting for Jesse to respond Archer continued, "Jesse – may I call you Jesse?" Jesse nodded, "Jesse, Archer Blake is one of Boston's oldest financial services firms. Because of our long-standing success with some very wealthy clients, we are able to provide 'pro-bono' – free – services to a number of charitable organizations. It is our way of giving back to a community that has been very good to us over several generations. My great-grandfather founded this firm and established our charitable services right from the beginning.

Anyway, to the point of this meeting. One of the charities we represent has received a very generous donation in the form of a charitable gift annuity. Are you familiar with CGAs?"

Jesse shook his head, "No, not at all."

Archer continued, "In simple terms, a donor contributes an amount of money to a charity with the understanding that the income earned by that money will be paid to the donor or the donor's designee for a specified period of time or until the recipient dies. It is a win-win situation for all parties. The charity receives a donation, the donor reaps certain tax advantages and the recipient benefits from the proceeds earned by the gift. When the term is up or the recipient dies then there are no further strings on the gift for the charitable organization."

Jesse nodded, "I think I understand, but I still do not see what this has to do with me."

"Jesse, you were named as the donor's designee to receive the income from this gift. Under the terms of the donation you will receive the income from the annuity for the full term of your life. On your death, the income and the principal will revert to the charity.

What we need to do today is the boring part: filling out forms, mostly for tax purposes since the income you will receive will be reported as taxable income. Then we can discuss how you would like to be paid."

Jesse didn't answer right away, then said, "I have no idea what this is all about. Who is the donor?"

"I'm sorry, Jesse, that is confidential. The donor made the gift anonymously and the charity as well as Archer Blake are bound by law to respect that anonymity."

Jesse looked at Ronald Archer, "Is this legal? I mean, should I have a lawyer?"

Archer laughed, "I can assure you this is all legal and not terribly unusual. We probably process a couple of hundred CGAs each year, although very few are this significant. Certainly, if you would like your attorney to review the paperwork that would be fine. If you don't have an attorney I can recommend several who specialize in this area. Of course, that will delay your first payment. We have been holding the check now for several weeks while we tried to reach you, so I suppose a while longer won't matter. By the way, the donor also stipulated that Archer Blake waive our usual fees if you would like to take advantage of our financial services to help you invest your income. Of course, that is strictly your choice. Perhaps you already have someone to handle your portfolio?"

Now Jesse laughed, "No. The only portfolio I have is the one where I keep copies of my résumé." He hesitated a moment then asked, "How much money are we talking about?"

"Your income will fluctuate some, depending on the income earned by the corpus of the annuity, but at today's rates I would think you could expect income of about ten thousand dollars."

"Ten thousand dollars? A year – for life?" Jesse said.

Archer nodded, "For life, yes. But not ten thousand each year; ten thousand each month, of course that could go up or down depending on the rate of return on the investments."

Jesse was dumbstruck. He could not imagine ten thousand dollars a month just magically appearing. He worked so hard for the money he earned now, and it took him months to earn ten thousand dollars.

The rest of the meeting was lost in a haze. Jesse signed a lot of papers, listened patiently but without really hearing as Archer outlined some possible ways to invest his newfound wealth, and in the end accepted a check for just over seventeen thousand dollars representing the first two months' income, less withholding taxes.

On the way back to Carlson's he stopped at his bank and deposited the check, half-expecting it to be denied by the teller. When it was safely deposited, he stopped at the ATM and withdrew a hundred dollars, to double check the balance on his account. Sure enough, the new balance was a lot larger than he was used to. He made one more stop on the way home to pick up a couple of rib-eye steaks for dinner. He knew they should celebrate but he still felt a bit uneasy about the whole matter, so he decided not to go hog-wild.

After dinner that evening, Jesse called Brother Clement to tell him the news. "Have you ever heard of such a thing?"

"Actually, I have Jesse," Clement answered. "A few years ago we were approached by a donor who proposed a similar kind of donation to the Priory. Remember when we were trying to rebuild our capital fund after spending all that money to update the well and septic system? This donor gave us a very generous gift with the provision that his elderly mother would receive the interest it earned until she died. We had an attorney look it over and set it up for us."

"So, it's OK then," Jesse said with some relief in his voice.

"It's perfectly legal, Jesse, but," Clement hesitated.

"But what?" Jesse asked.

"Well, to pay out ten thousand dollars a month in income earned, the amount of the gift must have been enormous – more than a million dollars I would guess. So that makes me ask two questions: Who do you know that would have that kind of money to give away and why would they choose to give it in an annuity just to help you?"

For days after they talked, Jesse could think of little else than Brother Clement's questions. Who indeed. The only name that he could come up with was Andrew Griffis, but such an act of generosity seemed a stretch even for someone as wealthy as Griffis. He tried to get Mr. Archer to confirm his suspicions, but either Archer was a convincing liar or he really did not know the donor's identity. Jesse thought about asking EJ's help with the mystery, but did not know how to broach the matter.

Jesse had planned to spend Thanksgiving at the Priory, but when Mr. Carlson told him EJ was coming home for the holiday, Jesse decided to stay. Brother Clement would understand.

EJ arrived the day before Thanksgiving. Jesse wanted to talk with him right away, but he yielded the first day to some catch-up father-son time for Mr. Carlson and EJ. Thanksgiving Day slipped past filled with food, football and the arrival of several other relatives for dinner.

Friday, Jesse invited EJ to supper at the local pub where EJ had been a regular when living at home. On their second pint of Guinness, the conversation turned in the direction Jesse had hoped.

"I have to tell you, Jesse, you made a big impression on SAC Granich," EJ said. "Ever since we got back from Nantucket he has been telling everyone who will listen about this amazing SAR team that broke the case open. I wouldn't be surprised if you get requests from other FBI field offices."

"Hopefully, some of his good feelings about us rub off on you," Jesse said. "After all, we would never have been there without your recommendation."

"Well, I'm still sort of a fringe operator in the office, but it does seem like my suggestions are listened to more than before. By the way, we found out a bit more about Scott Haffler's motivation for the kidnapping.

Apparently, he had spent one summer in the Middle East, on an archaeological dig in Lebanon. While he was there he fell in love with an Iraqi woman who was working as an interpreter on the project. He wanted to get married and bring her back to the States but her family would have nothing of it and she would not go against her family.

When he returned to the US, they stayed in touch. From letters we found in his home it was clear they were still in love with one another. However, when the Gulf War began they lost contact. He found out a few months ago that the woman and her family had been killed when a smart-bomb mistakenly struck the wrong building and a number of civilians died.

Haffler spiraled downhill after that consumed by wanting to do something but feeling powerless. When he learned that

Griffis had a vacation home on the island and that his company developed most of the guidance systems for these high-tech weapons he cobbled together this plan to strike back at Griffis and his company."

Jesse said, "So he wasn't a criminal or a terrorist, just a guy trying to take revenge for a senseless death."

"I guess so," EJ said, "but regardless of his motive, what he did was criminal and could easily have resulted in the death of young Andy Griffis."

Jesse nodded agreement, "Speaking of Griffis, I have another mystery that you might be able to help me solve."

Jesse described his conversation with Mr. Griffis about the reward and then told EJ about his meeting with Archer Blake, the anonymous donor and his windfall. EJ listened attentively, without reaction, until Jesse told him the amount of the first check.

"Wow!" EJ exclaimed, "that is serious money. The gift must have been huge to produce that kind of income."

"So, what do you think? Do you think it came from Griffis? I mean, I can't think of anyone else I have ever known that might have that kind of wealth."

"I don't know; I could do some snooping around. Moving that kind of money, even as an anonymous gift, has to leave a paper trail. I'll see what I can come up with." EJ paused for a moment, then continued, "Are you just curious about this or is it something more? What if I find out it is Griffis? What if I find out it is someone else? Will it change your decision about whether or not to accept the gift?"

"I wish I knew," Jesse said. "I keep asking myself whether I should accept the money or not. I guess I am hoping that once I know who is behind it and why, then I will know what to do. Weird, right?"

"Not for you, Jesse. You've always had your own way of looking at the world. I respect that about you. I don't always understand, but I respect it. I will do some checking and let you know what I find."

Two weeks later EJ called and told Jesse he had some information about his donor. He told Jesse to meet him for lunch at Webster's Oyster House in Boston.

When they were seated at a table near the raw bar, EJ said, "This place is expensive but you can afford it. I love having friends of independent means."

"Yeah, yeah. So what did you find out?"

"First we eat, then we talk. Those oysters look terrific!"

EJ polished off two dozen oysters on the half-shell and then ordered the swordfish special. Jesse tried the oysters but decided he didn't like food that was still moving when he ate it. He settled for chowder and a lobster roll. He tried, repeatedly to get EJ to tell him what he had found, but each time he asked EJ responded by ordering something more from the raw bar. Finally, Jesse decided this tactic was getting too expensive and decided to wait until EJ was ready.

Over coffee and Indian pudding, EJ said, "I'm pretty sure you were right; it's Griffis."

"What did you find?"

"I tried to track down significant gifts to local charities, but the reporting system is very protective of donor identities. Besides most gifts are reported annually so we could be waiting a long time for this year's reports. Then I tried to find records of large cash transactions, but no luck. Remember, I'm doing all of this as a private citizen; no way I could use Bureau resources.

Finally, I had another thought: what if the gift was not cash but securities? So I began to look for significant stock transfers and I started with Griffis Industries. Bingo! I found a large block of Griffis stock, transferred without voting rights a couple of months ago. Guess what firm handled the transfer?"

"Archer Blake," Jesse said.

"Correct-a-mundo," EJ replied. "I couldn't follow the stock any further, but there was no reaction in the stock market, at all, which makes me think it was a charitable gift. For that much stock to change hands and have no impact on the stock price, one way or the other, and for other stockholders to not even blink, I think that is the only explanation."

"Did the stock come from Mr. Griffis?"

EJ shrugged, "I couldn't tell for certain. The stock was officially held by a holding company and the ownership trail was pretty murky. But from what I could find in SEC filings, no one outside of the Griffis family holds enough Griffis Industries stock to make that kind of transaction. I'd say Andrew Griffis is your man."

EJ paused dramatically and then said, "So Sherlock, now what?"

Jesse did not answer at first. Then after a long silence he said, "OK. Thanks for your help, EJ. I'm convinced that Mr. Griffis is behind this as I suspected. He said he would find a way to help me and he did. The fact that he did it by making a very generous gift to a charitable organization makes me feel a little better. I guess I can live with what he did."

EJ laughed, "I'd say you could live rather well with what he did! Like I said, lunch is on you!

Seriously, Jesse, this is a great piece of good luck. Thanks to Griffis, or whoever, you are free to live the life you choose. Or is it the life that chose you? Either way, you have a gift, an amazing gift, one that can help so many people. Now you are free to be who you are without having to worry about scraping together the rent money every month. Don't think of it as a gift. Think of it as an opportunity: a fellowship that enables you to keep on helping those who need to be helped and finding those who need to be found. Griffis wasn't paying you back for saving his son, he was paying it forward so that you could be there to save other people's sons and daughters."

Chapter Fifteen

Winter held the Northeast relentlessly with frigid temperatures and almost daily snowfall until the beginning of April. Two weeks before Easter, the days warmed slightly and the promise of new life began to stir beneath the melting snow.

Jesse stood in the kennel watching the pack behavior of the newest group of young dogs to be trained. Watching them play-fight and tumble over one another, he wondered which of them might have the right make-up to excel at search and rescue work. He missed Brother Reuben's insights; Reuben seldom missed a talented dog and could spot, without fail, the ones lacking the right temperament; those destined for other things. Jesse trusted Reuben's judgement implicitly but still doubted his own, at times.

Carlson's voice over the intercom jolted him back to reality. "Jesse, please come to the house. You have an important phone call from the Priory."

Brother Clement's voice betrayed him from the moment he said Jesse's name. "Jesse, Sister Miriam had a stroke early this morning. I'm afraid it doesn't look good."

For a moment Jesse could not breathe. He opened his mouth but was unable to put into words the million questions forming in his mind. He struggled to draw a full breath but no air came in and no words came out for what seemed a very long time.

"Jesse?" Clement said, again.

Then, like a swimmer coming up from holding his breath under the water, Jesse wheezed loudly as both air and words came back to him.

"Sorry; how bad is it?" he said.

"We don't really know, yet. She is in and out of consciousness and seems to be paralyzed on the right side. The doctors say they should know more by this afternoon."

"Where is she?"

"They took her to Glens Falls, Jesse, but there is nothing you can do at the moment. I just thought you should know. If – "

Jesse cut him off, "I will be there this afternoon. If anything changes call me, please."

Jesse arrived at the hospital mid-afternoon. Miriam looked to be peacefully sleeping but he could tell her condition was serious from the worried expressions worn by Brother Clement, Brother Marcel, Sister Hannah, and Brother Seth. After exchanging hugs and greetings with everyone, Jesse went to the side of the hospital bed and took Sister Miriam's hand. He did not know what to say, so he just sat there, holding her hand and trying not to cry.

He thought about the bond between them, one that had been apparent from the very beginning. It was not a maternal bond but more like the one between a child and a fiercely protective grandparent. At first, Miriam had a professional responsibility to ensure Jesse's welfare. However, as time passed and she became comfortable with the Priory community, she began to take a more personal interest in the boy. She helped with his care as a child, questioned anything in his life that did not ring true with her very high standard of appropriateness, and lavished her own brand of love and affection on him. To this day, it took only a brief conversation about Jesse to cause Miriam's eyes to well up and, at times, overflow with emotion. This from a woman whose professional demeanor on behalf of children was stern enough to put the fear of God into even the most neglectful or abusive parent; enough to leave law enforcement officers from New York City to upstate New York looking for the nearest exit to avoid going up against her when she was on a case.

Somewhere along the line this boy, whom she watched over with such unaccustomed warmth, began to choose her, too, as the recipient of his affection. Hannah and Adam ostensibly served in loco parentis for Jesse, while the entire community shared the duties and the joys of raising him. However, when Miriam joined the Priory community, the bond between them solidified. Soon, whenever Jesse wanted to be held or comforted after a fall or a scraped knee or for no particular reason at all, he looked for Sister Miriam.

Jesse sat motionless, lost in thought until he felt Brother Clement's hand on his shoulder. When he looked up, he noticed three medical staff in the room, all waiting by the door.

"Jesse, they need to take Miriam for a brain scan. Let's go down to the cafeteria and get a bite to eat."

Clement led Jesse to a small table for two in the rear of the hospital dining room. The others found a table nearby, but out of earshot, taking Clement's hint to give him some alone-time with Jesse.

"Thank you for coming. I know it means a lot to Miriam," Clement said.

"Do you think she knows I'm here – we're here?"

"I do. The doctors told us that even if she doesn't respond she probably can hear and recognize our voices. The sense of hearing remains long after other senses shut down."

"What else do they say about her condition?" Jesse asked.

"Not much, yet; it's too early to tell how much she will recover, if at all. The brain scan may give them a better idea of how much damage has been done. How are you doing, Jesse? You look worn out," Clement said.

"I'm OK; just worried about Sister Miriam."

"I hear you have had a tough winter," Clement said gently.

"Did Mr. Carlson call you?"

"We talk once in a while."

Jesse stirred his coffee silently without making eye contact.

"Yeah, it's been a tough winter. He told you about the Maine search in January? That one took a lot out of the team. I mean, we know we aren't always going to bring them home alive, but we were so close, and we missed him. How could an old man get so lost? An old man with Alzheimer's no less; we should have been able to find him before..."

"Jesse, you know the dogs sometimes struggle in frigid conditions like that. It's something about the way airborne scents travel on cold air. Sometimes the dogs miss them – "

"Not Sara; we've done hundreds of cold weather searches."

"Jesse, even Sara can have a bad day. Besides, she is getting older. What is she – 11 years old? I don't know how much longer she can continue."

"Sara's fine. I know she is older than most, but she is still the best dog on the team. And I know you are right about cold weather searches. It just hurt so much that they found his body within a hundred yards of the grid. The Staties said he was hunkered down, maybe even hiding from us, but we still should have found him."

Clement sipped his tea and then said, "Tell me about the runaway."

Jesse looked at Clement with surprise, "I guess you have been talking to Carlson. He was convinced that case bothered me more than losing the old man."

"Did it?"

"Maybe, in a way; I've never had a case like that. I mean, she was mad – really angry – that we found her. It wasn't like she was being abused at home or anything. She was just a really pissed-off kid determined to have her own way. Fifteen years old, sure that Mom and Dad are completely useless, put on this earth to make her life miserable."

Clement nodded in understanding. "Where was she headed when you found her?"

"She had met this twenty-year old guy at a concert and concocted a scenario in her head of them being together. She wasn't in love with him; she just saw him as her ticket out of her parent's life. In her eyes, we ruined everything when we found her."

"What do you think would have happened if you didn't find her?" Clement asked.

"Nothing good. The guy had a police record and when he was questioned about whether he encouraged her to run away, he claimed he didn't even remember meeting her," Jesse said. "I guess what bothered me the most was knowing that whatever we saved her from, it's only temporary. She'll run again and who knows what will happen then."

"Jesse, you can't save them all. I know you have a big heart and you want to fix the world, but it is not always going to work out the way you want. Sometimes people who are lost, stay lost. Sometimes people who are found didn't think they were lost to begin with. That doesn't change what you do; you just keep doing what you do best and trust the rest to God. You have a gift, a wonderful God-given gift, but it is not always going to be enough to do what you want. In the end, we live this life trusting everything to God; putting every moment of every day and every person we care about into God's hands."

"Like Sister Miriam," Jesse said; more a statement than a question.

"Especially, Sister Miriam; her life has been in God's hands for a long time – long before she came to us. She might not have described her life that way but I saw it the first time she came to the Priory to rescue this little baby boy left on our doorstep. I knew right then that she was one of the ways God was at work in this world and I thanked God that she had come for you."

Jesse said, "Is there a chapel here, in the hospital?"

"There is a 'meditation room' – a chapel by any other name. It's just down the hall. Shall we go together?"

Jesse sighed and nodded his head.

Six days later they took Miriam home to the Priory. The hospital wanted her to go to a nursing home but eventually agreed that the Priory would be able to give her the same care and in familiar surroundings. The stroke had done irreversible damage and the best that could be done for Miriam meant keeping her comfortable and making the best of the time she had left.

Jesse drove back to Carlson's to pick-up Sara and then returned to the Priory, determined to help care for Miriam. By the time he arrived, Sister Hannah had established a medical care plan and a rotating schedule of caregivers so that Miriam would always have someone nearby.

Jesse set up a cot in the corner of Miriam's room and took the overnight shift. The Priory had always had a strict rule about no dogs in the residences but when Sara curled up on the floor at the foot of Miriam's bed no one said a word.

Miriam's medications caused her to lapse in and out of consciousness, seldom being awake for more than an hour or two. Even in the daytime hours Jesse stayed nearby determined that anytime she opened her eyes she would see a familiar face, preferably his, smiling at her.

Sister Hannah suggested some soothing background music, mostly classical recordings: Itzhak Perlman, Yoyo Ma and others. Jesse noticed, however, that Miriam's own CD collection tended more toward 50's music: early rock and roll and doo wop. At night, when the others had gone for the day he would play her music and they would "dance". Miriam still had use of her left hand so Jesse would take her hand in his and they would let their fingers bop to the rhythm of the songs. Every time he played *"In the Still of the Night"* he could see her lips trying to form words, as though singing along, and he was sure he could see a smile in her eyes.

Easter came and went. The early weeks of Spring struggled to warm the days and give new life to the land. One sunny day in late April, Hannah, Adam and Jesse managed to get Miriam onto a gurney and outside onto the patio. She had become less responsive in recent days, but something about the sun seemed to reinvigorate her. She lay there propped up on a stack of pillows and soaking in the warmth looking like an old-time movie star in her wide-brimmed straw hat and Clement's sunglasses. Jesse sat by her side talking non-stop, describing every sign of springtime in sight.

When they moved Miriam back inside, Clement asked Jesse to come with him back to the office, "How are you holding up, Jesse?"

"Good. I'm good," Jesse said. "You don't have to worry about me. I know she is failing, but I really believe we are making things better for her. She knows we are there and she knows how much we care for her."

"I'm sure you are right," Clement said. "I want to show you something."

Clement opened the bottom drawer of the desk and took out a thick blue binder. Even upside down, Jesse could read the words on the cover: *The Book of Jesse*.

"I started this book a long time ago, when you were just a baby. Actually, it was Miriam's idea. She said that not knowing your biological family would make it especially important for your adopted family to help give you a foundation, a history, a sense of who you are. So I put this book together – *The Book of Jesse*. It is your story, Jesse. I write in it regularly and include pictures and some of your many press clippings, too. Over the years, others in the community have added their own contributions to your book, including Miriam. I don't know if you understand how important you are to her, Jesse. You changed her life."

Clement opened the book and flipped to a page marked with a fabric bookmark.

"I don't know if this is the right time for you to read the whole book," he said, "but I think you should read what Miriam wrote just last month."

The Book of Jesse   *March 15, 1993*

Jesse – Do you know what love is?

I hope you do. I hope you know that love is so much more than most people ever understand. I've heard all the clichés about how love means "I get weak in the knees when I look at you" or "I can't live without you" or "You complete me". It's true that love can make you feel that way, but that is not what love is. All of those statements and the millions more like them are all about "me" – about how I feel, about what I want to get from love. But love is not about getting, it's about giving. It's not about "me" it's about the person I love. It's when you want only the best for someone else, even if it means that what is best for them may not be best for you. Love like that means always hoping and working for good things in the life of the person you love. It means putting someone else first; putting aside your own wants, if necessary, to help the one you love.

Most parents come to understand that kind of love the first time they hold their child in their arms. The lucky ones come to understand that all love is like that, not just parental love but all love: romantic love, the love of friends, Biblical love, even God's love. All love is about wanting only the best for the one you love.

You taught me that, Jesse, and now that is how I love you, with love that wants only the best for you. I never had children of my own. When I was young I wanted to be a parent but no matter what my husband and I tried we could not conceive. In retrospect, I can't help but wonder if my work with abused and neglected kids had something to do with our problems. All day, every day, I worked with children in pain. Children who suffered all kinds of things that children should never have to endure; children who never knew what it felt like to be loved. At first, I wanted to bring every one of them home with me. Later, I became so discouraged that I questioned whether I was capable of loving them any more than the parents who treated them like worthless nuisances.

When I had my "melt-down" in the city and walked away from my job to move to the mountains, I didn't know what to expect; I just hoped things would be better. But people are the same everywhere – there are just more of them in the city. If you and the Priory had not come along when you did, I don't know what I would have done. You taught me about love and my brothers and sisters in the Priory restored my faith in God and gave me a reason to hope for humanity.

I realize I am rambling a bit, but I hope you will understand how much you mean to me and how I only want the best for you. When you dropped out of college I was pretty hard on you. I've always been a big believer in education and I wanted you to have that opportunity. Maybe someday you will go back to *college, maybe not. But whatever you decide I want you to know how proud I am of you and how much I love you. I am not proud of you because of what you do. I don't love you because of what you have accomplished – and you have accomplished so much in your young life! I am proud of you and love you because of who you are – Jesse Tobias, the gift of a good God. I give thanks for you every day and I give thanks for who I have become because of you.*

All my love,
Miriam

Jesse put the book down and dragged his sleeve across his eyes. He looked at Clement but had no words.

"Miriam worried about you, so much, when you left school. For her, education has always been the way to a better life. She didn't talk much about her work, the children she tried to help, but I remember her saying education was the key. If she could help a child get an education, then she knew they had a fighting chance. Whether it was to get out of poverty or away from gangs or stay off drugs or at least to break the cycle of family abuse that many of them suffered. She believed education would give them that chance.

She didn't worry about those things in your life, but she wanted so very badly for you to have the best life possible. In her eyes, that meant going to college."

Jesse thought for a moment then asked, "What did she mean by her 'melt-down' in the city?"

"She never told me the whole story, but apparently she had a string of especially bad cases. The final straw came with a newborn baby abandoned on the steps of a church. Apparently the mother was a heroin addict because the baby immediately began going through withdrawals. Miriam sat with the baby for three days in the hospital until she knew the danger had passed.

She placed the child in foster care but two weeks later a woman came forward claiming to be the mother's sister. After a protracted hearing in family court the sister was awarded custody of the child. Miriam feared the worst and only a few weeks later her fears were realized. The baby was shaken to death by the sister's boyfriend who was also a heroin addict.

Miriam never went any further with the story. She never described her 'melt-down' but whatever happened, she left the city and a few months later found her way here to County Protective Services."

A knock at the door interrupted their conversation.

"Come in," Clement called. "Yes, Sister Adina, what is it?"

"Brother Clement, the Rabbi is here. Shall I take him to Sister Miriam?"

"Yes, please do. I will be along in a moment," Clement answered.

"Jesse, did you ever meet Rabbi Shulman?"

Jesse shook his head no.

"He's a good man; I think you would like him. Why don't we go over and I will introduce you?"

"OK," Jesse said, "but why is a Rabbi here to see Sister Miriam?"

"I'll explain as we walk. Let's go," Clement said.

On the way to the infirmary, Clement explained, "Miriam is Jewish, at least, she was born into a Jewish family. She had not lived an observant life since she was a teenager. When she decided to join us as a member of the Priory community we encouraged her to consider how she would live out her faith tradition. We had never had a community member who was not Christian, but we knew Miriam belonged here, however she chose live in relationship with God.

I knew Rabbi Shulman from the Mountain Interfaith Alliance so I introduced him to Miriam. He comes to visit regularly and has been a great help to her in spiritual matters."

Clement and Jesse stood by the door to Miriam's room. Inside Rabbi Shulman sat by Miriam's bedside chanting softly in Hebrew.

Clement whispered to Jesse, "Didn't you ever wonder why Miriam kept her own name when she joined the Priory community?"

"Not really; she had always been Miriam so I guess it never occurred to me. Besides, Miriam is a good Biblical name."

"True, but the reason community members take a new name is to represent their new life in Christ, in the same way that some traditions take on new names at baptism. Since Miriam was not entering into a Christian life we agreed she should simply remain Sister Miriam."

When Rabbi Shulman came out, he and Clement embraced one another then Clement introduced him to Jesse.

"So, we finally meet," Shulman said. "I feel as though I already know you; Miriam spoke of you every time we met. She loves you very much, but I'm sure you know that."

Jesse smiled and nodded his head.

"Brother Clement, thank you for calling me. I'm saddened to see Miriam like this, but I appreciate the opportunity to pray with her. She has a strong spirit but I am afraid she won't be with us much longer."

Clement said, "Her doctors told us to expect another stroke, but it's impossible to know when."

Shulman placed his hand on Clement's shoulder, "You have been such a gift in her life, all of you. I think Miriam came to the mountains hoping to hide from all the pain and suffering she had seen in the world. I don't think she ever expected to find a new life for herself, especially not in a religious order. But nothing could have been better for her. To live here, and to die here, surrounded by the love of this community – well, we should all be so blessed."

Ten days later, Miriam died peacefully in her sleep. Rabbi Shulman led her funeral service in the Priory Chapel. One by one, the members of the community shared their stories of Miriam's life and how she had touched them. Most of the stories revolved around Miriam's love for Jesse, the child who had first brought her to the Priory more than twenty years earlier.

When Jesse stood to speak, Clement stood at his side.

"Miriam has been a part of my life from the very beginning, but I never really appreciated how much I was a part of her life until she had the stroke. I guess I took her for granted, the way children just assume that their parents and grandparents have always been there and will always be there. I am who I am because of all of you and because of Sister Miriam.

Not long before her stroke, Miriam wrote some words of advice for me about love. She included a copy of a poem by e.e. cummings that includes this couplet:

'i carry your heart with me (i carry it in my heart)
i am never without it (anywhere i go you go, my dear')

Wherever I go, she will go with me; I carry her heart in my heart. And I know one place I am going: in the fall, I am going back to college, just as Sister Miriam hoped. A few days before she died, I promised her I would go back and finish. I intend to keep that promise. I will keep my promise just as Miriam always kept hers."

Chapter Sixteen

True to his word, Jesse returned to Devoe College in the Fall and for the next two years dedicated himself to his studies in a way he had not done before. The results reflected his concerted effort as he regularly made the Dean's List for academic achievement.

One Wednesday morning about six weeks before graduation, Jesse was up early working on his senior project when his phone rang.

"Jesse, it's SAC Calvin Granich from the FBI. I know I promised not to call you during the school year, but we have an emergency. There has been an explosion at the federal building in Oklahoma City; nearly the whole building is gone. We are mobilizing all available resources to help rescue survivors. Normally, I wouldn't call you, but EJ Carlson and Delores Greenway are among the missing. They were there working with a joint agency task force and we have been unable to reach them. Can you go?"

Jesse's mind spun out of control. He tried to speak but discovered he had no voice.

"Jesse?" Granich said.

Jesse snapped back to attention, gulped down a huge lung-full of air and then said, "Just tell me where to go and I'll be there."

"Our old friend Mr. Griffis has once again offered his corporate jet. How soon can you be ready?"

An hour later, Jesse and Sara were airborne and three hours after that they were rolling down an Oklahoma interstate in the backseat of a FBI SUV. As they approached the city, an ominous gray- brown haze hung in the sky muting the midday sun. The streets swarmed with people on foot and in vehicles in a kind of quiet chaos. As they moved closer to the heart of the city, a heavy silence seemed to stifle all sound except the piercing wail of emergency vehicles.   Although the buildings surrounding the first checkpoint were still blocks away from the disaster site, they clearly bore scars of the explosion: shattered windows, pockmarked facades and debris littering their sidewalks and entrances.

Inside the first perimeter, traffic moved slowly. They passed through two more checkpoints where heavily armed police wearing military style helmets and body armor not only checked their FBI credentials but peered through the window glass and scanned the undercarriage with mirrors. This scene was unlike anything Jesse had ever encountered.

The agent driving their SUV, Jesse never did get his name, parked behind a long line of identical vehicles. He turned to Jesse in the back seat and handed him a black Kevlar vest with "FBI" in gold letters printed on the front and the back.

"I don't –" Jesse started.

"Sorry, sir; you can't exit the vehicle without the vest. You need to wear the cap, too, and be sure your credentials are visible."

Jesse did as he was told. He also pinned a special FBI patch to Sara's work vest. Properly outfitted, they followed the agent toward a trailer identified as the "Incident Command Center" and bearing the logo of the Oklahoma State Police. The remains of the Federal Building, two blocks away, were still out of sight.

Jesse showed his credentials to the officer at the registration desk who pointed him to another desk labeled "SAR" at the far end of the trailer.

The SAR liaison, Albert Turner, appeared to be one of the few people in the command center not identifiable as law enforcement. He looked surprised to see Jesse and Sara walking toward him.

"I didn't know the FBI had a SAR team of their own."

Jesse smiled at him, "They don't. I'm Jesse Tobias and this is Sara. We are sort of official FBI, unofficially."

"I'm not sure what that means, but we can use all the help we can get. How many are on your team?" Turner asked picking up a clipboard from the desk.

"No team; just us," Jesse answered. "Like I said, we are kind of unofficial."

"I don't know about this. Are you sure you're supposed to be here? Who told you to report –"

"Jesse?" interrupted a geeky looking older man in an FBI vest. Without waiting for a reply he extended his hand and said,

"I'm Agent Wilson Taft. You got here fast, but I heard they were sending a private jet for you."

"Yeah, we made good time," Jesse said.

"Wait a minute," Turner said. "Who are you? A private jet for a SAR handler? You're kidding, right?"

"No, we're not kidding but there's no time to explain now," Taft answered. "Please give Jesse a quick overview of the search grid. I'll take it from there."

Turner was still somewhat befuddled but he briefed Jesse on the grid and the progress. Several dog teams were on the way, but so far only two K-9 units were working the scene.

When Jesse moved on to Agent Taft's desk he asked, "What happened here? SAC Granich said there was an explosion. I've never seen so many law enforcement agencies in one place, so I'm guessing this was no accident."

"We can't be specific at the moment, but we are treating the whole site as a crime scene. We've had multiple bomb threats phoned in since the explosion, but nothing else has turned up. Right now our priority is finding and rescuing victims while disturbing the crime scene as little as possible."

"SAC Granich asked me specifically to follow-up – "

"The Task Force, I know," Taft finished Jesse's sentence. "Greenway is a good agent; I didn't know Carlson –"

This time Jesse finished Taft's sentence, "I knew – know – them both. Can you show me where on the grid the Task Force was meeting when the explosion occurred? I want to begin working that area."

Jesse and Sara followed Agent Taft out of the trailer. Albert Turner ran up behind them.

"You're him, aren't you – the boy wonder from the East coast? Everybody's been talking – "

"Albert, I'm sorry, but I've got to go. Maybe we can talk later," Jesse said.

"Yeah, later," Turner said. "Hey, look, there's broken glass everywhere. I can get you some booties for your dog."

Jesse smiled, "Thanks for the heads-up; I've got booties in the pack. We'll see you later."

Agent Taft let them through the escalating chaos that surrounded the site of the explosion. When the remains of the building came into view, Jesse stopped dead in his tracks. He felt sick to his stomach. The scene looked like something out of a war movie: the skeletal remains of the twelve-story building seemed to lean precipitously to one side propped up by mountainous piles of debris on all sides. What remained standing looked precarious, as if it, too, might crumble to the ground at any moment. Firefighters, EMS personnel and other rescuers swarmed over the entire site.

"Jesse," Agent Taft called, "it's over here."

Minutes later, Jesse and Sara began picking their way among the rubble looking for any sign of life. Jesse gave Sara a good whiff of an old baseball cap of EJ's and asked her to find more. As he gave the command he thought to himself even Sara would need a miracle to find EJ amid such widespread destruction. Jesse kept Sara on the lead partly for her own protection and partly for his own peace of mind. As they walked, they passed rescue workers digging, EMS personnel doing battlefield medicine for survivors pulled from the rubble and others standing vigil over the remains of the dead. Jesse would not allow himself to think about anything other than finding EJ alive and well. He was not prepared for any other possibility.

An hour into the search, Sara showed heightened interest in a pile of debris just below the lurking hulk of the blown-out building. She strained at the lead, occasionally turning to give Jesse a look that said she was on the scent. Normally he would let her go off-lead and she seemed surprised that he did not release her. Climbing over slabs of concrete and twisted rebar took time, but gradually they made their way to the base of the building.

At first Jesse did not see it. Sarah sat unmoving and staring at the bottom of a pile of debris about eight feet high. Jesse scanned the pile from every angle and saw nothing. Then he moved a few steps to the side and saw what Sara saw: it was twisted, bent and broken but it was, without a doubt, EJ's wheelchair. His monogrammed seat pad lay on the ground next to one of the wheels partially hidden beneath a slab of concrete.

Jesse moved slowly forward, afraid of what he might find, but knowing he had to look. He gave Sara the command to stay and began removing chunks of concrete and other debris from the chair. Two other rescuers saw him digging and came to help. In a few minutes they had pulled the entire chair from the wreckage but found no sign of EJ or any other victims.

One of the workers said to Jesse, "I don't see anything here, and there is no blood or human remains on the chair. Maybe he got away somehow."

The other one pointed at Jesse's leg and added, "You really should get that looked at. The medical tent is over there next to the EMS command center."

Jesse looked down and saw that his left pant leg was ripped open and his leg was covered in blood. He felt a burning sensation radiate down his thigh as if seeing the injury made it real. He pulled a gauze pad from his daypack and pressed it against the wound. Red hot pain shot through him; it felt as if whatever had cut into his leg was still there. Reluctantly, Jesse left the broken wheelchair behind and began limping toward the medical tent.

Two EMS personnel stationed outside the tent did triage. Jesse waited his turn behind a firefighter who carried a small child covered in dust and blood; the child's left foot dangled at an awkward angle below a torn pant leg. The little boy never made a sound as the paramedics first examined him then quickly admitted him into the tent.

As the firefighter turned to go back to the search, Jesse heard him say to the others, "There's more…too many more."

Jesse started to walk away and one of the paramedics took his arm, "Not so fast, friend; it looks like you need some help."

"No, it's nothing," Jesse said. "You've got more serious injuries to deal with."

"Why don't you let us be the judge of that," the paramedic said. "Have a seat."

Inside, the tent bustled with activity but with an underlying sense of order that Jesse found reassuring. He sat in a chair off to the side and kept his head down partly to avoid staring at other injured victims and partly because he was afraid of what he might see. It took a while, but an EMT washed out the gash on Jesse's leg and removed a two-inch long shard of glass from the wound. He expertly sealed the cut with something that he said would work like crazy glue and then he bandaged Jesse's leg from the knee to the ankle.

"I would tell you to go home and rest, keeping your leg elevated if I thought you would listen to me. But I'm guessing you are like all the rest and are going back out there," she said.

Jesse nodded, thanked her for her help and stood up testing his mobility. As he turned to the door, he heard a familiar voice call his name.

"Jesse! Jesse! Over here!" EJ Carlson called waving his arms in the air as he lay on a gurney on the other side of the tent.

As Jesse approached EJ said, "What are you doing here? Are you OK?"

The two men embraced.

"I'm fine; man, am I glad to see you!" Jesse said.

"Let me guess, Granich called you, didn't he? But how did you get here so fast? Don't tell me Griffis flew you out here!"

"SAC Granich said he couldn't reach you or Agent Greenway. EJ, is she…" Jesse searched for the right words.

"Greenway is fine; well, she's a little banged up but she'll be OK. We got separated in here, but she's here somewhere. She saved my life, Jesse. When the bomb went off – it was a bomb, wasn't it? They won't tell us anything."

"I don't know for sure, but I've never seen so many law enforcement people in my life and they are treating the entire area like a crime scene. Are you OK?"

EJ nodded, "Yeah, I'm OK. They want me to get checked out for internal injuries but so far so good. A lot of people are worse off; I won't get to a hospital for long time."

"Do you remember what happened?"

"It had to be a bomb. The explosion threw me out of my chair and the whole front of the building just kind of slid away, in slow motion, you know? I saw the whole thing and I could feel the floor under me starting to go. Then Dede – Agent Greenway – grabbed my arm and started dragging me back from the edge. She was incredible! She got hit in the face by flying debris and she couldn't see, but somehow she got me on her back and carried me out of there, down six flights of stairs. I was her eyes and she was my legs. If not for her, I don't know what would have happened to me...

Whoa, the drugs they gave me are kicking-in."

Jesse rested his hand on EJ's shoulder, "Get some rest, brother. I'll check back later."

"Thanks for coming, Jesse. I always said if I was lost I would want to know you were looking for me," EJ mumbled as he drifted off.

Jesse and Sara worked the site non-stop until dark. Then after a quick supper they were back on the job working under the glare of portable Klieg lights. They assisted in seven rescues and helped uncover twice as many who did not survive.

Around midnight Sara stopped walking, turned to look at Jesse and then sat down. Jesse knelt down next to her and felt a wave of exhaustion sweep over him.

"You're right, girl, we need some rest."

A respite center had been set up by the Red Cross in a nearby building. Jesse found an empty cot near the wall, lay down and closed his eyes. As weary as he was, sleep would not come. Instead a steady stream of agonizing images tormented him. Ghost-like hulks of buildings with blown-out windows like eyes that stared, unseeing. Piles of dirt and concrete littered with the detritus of anonymous lives: torn and tattered photographs, chairs broken and empty amid shards of shattered glass and twisted steel. And broken bodies, everywhere; lifeless forms battered and bloodied. Men, women, children – so many children – with empty expressions frozen in time. Jesse tossed and turned but he could not escape the procession of death and destruction that moved before him. He woke in the morning feeling more exhausted than when he lay down the night before.

The next nine days followed the same pattern: work the scene until they could no longer walk then stumble into shallow and unsatisfying sleep. No time to think of anything else, no break from the search. Jesse did manage to see EJ once more before he was transported to a hospital in a nearby town. Delores Greenway went with him.

Each day, Albert Turner managed to find Jesse wherever he was on the site when his own liaison shift ended. They would sit together on a debris pile and eat the sandwiches that Albert's wife packed for them. Once he got over Jesse's quasi-celebrity status Albert proved to be a good friend. Each day he would give Jesse an update on the investigation and each day he would try to get Jesse to take some time off.

"I know I sound like a broken record, Jesse, but you can't keep going like this, day after day. You look terrible and Sara does too. No matter how many sandwiches I bring, it seems like you both get thinner by the day. You can't do it all by yourself, Jesse, let the others take the lead."

Jesse would nod and agree that Albert was right, but nothing changed. He kept going day after day after day.

On day ten, Jesse and Sara were reworking the southwest part of the grid when Sara suddenly stumbled and dropped to the ground. She lay still, except for the rhythmic heaving of her ribs as she breathed. Jesse squatted beside her and stroked her head gently.

"Sara, I'm sorry girl. Take it easy; a little rest and you'll feel better."

They were still there when Albert came, "I know a good vet. If I call him – "

Jesse interrupted, "No, thanks Albert but this is my fault. I'll take her home."

Albert drove Jesse and Sara to a hotel by the airport and checked them in for the night. He brought Jesse a change of clothes for the flight home the next day and insisted on taking them both out for burgers at a nearby fast food restaurant. Jesse ate his sandwich without enthusiasm; Sara sniffed at hers but did not eat.

Carlson met them at the airport and drove them straight to the veterinary clinic that he and the rest of the SAR team used. While they waited for Sara's test results Carlson updated Jesse on EJ's condition.

"He expects to be discharged from the hospital tomorrow and then he's coming home for some recuperation time," Carlson said. "Jesse, thanks for going to find him. I don't know what I would do if..."

"I know; he's like family to me, too," Jesse said and then they both sat in silence seemingly lost in thought.

After a while, Carlson spoke again, "What are you going to do, now? I called the college to let them know why you were gone. They understood completely. Dr. Shumway said as long as you submit your senior project you will graduate with your class. Even if it comes in late, they will still include you in the class of 1995."

"Thanks; I never even thought about school. It seems so insignificant now, after –" the vet came into the waiting room interrupting their conversation.

"Jesse, it's not good," the vet said. "Sara's kidneys are failing. I don't know if she can pull through this; her age is against her. I can give you some medication but I really doubt it will be enough. You might want to think about putting her down."

Carlson dropped his head and walked away, but Jesse never flinched, as though he expected to hear exactly what the vet said.

"No. Thank you, doctor, but we will figure this out."

On the way back to the house, Carlson asked Jesse, "What are you going to do? It doesn't sound good for Sara."

Jesse only took a moment to respond, then said, "I know. It's my fault; I pushed her too hard. She would never stop on her own; she wouldn't want to let me down. But I let her down, I let everybody down. I tried, but I couldn't do it. It was too much – "

"Jesse –" Carlson interrupted.

"No – I can't do it anymore. I'm done; Sara's done. We're going home. We're going back to the Priory."

Home Again

I'll travel old familiar roads

To the source of my life

And lay down my burden

Where the mountains meet the sky.

Chapter Seventeen

Carlson looked long and hard at the photograph and then handed it back to the young woman sitting across from him on the porch. She had such a sweet smile and he wanted to trust her, but the years had made him skeptical, even cynical EJ said.

"Ms. Madison – "

"Leah, Mr. Carlson, please. I assure you I mean no harm. The man in the picture – you know him, right?"

"Tell me, again, why you are looking for him," Carlson said.

"That photograph touched me – "

Carlson interrupted, "You and half the people in the United States. That picture was everywhere; those were difficult days. That photograph seemed to capture the emotion we all felt."

"I remember," Leah said. "But it was more for me. It changed my life. When that picture appeared, five years ago, I was a college student back home in Virginia. I remember the day the building blew up in Oklahoma City – I just sat with my dorm mates glued to the television, watching the rescue workers digging through the rubble, feeling scared but mostly feeling helpless. I wanted to do something. I couldn't just sit by after that bomb went off and killed all those people. But what could I do? I was nobody, nothing, just a kid in college and not taking that very seriously.

Then a few days later that picture appeared. I don't know where I saw it first – on TV or in the newspaper, but suddenly it was everywhere. It was on every bulletin board on campus. It was taped to the door of every room in my dormitory. This picture of a young man – he didn't look much older than me – sitting, covered in dust leaning against the crumbling remains of a wall. And the dog, sitting so patiently, looking right at him as if to say, 'I know you're tired, but we've got work to do. So when you're ready, I will be here'.

I know how silly that sounds, to imagine all of that from looking at a photograph, but I swear that is exactly what I was thinking. I looked at that picture and I smiled – I still do – every time I look at it, I smile. Back then, I don't think I had smiled since that bomb went off. But as bad as I still felt, that picture made me feel that somehow we were going to get through this.

And that was when I knew what I was going to do with my life: I was going to be a photojournalist. Well, actually, I didn't even know photojournalism was something you could do, but I knew that if a picture could be that powerful, then I wanted to take those kinds of pictures.

My parents thought I was crazy, but I changed my major, talked my way into the school of journalism and, well, here I am."

Carlson said, "That's quite a story but why are you looking for this man now, after all these years? Why bring up all those bad memories again? People have moved on, forgotten about that terrible day. Why not just let it be?"

She answered, "It's simple, really. The fifth anniversary is coming-up and with the dedication of the memorial, like it or not, the media will bring it all up again. What I want to do, what my magazine wants to do, is to focus on the positives that emerged from the tragedy. That picture is an icon for so many people, including me, but no one has ever told the story behind the picture. I understand reporters tried to find the man in the photograph but they never could. He apparently was not signed-in on the job and he had no ties with the search and rescue teams working the site. Everyone remembered seeing him, but nobody knew who he was or where he came from. Or if they knew, they weren't talking to people like me."

Carlson looked at her hard, "So what brings you here? What makes you think that I know who he is or where he is?"

Leah took a deep breath and said, "I tracked down Albert Turner, the SAR liaison officer on the job. Albert refused to tell me who the man was although I know he knew more than he let on. He did mention something about the handler being injured. So I magnified a digital copy of the photo about ten times and if you look close enough you can see a bandage on his leg.

I talked with several of the medical personnel who worked on site. One of them remembered bandaging the leg of a guy with a SAR dog and then seeing the guy hugging an injured FBI agent; an agent who was a paraplegic *before* the explosion. Do you know how many paraplegics work for the FBI? Not many, but one of them is your son, EJ, and you have a long and respected history with search and rescue dogs. I just put the pieces together. How did I do?"

Carlson chuckled, "I don't know how good a photojournalist you are, but you would make a hell of a detective. I've got good news and bad news for you. The good news is that I do know the man in the photo; he lived here in those days. The bad news is that he doesn't live here anymore, in fact, he doesn't do search and rescue anymore and I doubt if he will be interested in talking to you.

That job took a lot out of him. Truthfully, it broke him. He was one of the kindest most genuine people I ever knew. When he came back from Oklahoma City he was in tatters. He was one of the top search and rescue handlers and trainers in the country – probably in the world – but after that job he had no heart for the work. Did you know his dog died shortly after getting back from that search? When she came back it was as if that last search was more than she could handle. And when she died, something seemed to die in him, too.

I would like to help you, but I don't think he will want to relive all of that again. He just came back to work last year and I – "

Leah said, "So he is here, in this area, and you know how to reach him! Please, Mr. Carlson, I understand what you are saying, but shouldn't you let him make that decision for himself? I can't explain it, but I think somehow I am meant to tell his story or at least learn his story for myself. Would you please contact him, tell him about me and ask if he will meet me – no strings attached. If we meet and he decides not to cooperate, I will walk away and never bother him, again. I promise and I always keep my promises."

The next day Carlson sat across from Jesse in the back booth of Carm's Coffee. Before he could finish telling Jesse the whole story Jesse began shaking his head.

"No. I'm sure she is a nice person, but I've had enough of the media. Thanks, anyway, but I'm going to pass."

"I understand. I told her you would probably not be interested. But Jesse, there is something about this young woman; I can't put my finger on it but she is not like the others. She's not all ego and fluff; there is something substantial in her character. But I understand; you're not interested."

Jesse was quiet for a moment then said, "I know it's been five years, but it still seems like yesterday. I will never get those images out of my mind. How can people do something like that?"

Carlson shook his head, "I don't know, Jesse. But what keeps me going is knowing that for every one of them there are thousands of others like you and the other members of the team who come running when something happens. As bad as the others are, you guys make this world livable."

Carlson sipped his coffee before continuing, "You know, Jesse, with the dedication of the memorial the press is going to be all over this again. Leah may be the first but she won't be the last to come looking for you with that picture in their hand. Maybe you can get out in front of the story by working with her. Maybe if she tells the story the rest of them will lose interest."

"This woman must really be something. She's got you wrapped around her finger," Jesse said.

Carlson laughed, "Like I said, I don't know just what it is, but she's different. Why don't you at least talk with her? She promised to back off and leave you alone if you decide that is what you want."

Jesse said, "I don't know. Let me think about it."

Carlson slid a piece of paper across the table, "Here is her number. She said she would be in town until Friday."

On Friday morning Jesse was back in his usual booth at Carm's, only this time Leah Madison sat across from him. After a couple of minutes of awkward conversation Leah put the photograph on the table in front of Jesse.

Jesse drained his coffee cup and, without even a glance at the photo, said, "I didn't even know about that picture until I saw a newspaper on the plane ride home. By then it had been on the front page of papers all over the country."

"What do you remember about that day?" Leah asked.

Jesse waited while Carm refilled their coffee cups, then said, "Everything and nothing. Those days all run together in my memory. But I remember it all. I remember too much, too often. Five years might as well be five minutes. I can still taste the dust in the back of my throat. Just looking at that picture takes me back to a place I would rather forget, but I can't. After all the searches I had done, all the things I had seen, I thought I was ready for anything. But that," Jesse's voice cracked, "I wasn't ready for that."

"Mr. Carlson said you stopped doing search and rescue after Oklahoma City. Was it because of what you saw there?"

Jesse looked at her hard, "I thought you wanted to talk about the picture. That's all I agreed to, nothing else. The rest of my life, what I'm doing or not doing, is off limits."

Leah looked down at her coffee, "I'm sorry. I've looked at that picture so often and wondered about you and your dog –"

"Look, there is nothing heroic about me or what I was doing there. Honestly, I shouldn't have even been there. I went to find a friend and when I found him I should have just gone home. Don't pretend I'm something I'm not. There were no heroes on that site just people not smart enough to give up."

Leah stared at Jesse, "What about all the people you rescued?"

"What about all the people we didn't rescue? What about them, huh? What about all those who died? We weren't any help to them or their families. What about all the children from the day care –" Jesse stopped. "No. That's it, I'm done."

Jesse stood to leave but Leah grabbed the sleeve of his jacket. "Please, don't go. Please…"

"What do you want from me?"

"I don't know, Jesse. I've wanted to talk to the guy in the photograph for so long but I don't know what I really want. Please, just stay and talk to me a little more."

Jesse sat down again. Carlson was right, there was something about this young woman that set her apart. An urgency in her voice that made him believe this was about more than a photograph; more than a story.

"What do YOU see when you look at that picture?" Jesse asked.

Leah picked up the photo and looked at it intently, almost as if she was projecting herself into the picture. Her eyes glistened and her voice took on an ethereal quality.

"It's as though the entire world has crumbled. All the things that seem solid and dependable have been blown apart. I mean, what is more solid than concrete but here it is nothing but dust and rubble. How are we supposed to feel safe when the very things that we think are indestructible lay in ruins around us?

But then, in the middle of all this destruction, there sits this young man and his dog, obviously exhausted but no less determined to carry on the search. He – you – change the emotion from despair to hope simply by being there. You are leaning up against what's left of that wall and I can't be sure if the wall is holding you up or if you are keeping the wall from falling down. But either way, I feel a new sense of confidence that because of you, things will be alright."

Jesse shook his head, "I don't know where you get all of that; you're reading a lot into that picture that just isn't there. I think you're seeing what you want to see."

"Maybe so," Leah answered, "but tell me – did you get up and go back to the search after that picture was taken?"

"Like I said, I didn't know – "

Leah interrupted, "Yeah, you didn't know about the picture, but you remember sitting there, leaning up against that wall, don't you? So what did you do, that day?"

"I don't know," Jesse said.

"The picture was published two days after the explosion. How many days did you spend on the search?"

Jesse sighed heavily, "OK, you made your point. I went back to the search. I probably shouldn't have. If I had given-up that day instead of a week later maybe my dog wouldn't have died, maybe I wouldn't have walked around for months with an empty ache inside that felt like it was going to rip me open. If I hadn't stayed, maybe I could just forget all I saw and all I did five years ago and get on with my life. Maybe I wouldn't have to explain myself to people like you who…"

Jesse stopped talking abruptly, got up and headed to the door.

Leah jumped to her feet, dropped some bills on the table and followed Jesse out onto the sidewalk. Half walking, half running, she caught up with him and took hold of his elbow but Jesse kept moving purposefully ahead.

"Jesse, wait! I'm sorry if I pushed too hard. We don't have to relive everything. Jesse, please!"

Jesse turned to face her, "Look, what more do you want? I'm still hurting, is that what you want me to say? I still have bad dreams, I still can't go back to doing the work I love, the work I was born to do, because even the thought of searching reminds me of what I found in the ruins of that building.

That photograph changed your life for the better; it gave you a purpose for your life. Great! But what you see in that photograph changed my life, too, and not for the better. So, go away! Go write your story about how the guy in the photo, who everyone called a hero, is no hero at all. He's just some pathetic loser who can't forget, who can't let go of something that happened five years ago."

Jesse turned to walk away, and Leah wrapped her arms around him, pressed her face into his back and held on tight. Jesse could feel her sobbing against his shoulder. The two of them stood together, without moving, without speaking, until Leah's sobs faded. Then Jesse pulled apart her hands, breaking her hold on him and turned to face her.

She would not look at him; her gaze downward staring at her feet but Jesse could see the tears on her cheeks. He wanted to say something to make her feel better but he had no words. He realized he was still holding her hands and he did not want to let go. Jesse leaned forward and gently rested his forehead against hers.

Finally, he spoke, "Let's go for a walk. There's someone I want you to meet."

They walked the three blocks to Jesse's house still holding hands and still without speaking. The house, a craftsman-style bungalow sat on a dead-end street surrounded by other houses like it, built in the years before the Great Depression. Most of the homes in the neighborhood, like Jesse's, were well-kept and maintained the distinctive style of the architecture. Jesse led Leah to the side of the house where a gate opened to the fenced-in backyard.

Standing before the gate, Leah was startled to see the head of a large dog suddenly appear above the fence. The dog's ears were back, his tongue dangled out the side of his mouth and he looked at both of them with what could only be described as a silly grin on his face.

"Sacha! Down, please," Jesse said as he pushed the gate open and stepped into the yard.

The dog sat obediently, his eyes intently focused on Jesse, waiting for another command. Although he sat without moving his body virtually rippled with kinetic energy, an outburst waiting to happen. His muscular torso coiled, ready to bound forward on command; the only visible movement coming from the tip of his tongue as it flicked saliva from the side of his mouth.

"Leah, this is Sacha. Sacha, this is Leah," Jesse said with mock formality. "OK, boy, come, please."

Jesse's words still hung in the air when Sacha exploded out of his sitting position and charged toward Jesse. In a furious sequence of movements that blended into one single motion, Sacha greeted Jesse, circled him twice sniffing around his pant legs and moved on to proffer Leah the same cursory inspection.

Leah, laughing, dropped down on one knee trying to stroke Sacha's head, but he would not stand still long enough. The dog bounded around both of them, a frenetic bundle of energy seemingly out of control.

Jesse said, "You would never guess, to look at him, that Sacha is one of the most promising search and rescue dogs I have ever trained. Here at home, he is pure goof-ball but – "

Sacha stopped still as a statue, ears perked forward and head tilted; his eyes locked on Jesse.

"Uh-oh – I said the magic word. The word that refers to a spheroid shaped object made of rubber? I can't say it, or even spell it, without Sacha going nuts."

Jesse chuckled and pulled a red ball about the size of a baseball from his jacket pocket. Sacha locked his gaze on the ball, the muscles in his haunches twitching. He did not seem to be breathing but streams of drool flowed from the corners of his mouth.

Jesse tossed the ball in a gentle arc over Sacha's head. The dog did a neat back-flip as he tried to snatch the ball out of the air but missed. When the ball sailed untouched over his arched airborne body, Sacha hit the ground in full stride and in seconds pounced on the ball, brought it back to Jesse and dropped it at his feet glistening and dripping with drool.

"Dog slobber," Jesse said to Leah. "If you love dogs you gotta love dog slobber."

For the next ten minutes Sacha chased the ball relentlessly, wherever Jesse threw it. Leah laughed, watching the two of them so thoroughly engrossed in play that neither of them noticed her taking out her camera and snapping pictures.

Finally, Jesse said, "Enough, Sacha. Sit, please."

Sacha walked close to where Leah stood, his ribs heaving with each breath that wheezed through his jaws clenched tight around the ball. He sat and dropped the ball at Leah's feet, with an obvious hopeful expression on his face.

"Well," Leah said looking at Sacha and the ball, "I guess he likes me."

"Maybe," Jesse said, "but don't read too much into it. Sacha would like the neighbor's cat if it would play ball with him."

An hour later, Jesse and Leah sat on the front porch, talking. Sacha lay stretched out at their feet, his head contentedly resting on Leah's foot.

"Maybe he does like you," Jesse observed.

"Tell me about him," Leah asked.

"Sacha is the reason I'm back here and back at work, at least, as a trainer. He is nearly three years old. He is a grandson of the dog in the photograph, Sara. She was my first SAR dog – well, the first one that was mine alone. I raised her from a pup and trained her myself. She came from a great line of SAR dogs and Sacha is helping keep that bloodline going."

"So, dogs are bred to do search and rescue? I thought it was training," Leah said.

"It's both. Some dogs have the aptitude, some don't. If a dog doesn't have the basics – the temperament, the innate curiosity, the trainability – then you are wasting your time trying to teach them. But breeding is no guarantee, either. So, you breed, you evaluate, and then you decide if training will work. Sara's bloodline is more productive than most, but we still can't assume that all her pups will be SAR dogs."

"Wait – the dog in the picture, Sara, was a yellow lab wasn't she? Sacha is, I don't know what color you call that, but he is not yellow. How is that possible?"

"Sacha is what we call Brindle – a kind of mottled brown and black coloring unusual in Labs, but not impossible. Coloration is another one of those things that breeders sometimes worry about, but it has nothing to do with aptitude or trainability."

Leah nodded, "So, you saw Sacha's aptitude for SAR and decided to start training again?"

"Sort of," Jesse said. "After Sara died I didn't know what to do. I took some time off. I traveled and spent some time thinking, trying to figure out what a different life might look like. After almost two years I came up empty. I could not imagine another life for myself.

I came home the same week that Sacha's litter was born. As soon as I saw this runty brindle-colored pup I knew he was for me. I didn't know if he would be SAR material or just a pet but, either way, he would be mine.

When he turned out to be right for SAR he forced me to decide whether or not to train him, which also forced me to decide whether or not I was ready to face my demons. I think what pushed me over the edge, what gave me the willingness to try again, was his personality. He is so goofy, so easy going he just makes me feel good being around him. When I'm having a bad day, when the memories come crashing in, he chases the bad stuff away. That's why I brought you to meet him; I thought he might be able to do the same thing for you. I made you cry, but I hoped he would make you laugh. And he did, so..."

"Thank you, Jesse."

"Don't thank me, thank Sacha," Jessed said. He paused for a moment then continued, "What time is your flight?"

"Actually, I took the train. I go back at five this afternoon."

"I don't suppose you would want to stay a little longer. I'm teaching a class tomorrow for some new SAR handlers. You might find it interesting."

"I would. Let me call my editor and see if she will approve another night in the hotel."

"Ask for two nights – maybe we could do something, together, on Sunday," Jesse said.

Leah smiled at him and nodded.

Chapter Eighteen

Leah arrived at the County Fire Training Academy on Saturday in time to see Jesse lead eight handlers and their dogs through a quick obedience test. Three of the dogs, distracted by a room full of canines, resisted simple commands. One black lab, in particular, pulled at the lead, ignoring his handler's instructions, determined to sniff the tail of every dog in the room. Jesse watched as the handler tried, without success, to gain control. Finally, Jesse stepped in. He took the lead from the handler, pulled the dog up short and turned away. After two steps, he turned again. He repeated this maneuver several times without speaking, but with each turn he firmly used the lead to bring the dog alongside him. The dog followed each turn obediently until they returned to their original position in line with the other dogs. Jesse gave the command to sit and when the dog sat, he handed the lead back to the handler.

"He's a little scatter-brained, but he will get it," Jesse said. "Just remember, he takes his cues from you. If you are locked-in, he will be too. If you get distracted by him being distracted it will be impossible to keep him focused."

The handler nodded, sheepishly and took her place next to her dog.

Jesse noticed Leah in the doorway, smiled at her and said, "Class, this is Leah Madison. Ms. Madison is a photojournalist and is here to observe and to take some pictures for a magazine article. If you would prefer not to have your picture taken, please inform Ms. Madison. I'm sure she will honor your request. Now, where were we?"

Jesse smiled at Leah, again, then said, "Sacha, come please."

Leah could not believe it was the same dog. Sacha walked calmly across the room to stand at Jesse's side. He walked with purposeful strides, his head and his tail held high, with what could only be described as precision and dignity. Sacha wore his SAR vest and a red-and-white-checked bandana tied around his neck. The other dogs watched him but Sacha ignored them all, his eyes locked on Jesse.

"Sacha still has a lot to learn about the finer points of search and rescue work," Jesse said to the class, "but when he wears his SAR vest he is all business. He gives me his full attention and that keeps him from being distracted. Believe me, he would love to sniff every one of you and roughhouse with your dogs, but he is working, now, and the job is all that matters. With continued work and diligence, your dogs can get to this point, too. If they don't, SAR work is out of the question."

For the next two hours, Jesse put the class through their paces, often using Sacha as a teaching aid. Leah moved about the room snapping hundreds of pictures with her digital camera.

After lunch, Jesse spent time with each of the handlers and their dogs individually. Watching him work reminded her of a master class she had taken a year ago with a veteran combat photographer who worked for the Associated Press. He shared his experiences and pointed out the nuances that separate a photojournalist from a photographer and a photographer from someone who takes family snapshots. Leah had marveled at the depth of his knowledge; he had forty years of real life experience to illustrate his lessons. She saw Jesse doing much the same thing with these handlers despite the fact that he was only a few years older than her and younger than most of the handlers he was training. Still they hung on his every word, knowing they were learning from a master.

Late in the afternoon, as the class neared its conclusion, Jesse said to Leah, "How would you like to earn your keep for the day? I need a volunteer to hide and be found by the dogs."

Leah agreed and, after giving Jesse the woolen scarf she wore around her neck, one of the observers from the training academy led her outside to a pre-arranged hiding place in the woods behind the academy. Three other volunteers also hid in places nearby.

Jesse led the class outside and explained the exercise. "Four volunteers have hidden somewhere on the grounds of the academy. They are not inside any of the buildings but they could be anywhere else on the ten acres of this property. The object of this exercise is to find Ms. Madison. I have her scarf here; one by one, each of you will show the scarf to your dog then give your command to 'find more' and begin the search. Please spread out, maintain your distance from one another and follow standard SAR protocol for group searches. When your dog indicates, raise your hand. All the others will stop searching and wait for your dog to complete the search. If your dog loses the scent or fails to locate Ms. Madison, the exercise will resume until someone successfully locates her.

This is not a competition; it is a training exercise. On actual SAR missions the goal is never about proving your dog is better, faster, or smarter than any other dog. The goal is always to rescue the person who is lost. When that happens, regardless of which dog makes the find, all dogs are rewarded and all handlers share in the success. Let's begin."

The search began with some chaos as the dogs and their handlers moved out across the grounds. Leah had not followed a direct route to her hiding place but had made several turns and switchbacks to provide the dogs with a complex scent trail. Once the dogs were searching in earnest only three or four minutes passed before two handlers raised their hands simultaneously. Jesse gave one of them the signal to proceed while the others waited.

Leah could not see anything from the camouflaged blind where she crouched behind a cluster of bushes. She was wiping some moisture from the lens of her camera when she had the distinct feeling she was being watched. Turning to her right she saw a large yellow lab sitting motionless and silently staring at her. A moment later the dog's handler, a woman of about forty, pushed aside camouflage tarp and smiled at her.

"Ms. Madison, I presume?" she said.

Leah stood up, but not before snapping a photo of the dog; a close-up in which the dog's faced filled the entire frame, its snout so prominent his nose seemed to poke through the camera lens.

The other handlers gathered around, rewarding their dogs and congratulating one another on a successful search. Jesse waited until the talk died down and then gave each handler a quick critique of their performance on the search.

"I was very impressed with the way all of your dogs responded to the exercise. I have no doubt that, given time and opportunity, any of them would have found our missing photojournalist. Well done! Keep up your practice routines and I will see you here, again, next month. Thanks, everyone."

Leah waited and watched as each of the handlers made a point of speaking with Jesse individually. Jesse took time with each one, answering questions and offering encouragement. Sacha sat patiently at Jesse's side.

When the last handler walked away, Jesse said, "Are you hungry? I know a place near here that makes great pizza and they have a soft spot for SAR dogs."

Ronnie at Village Pizza greeted Jesse and Leah at the door, "Jesse! I figured we might see you tonight. How did the class go?"

"You mean how did your niece do, right Ronnie?" Jesse said. "Angie did great; I think Turbo is starting to get it. They will make a good team."

"I know they will be OK with you. Look, we are full-up at the moment, but have a seat and I will get you a table ASAP. You want a beer?"

Jesse and Leah nodded and by the time they hung up their coats, Ronnie was back with two Sam Adams Winter Ales. "I should have asked the lady what she wanted, but I took a chance and brought her the same as you."

"Ronnie, this is a friend of mine, Leah."

"Leah, nice to know you. Any friend of Jesse's is welcome here."

"Thank you, and Sam winter is perfect," Leah answered.

Halfway through their first beer Ronnie moved them to a booth, brought out a plate of snacks and took their order. Jesse and Leah sat next to each other on one side of the booth while Sacha, still in full SAR dress stretched out on the other bench and promptly went to sleep.

"So is service always this good here? I feel like we're getting the VIP treatment," Leah said.

"Ronnie takes good care of anybody who is a first responder. He was a volunteer firefighter for years, right up until he had a lung removed. His niece Angie is the second SAR handler in his family."

Leah smiled at him, "Are you really that humble or don't you get it? People love you. Mr. Carlson, the handlers, the people at the training academy, Ronnie, everybody I have spoken to about you – they all think you are something really special."

Jesse shook his head, "No, they are just being nice. It's got nothing to do with me."

Leah laughed, "Yeah, right."

"So, can I see the pictures you took?" Jesse asked.

"Changing the subject, are we? You don't like it when we talk about you."

"Yeah, yeah, yeah, Dr. Freud. Can I see the pictures or not?"

Leah scrolled through the pictures from the training. They both laughed out loud when they saw the close-up of the dog that found Leah during the search exercise.

"That's your cover shot!" Jesse said.

"You would say that since it is a photo without you in it!" Leah replied and then went back to scrolling through the other pictures she had taken including the ones of Jesse playing ball with Sacha the day before.

When Leah put away the camera Jesse said, "I'm impressed. Really. You got some great shots."

"So, Jesse, now that you know me better, will you let us do the article? My editor is pressing me for a decision. She needs to schedule the photographer, assign someone to write the copy and get everything done in the next ten days to meet the deadline for the April issue."

"Wait a minute, I'm lost. What is all this about scheduling a photographer and a writer? I thought you were going to do the story."

Leah chuckled, "Me? No – I'm just an intern. I get to do the grunt work: tracking you down, getting your approval and maybe even developing a point-of-view for the story. But the actual article will be done by a real photojournalist and a copy writer.

So, can I tell them you are in?"

Jesse took a long sip of his beer and then said, "I'm in, but only if you do the story. I want your photographs in the article and I don't trust anyone else to write the copy. It's got to be your story or I won't do it."

"Jesse, I'm flattered but they won't go for that. I'm just an intern and this is a big story, maybe even the lead story for the issue. They won't let an intern do it."

"Well, that is up to them. I won't tell them how to run their magazine," Jesse said, "but I won't do it with anyone else. I've had enough bad experiences with the press. You got me to trust you, so you do the story or I'm out. Don't let them blame you; put it all on me. Tell them I am temperamental or egotistical or whatever you want but I'm not going to budge on this. It's you or nothing."

Leah stepped outside to call her editor. When she returned the pizza had arrived and Jesse was talking to a young woman that Leah recognized from the training.

"Angie?" Leah asked.

"Yeah, she works here on the weekends helping Ronnie out. What did your editor say?"

"I left a voice message. She is a workaholic but even she takes off Saturday nights."

"OK, then," Jesse said. "She's not working so neither are you. Let's forget about the article, this pizza is calling my name!"

When they had finished eating Jesse said, "So, do you have plans for tomorrow?"

"Not really. You mentioned maybe doing something together. What do you have in mind?"

"No work, no dogs – sorry Sacha – and no SAR. Maybe church in the morning and then go for a ride in the afternoon."

Leah looked surprised, "Church in the morning? I, uh, don't, uh, do you usually go to church?"

"Just about every Sunday, at least when I am in town. I'd be happy to have you come with me, but if you would rather not..."

"I don't usually go to church. Maybe we could meet after?" Leah said.

Jesse looked disappointed but said, "Sure. No problem. How about if I pick you up at your hotel around twelve-thirty?

Dress comfortably, like today, only bring an extra sweater just in case."

"Where are we going?"

"It's a surprise. I'd tell you but you might not come and you would miss out on a nice afternoon. Trust me," Jesse said with a warm smile.

The next day when Jesse pulled up to the hotel, Leah was waiting just inside the lobby door. Watching her step outside took his breath away. She was dressed in boots, jeans and a pea coat with a long scarf and a knitted tam-o-shanter of brilliant fuchsia that accented her long reddish-brown hair. She waved and smiled at him with such radiance he had to squint his eyes. Even dressed for a casual afternoon outing, she was stunningly attractive. Jesse struggled to regain his composure before she reached the door of his Jeep. A light snow began to fall as they headed out of town.

"OK, you can tell me now, right? Where are we going?" Leah asked with a chuckle.

"I thought today is a perfect day to go to the beach," Jesse said with a chuckle of his own.

"The beach?" Leach said, "You're kidding right? It's winter!"

"Right! It's perfect! Think about it: no traffic, no crowds, no need to slather on all that sunblock and we will have the beach all to ourselves!"

Leah looked at him with an expression that made it clear she was not convinced. Jesse glanced at her and caught the look on her face.

"Seriously, this is one of my favorite times of the year to go to the beach. Don't knock it until you've tried it. Trust me, this will be great!"

They drove on in silence for a few miles, then Jesse said, "So, how was your morning? Did you hear anything back from your editor?"

"No, nothing yet, but knowing her I imagine she will be checking email today so I may get an answer this afternoon." Leah paused for a moment, then continued, "So, how was church this morning?"

"Good, or as good as a Sunday in Lent can be," Jesse said.

"Lent?"

"Yeah, Lent – the weeks leading up to Easter. It's a time of introspection and repentance so it tends to be quieter and more somber that the rest of the year."

Leah looked at him, "Repentance like confessing your sins?"

Jesse smiled, "Sort of, repent means to turn around. So during Lent we are called to think about our lives, what we are doing right and what we might need to do differently and then turn away – turn around – from the things we think are not right in our lives. There's no sackcloth and ashes anymore, if that is what you're thinking; just a serious look at your own life."

"And you do this every year?" Leah asked.

"Well, we probably should do it every day, but it is part of our preparation for Easter every year. I take it that you are not a church goer," Jesse said.

Leah shook her head, "No, not anymore. My Mom and Dad were raised in the church and we used to go whenever we visited my grandparents because they expected us to go with them. But we never went on our own. I went a couple of times with friends from college, but it all seemed so foreign to me. I did not understand what they were doing or what it had to do with my life."

"So you don't believe in God, either?" Jesse asked.

"I don't know. I don't believe in some old man in the sky who controls the universe, but I believe in something. I don't know if I'd call it God. It's more like – don't laugh – remember the movie 'Star Wars'?"

Jesse laughed, "The force! May the force be with you!"

Leah punched him in the shoulder, "I told you not to laugh!"

Jesse laughed some more, "I'm not laughing at you. I loved those movies and I agree with you! I think in some way God is a lot like the force. I don't think of God as some old man in the sky either. God is more spirit, like a life-force moving throughout the universe. We are not that different in what we think."

"Maybe not, but that's not what I heard in church. They had a different way of thinking and they made it very clear that if you didn't believe what they believed then you were going to hell. Somehow that didn't seem very Christian to me; it didn't sound like God was about love and forgiveness if all it took to send someone to eternal punishment was a different opinion."

Jesse nodded, "I understand, but all churches are not alike. Maybe you just didn't find the right one for you."

"Did you grow up going to church? I mean, did your Mom and Dad take you to Sunday school and all that?" she asked.

Jesse didn't answer for a moment, then he said, "That's complicated. I didn't have a normal childhood, but let's not go into that right now. Here's our exit."

Bufflehead Cove sat gray and still in the February chill, the stately summer cottages shut tight against the winter weather.

Jesse parked the Jeep on the road. They followed a narrow path that cut through a ragged stand of over-grown boxwoods and then wound between the sand dunes that separated the shore from the road.

The beach stretched wide and empty in both directions Beyond the shelter of the cove whitecaps dotted the waves but here the retreating surf gently broke on the wet sand. Sandpipers and seagulls pranced along the water line, the only signs of life on the entire beach.

"See, no crowds," Jesse said with a smile. "Come here in the summer and you have to elbow your way in, that is, if you can find a place to park in the same ZIP code."

Leah nodded, "I see, but if you think I'm going into the water you are out of your mind."

"That's right, you are a Southern girl – "

"Mid-Atlantic," Leah interrupted. "We Northern Virginia debutantes prefer Mid-Atlantic."

"OK, Mid-Atlantic, but those of us who frequent the beach in the great Northeast spend more time looking at the ocean than wading into it. The water is just too cold most of the year for swimming, but there is something primal about being near the sea. They say we all came from the salt water, right?"

"I thought your God created us from a little mud."

"I see I've got my work cut out for me. Just because I have faith in God doesn't mean I have to disbelieve scientific research. My intellect is a gift from God, too," Jesse said.

Leah smiled at him, "Sorry. I was just trying to be clever but I am clearly out of my league with you."

"Anyway, life here in New England certainly emerged from the sea. Pilgrims, fishermen, whalers, explorers all went down to the sea in ships. I don't really believe in reincarnation, but I have this recurring dream of being on an old-time whaling ship. It is so vivid that it seems more a memory than a dream. The odd thing is that I love being on the ship but I hate the idea of whaling so I'm always hoping for the whale to escape us."

"So if you don't plan to go into the water, you can come to the beach anytime, even in winter," Leah said.

"Let's walk," Jesse nodded.

He took Leah's hand as they set off toward the rocky point that defined the south end of the cove. They walked without speaking for several minutes watching the sea and the birds. Jesse took it as a good sign that they were comfortable enough with one another to be able to let the quiet hang between them and not have to fill it up with small talk.

Stopping to explore a tide pool, Leah crouched down close to the rocks and carefully picked up a small coral-colored star fish. She held it close to examine it and Jesse found himself staring at her. As much as he loved the ocean in winter, on this day he could not take his eyes away from this young woman who walked with him.

Leah gently returned the starfish to the pool and Jesse offered his hand to help her to her feet. She rose and in one smooth motion pressed up against him and filled his arms. It was unclear whether she had done it intentionally or if Jesse had pulled her close but neither of them appeared to care how it had happened. They held the embrace until again, with no apparent forethought, they stood face to face and their lips met in a kiss so tender and sweet that it seemed completely natural, as if they had kissed hundreds of times before.

Still holding her close, Jesse said, "You must be cold; you're trembling. Let's head back."

They walked back up the beach; Jesse's arm around Leah's shoulders and her arm wrapped around his waist. They stopped twice along to way to share kisses, each one slightly more passionate than the one that preceded it.

Back in the Jeep Leah said, "You were right. I like going to the beach in winter."

"Oh, but you haven't had the best part, yet," Jesse said as he started the engine and drove up the road.

The small, easily missed sign over the door to the nondescript wooden shanty read "Bapi's Chowder Pot". Jesse parked on the side of the road with two other cars.

"I know it's not much to look at, but Bapi makes the best clam chowder in New England."

Inside, they settled at a table near the woodstove in the back. The warmth from the stove washed over them and quickly chased the chill of the beach.

"So, you have a difficult choice to make," Jesse said. "Bapi makes two kinds of chowder: traditional New England chowder and a clear chowder with Portuguese sausage. What kind of chowder do you like?

"I've only had one kind, Manhattan," Leah said.

"Oh, don't say that too loud. People around here don't believe Manhattan clam chowder is chowder at all. On a day like this, I suggest the New England chowder but I'll let you taste my Portuguese version."

Jesse placed their order at the counter and was back at the table with two steaming bowls of chowder by the time Leah had taken off her coat. They ate without much conversation beyond exchanging comments about what a genius Bapi must be to be able to make something so delicious out of a few clams and potatoes.

When they had finished eating Leah said, "Jesse, what did you mean before about your childhood being complicated?"

"It's not important."

"But, Jesse, I want to know everything about who you are," Leah said.

"Well, maybe there are some things I'd rather not talk about."

"I understand you wanting to keep some secrets from a journalist, but things are different now, right?"

"Not everything. There are still some things I would rather not see end up in your story."

"My story?" Leah said louder than she intended. "You think this is about my *story*? You think I came out here with you, froze my butt off on a beach in February, for my *story*? You think what happened out there on the beach was about getting you to give me some juicy details for my *story*? I thought you knew me. I thought we had something happening between us, but apparently you think I would do just about anything for some *story*!"

"Leah, I'm sorry. I didn't mean – "

"Jesse, take me back to the hotel. I want to go back, now!"

They made the trip back to the hotel without speaking. When Jesse pulled into the parking lot, Leah opened the door and stepped out into the cold night.

"Leah, wait," Jesse said. "I didn't mean to hurt you. I'll tell you anything you want to know, just don't go"

"Goodnight, Jesse. I don't want to know anything more. I will let you know when I hear from my editor who she has assigned to finish the story.

Chapter Nineteen

"So, you and Leah!" Carlson said. "I'm not surprised. I told you there was something special about her the first time I met her. So you had a good day, yesterday. Where did you take her?"

"Bufflehead Cove and – "

"Let me guess, chowder at Bapi's, right?" Carlson nodded his head with approval. "Good choice; give a Southern girl a genuine taste of New England."

"Mid-Atlantic, actually."

"What?"

Jesse chuckled, "It doesn't matter. Anyway, we had a nice day – a sensational day – right up until I blew it. She wouldn't even talk to me when I dropped her off at her hotel."

"Oh, Jesse, I'm sorry. I can tell you really like her. What happened; what did you do?"

"She wanted to know about my family and my childhood."

"And you didn't want to tell her. Jesse you have nothing to be ashamed of, in fact, I think your story is something to brag about. You grew up in a great place with one of the best extended families I have ever seen."

Jesse shook his head, "I'm not ashamed of them, but I never know how to tell someone that my mother abandoned me at birth without sounding like some pitiful loser."

"So go see her and tell her everything. I bet Leah is someone who will get it. I doubt she will end up feeling sorry for you."

Jesse scoffed, "No, she won't feel sorry for me. I didn't only not want to talk, I made it sound like she was only pretending to be interested in me for her story."

"Uh oh; that may take some work to make right," Carlson said, "but if you want my opinion I think she is worth the effort. Go see her, Jesse, and do whatever you have to do. Apologize, grovel, whatever, and then tell her the whole story. Don't leave anything out."

Before Jesse could reply, his phone rang and he recognized Leah's number on the display, "Hello?"

"Jesse, it's Leah. My editor called this morning and, I don't believe it, but they agreed to have me do the story. There's one catch: the story has to be in by Friday, otherwise, they will drop the whole thing and go with another angle. If you are still willing to do it, I will work out a plan this afternoon and we can get started first thing tomorrow morning."

Jesse said, "Yeah, I will do whatever you need. Can I see you later?"

"No. I need to work today. I've got to go through all my pictures and decide what shots I still need and I need to begin writing a draft of the narrative."

"I understand, but I feel terrible about yesterday and I want to make it right," Jesse said, pleading a bit more than he intended.

"Jesse, I can't deal with all of that right now. The story has to be my priority or my first shot at a byline will be my last."

"What about after the story is done?" Jesse said.

Leah answered quickly, "Maybe, I don't know. Ask me again on Friday."

The rest of the week passed quickly. Jesse and Leah were together every day, as Leah took more photos and asked question after question to help her build the narrative that would go with the pictures. Leah kept everything very professional; working together but not allowing anything social, not even a shared meal.

By Friday, Leah was showing the effects of stressful days and sleepless nights. When Jesse met her at the hotel after lunch he thought to himself that even looking exhausted and a bit disheveled she was still beautiful. He wanted to tell her but sensed the time was not right.

Leah looked at him and said, "It's done. I've been over it a dozen times and I can't do any more. Do you want to see it before I send it in? It's not good journalism to show a story to the subject before publication but I feel like I owe it to you."

Jesse shook his head, "I trust you. Whatever you have done is fine with me."

Leah smiled at him for what seemed to Jesse like the first time since Bufflehead Cove.

"Thanks for that, Jesse."

"Do you have plans for the weekend?" Jesse asked tentatively.

Leah looked away from him, "Jesse – "

"Leah, you said I could ask when the article was done. Well, it's done and we have some unfinished business. If I don't at least try to make this right, I will never…" his voice trailed off. "Anyway, do you have plans for the weekend?"

"Yeah, sleep! I am going to sleep the sleep of the dead until I feel human again."

"Great," Jesse said, "I'll pick you up around nine in the morning and you can sleep in the car while I drive."

"I don't know, Jesse, maybe we should –"

"Please, Leah. Come with me. Give me a chance to earn your trust again. If you are not convinced, I will leave you alone, I promise."

"Where are we going?" Leah asked warily.

"Home. I'm going to introduce you to my family and tell you the whole sad story of my life."

"Jesse, you don't have to," Leah said.

"I know, but like I said, I trust you and I want you to know so maybe you will trust me again. But mostly I want to convince you to give me another chance."

"Alright, but make it ten in the morning," Leah said with a half-smile.

"Nine-thirty," Jesse said, "we have a long drive. Oh, and pack an overnight bag."

True to his word, Jesse drove the first couple of hours in silence as Leah napped beside him. He took his eyes off the road every so often to glance at her sleeping peacefully. He wanted to know more about her; he wanted to know everything but he knew that first he had to let her into his life. Each mile that ticked off on the odometer marked a step in that direction. After this weekend, she would know everything and maybe, if all went well, he would know more about her, too.

When Leah awoke, Jesse began talking. By the time they began the climb into the Adirondack Mountains, he had told her the whole story: how he had been abandoned at birth, how he never knew his mother or father, how he had been raised in a religious community. He even told her about being teased as the dog-boy in school.

Carlson was right; Leah did not react like the others. She listened intently and she asked probing questions when she needed to understand something better. Never did she show any sign of pity or feeling sorry for Jesse. When he finished, she sat quietly watching the mountain road for several moments.

"Thank you, Jesse. I feel like I understand you much better, now. Your life really has been shaped by how you grew up."

Jesse said, "Brother Clement always said that who we are today is the product of two things: where we came from and where we are going. We can't change where we came from but we can choose where we go next. He would say that at any moment in life we have an almost infinite number of possible next steps and the one we choose will change our present. If we choose well, then good; but if we choose poorly we should simply take it as a learning moment because we always have that wide range of next steps in front of us. We choose one and move on, then choose another and then another and so on. Each choice builds on our past, redefines our present and opens up a new future."

Leah looked at him, "So there are no wrong choices in life, and no right way to go?"

Jesse chuckled, "No, there are plenty of wrong choices, we pick them all the time, but for the most part they are not fatal or unable to be overcome. There is a right way – a best way – to go, but only God knows that way."

"So, God knows and we are just out of luck? God watches us and then hands out the punishment for our bad choices?" Leah said sarcastically.

"Not the God that Brother Clement knows. He would say that God walks with us down whatever path we choose and that God is always ready to help us find the best way. That is where faith kicks in. All we need to do is follow where God leads us."

Leah shook her head, "I've got to think about that one."

"Brother Clement explains it much better than me. You can ask him yourself soon. We are almost home," Jesse said as he turned the Jeep onto the steep dirt road that leads to the Priory.

Jesse had just turned off the engine when they were surrounded by a welcoming committee led by Brother Reuben, Brother Marcel and Sister Hannah. Everyone lined up to hug Jesse and then to embrace Leah in the same way.

"It is so good to have you home, again, Jesse," Reuben said, "and Leah we hope you will be at home here, too. Brother Clement wanted to be here when you arrived but he had to go into Saranac Lake. He will be back soon. Let's get you settled in your rooms then, Jesse, you can show Leah around."

Jesse still had his childhood room with Brother Adam and Sister Hannah anytime he came home. Sister Adina offered her guest room for Leah and when she had settled in, she found Adina waiting with tea and cookies fresh from the oven. The two of them were getting acquainted when Jesse knocked at the door.

The usual January thaw had done little to reduce the snow cover in the mountains. Brother Seth had become expert at plowing snow from around the main buildings and creating enormous snow banks at the perimeter of the Priory compound. Still, as Jesse showed Leah around they frequently found themselves slogging through several inches of snow. Jesse pointed out the main buildings: the residences, the communal dining hall, and the library. They lingered for a while in the stillness of the chapel, the place Jesse missed most when away from the Priory. He saved the kennels for last hoping the dogs would make a good impression on Leah. He was not disappointed; when she saw the puppies, she melted, dropping to her knees and picking up the nearest bundle of fur to cuddle.

"Jesse, how could you ever leave this place? It is magical!"

They played with the puppies for a while and then Jesse showed Leah the other dogs. Finally, they watched Brother Reuben put one of the dogs through a typical indoor training routine.

"Jesse," Reuben called, "You're better at this than I am. Do you want to give me a hand?"

For the next twenty minutes, Reuben and Jesse worked patiently with the dog, a six-month-old yellow lab named Scooter. The dog was eager but keeping his attention was not easy.

"What do you think?" Reuben asked.

"Well, he's smart and very affectionate but I don't see much progress since the last time I was here. He is still scatter-brained and easily distracted. I'm not sure he will make it in SAR," Jesse answered.

"That's what Marcel thought, too. But I really like him, so I hoped with a little more work he might make the grade. I guess not; you and Marcel know best."

"If you want, I could help you with him. Maybe if we worked together – "

Reuben interrupted, "Thanks, Jesse, but he will be on his way to companion dog training next week. I just had to try one more time…"

Just then Brother Clement's voice came over the intercom speaker, "Jesse, are you there? I'm back in my office and ready to meet your young lady. Jesse?"

Jesse pushed the talk button on the intercom, "Hi, Brother Clement. We will be there in a couple of minutes."

Brother Clement greeted them both with hugs and a huge smile, "Somehow I suspected you would be in the kennel. Once a 'dog-boy', always a 'dog-boy'".

Jesse laughed, "Don't blame me; I couldn't get Leah away from the puppy kennel. I think she would rather sleep there than at Sister Adina's!"

"They are adorable, Leah, aren't they? But Sister Adina can be pretty adorable, too, once you get to know her," Clement said.

Leah smiled, "She's been very kind and very welcoming – everyone has. Thank you."

"You know," Brother Clement said, "this is a new experience for us. This is the first time Jesse has brought home a young woman to meet the 'family'. We are all trying to be on our best behavior; we don't want to scare you away.

You can probably tell that Jesse is a treasured part of this community. I gather he has told you something about his life here with us?"

Jesse answered before Leah could reply, "Everything. I told her everything on the drive here this morning."

Clement smiled at Jesse then turned to Leah, "I'm sure he did – tell you everything from his perspective, but I bet I can embellish the story a bit. You know, fill in some of the juicy details Jesse left out."

"Ooh, that sounds interesting. Please go on, Brother Clement," Leah laughed.

"Did Jesse tell you I've been keeping a book about his life?"

"No, he never mentioned that," Leah said. "Can I see it?"

"By all means! It has some great baby pictures and notes about some of those little embarrassing moments we all have in our pasts. You will love it!"

Clement retrieved the Book of Jesse from the shelf, pulled a chair up next to Leah and began to tell her about Jesse's childhood, about Sheriff Hansford and Miriam Fossler, about Jesse's early years in the Priory and his gift for working with animals. Page by page Clement let the book illustrate his telling of Jesse's life story.

"Oh, here is an important moment in Jesse's young life – his first SAR rescue. A young family was lost on the mountain in a freak October snow storm and Jesse rescued their little girl."

Leah stared at the photo, "Jesse, is that you?"

"I know it's hard to believe that a dorky little boy like that could grow into a hunk like me, but yes, that's me. That's my dog

Sara, the first dog I trained on my own and the same dog you saw in the Oklahoma City picture."

"That's really you?" Leah said, again.

Brother Clement answered for him, "Yes, that's Jesse and Sara and the little girl they rescued on the mountain. What was her name, Jesse? What was her name?"

"Lulu," Leah said before Jesse could answer. "Her name was Lulu."

"Lulu," Brother Clement said, "that's right. Her name was Lulu. So Jesse already told you this story."

Jesse interrupted, "No, I didn't. I never mentioned the little girl. Leah, how do you know about the girl in the picture?"

Leah reached out and touched the photograph and said, "You're the one. That's you in the picture and that's me; Lulu. I am Lulu."

Jesse stared at her, "You're Lulu? I don't understand. Your name is Leah Madison – "

"McKinley," Leah added. "My full name is Leah Madison McKinley. I use the short version professionally. When I was little, my Dad nicknamed me Lulu.

I've seen this picture before. I vaguely remember being lost in the snow, but whenever my parents would show me this picture they would just say that I was walking in the woods and the boy and the dog found me and brought me home."

"Well, that explains it," Jesse said.

"Explains what?" Leah asked. "My fascination with the other picture of you and Sara in Oklahoma City?"

Jesse shook his head, "No. From the first time Mr. Carlson met you he said there was something about you. I felt it, too, the first time we met. I didn't know what it was but now I know. We knew each other from before; our lives intersected all those years ago and we have been waiting to meet again ever since."

Jesse looked at Leah and Leah looked at Jesse as if they were seeing each other for the first time.

Brother Clement smiled, "And they say God works in mysterious ways…"

Leah joined Jesse and the rest of the Priory community in church on Sunday morning. Brother Clement's message reflected on Jesus' teaching about being one in the spirit; a message well-suited for a gathering that felt more like a family reunion than a Sunday service. As the word spread among the community about Lulu's return, the members embraced Leah with even more warmth than before.

Their midday community meal was interrupted by the arrival of Sheriff Hansford. Brother Clement greeted him, and after a brief conversation asked for everyone's attention.

"Brothers and Sisters, Sheriff Hansford is asking for our help finding a man missing on Giant Mountain. He left home yesterday and has not returned," Clement paused before continuing. "Jesse, it's Rudy Talltrees."

"Rudy?" Jesse said with surprise. "Rudy is the last person I would ever expect to be lost in these mountains. He knows them better than any of us."

Sheriff Hansford said, "How long has it been since you've seen Rudy?"

"Several months, I guess. I ran into him in town last summer but we didn't have time for more than hello."

"Rudy hasn't been Rudy since he returned from his last deployment," Hansford explained. "I never knew him that well before, but I've seen too much of him in the last six months. We have picked him up three or four times for petty stuff, disorderly conduct mostly. His wife always comes to get him but she won't say much about what's going on. I know he's been out of work since the school district let him go in November."

Jesse shook his head in disbelief, "None of that sounds like Rudy. He was always quiet, private about personal stuff, but solid and dependable as anyone I've ever known. And nothing meant more to him than Loreen and the kids."

Clement spoke up, "Maybe we should leave the whys and wherefores until after we've found him. Jesse, I know you haven't been – "

Jesse interrupted, "Of course I'll take part in the search; this is Rudy we're talking about. My go bag is in the car."

"Actually, we need you and Sacha to lead the search. We don't have any dogs with actual SAR experience here, right now. We have a couple nearing the end of their training but they are untested in the field."

Jesse agreed and twenty minutes later he stood with a small group laying out the search grid on a topographical map in Clement's office. Jesse and Sacha would take the lead with Reuben and Sully on one flank and Marcel with Soto on the other.

"We only have about four hours of daylight. If Rudy went in here, on the backside of Giant, he could go anywhere in these three quadrants," Jesse said pointing to the map.

"That's a lot of ground, especially with the snow cover," Marcel said. "We need to narrow it down; make an educated guess about where he might go."

Jesse nodded, "I agree. Normally, I would let the dogs lead us, but I think we need to take a chance here. Rudy is not lost; he knows these mountains too well. So he is either hurt, in which case we need to find him quickly, or he is up to something and won't want to be found. If he doesn't want to be found, we could be out there for a month and never locate him."

Clement said softly, "Jesse, Loreen says he took his gun with him."

"A gun?" Jesse said. "That doesn't sound like Rudy."

"He hasn't been himself lately," Clement replied. "Anyway, just be careful."

"Rudy's not going to hurt anyone – especially not me," Jesse said and then turned back to the map. "When we were kids we used to explore some shallow caves not far from where the Giant trail crosses this small stream – right about here. It's a long shot, but it's a starting point. If he is not there, then we can work back up the mountain along the stream."

They each marked up their maps, set the portable GPS trackers they would carry and headed to the van. Leah and several others walked with them.

"I wish I could come with you but I know you will move faster without me," she said.

Jesse smiled at her, "Brother Clement suggested you could help out with communications. You can be that voice whispering sweet nothings in my ear."

"Be careful," she sighed as she kissed him on the cheek.

Jesse smiled again, "I'll be fine and I'll be back in time for supper."

After the short drive to the trailhead, the three handlers and their dogs set off up the mountain doing their best to maintain visual contact through the dense underbrush. The dogs scented frequently but showed no signs of recognition. If Jesse had guessed right and Rudy had gone to the caves, he clearly did not use this trail. Still, it was their best chance for a quick resolution to the search, so Jesse pushed on.

About forty-five minutes from the trailhead, Sacha stopped and stood still with his nose in the air. He turned to look at Jesse, just as he had a thousand times before. He had something. In other circumstances, Jesse would have taken Sacha off the lead but not this time. Rudy had a gun and although Jesse trusted Rudy with his own life, he was not sure he could trust him with Sacha's.

Sacha led Jesse off the trail, moving diagonally up the mountain, away from the stream and the caves that Jesse remembered. He thought about telling the others he had changed course, but decided to let them continue to work the grid until he had a clearer idea of where Sacha was leading him.

Twenty minutes later, Sacha stopped again, this time clearly indicating toward a recessed area in the rock face about fifty feet ahead of them. Jesse stood silently scanning the woods and the hillside but he saw nothing. Then he heard a distinct click; the unmistakable sound of a rifle being cocked.

Jesse switched on his com-link and whispered, "I've found him. Everyone hold your positions until I make contact."

Jesse stood motionless listening and looking for some sign but the only thing stirring was the afternoon breeze moving through the pines.

"Rudy! It's me, Jesse; Jesse Tobias," he called.

Nothing. No sound, no movement, nothing.

"Rudy, come on out. Loreen's worried about you. She asked us to come find you; make sure you are OK."

More silence.

Then Jesse heard Rudy's familiar voice answer, "Leave me alone, Jesse. Go back to wherever you came from. I don't need your help."

"OK," Jesse answered, "I'll go, but can't we talk for a minute?"

"You've got nothing to say that I want to hear."

"So, I'll just listen. You can do all the talking," Jesse said.

"Go home, Jesse. I've got nothing to say to you."

"Come on, Rudy, you know I can't do that. I have to be able to tell everyone that I've seen you and you are OK. Otherwise, Loreen is going to worry and the Sheriff is going to have to keep looking for you."

"They can look, but they'll never find me."

"I found you," Jesse said.

"Yeah, well I didn't count on you and your dog being here. I thought you were some big-shot over in Massachusetts."

"Ha ha, yeah, that's me: a big-shot in Massachusetts. Look, Rudy, I'm going to come up there so we can talk," Jesse said and then he heard that click, again.

"You heard that, right?" Rudy called.

"Rudy, you're not going to shoot me. We're blood brothers, remember? I can still see the scar on my hand. I'm coming up."

Jesse moved slowly up the mountain with Sacha leading the way. Rudy stepped out from under a moss covered ledge that sheltered what Jesse guessed to be another shallow cave.

Rudy carried the rifle in the crook of his arm and although Jesse knew it was him, he hardly recognized him. He had always been slightly built but he had lost about twenty pounds since Jesse had seen him last and he looked gaunt and tired. His eyes appeared incredibly sad and seemed to sit too deep in his skull. This was not the Rudy that Jesse knew.

Jesse started to reach out to him but Rudy recoiled, "Stay back, Jesse! I don't want to hurt you."

"I don't want you to hurt me, either," Jesse said with a forced smile. "I'm just happy to see you. I was worried."

"Yeah, well, now you don't have to worry. So you can go back down the mountain and leave me alone."

"What's going on, Rudy? What are you doing out here?"

"I'm just taking care of business, Jesse. Personal business. Business that doesn't concern you. The sooner you get out of here, the sooner I can do what I got to do."

"OK, it's none of my business, but what about Loreen and the boys? It's their business, isn't it? I mean, you are still their husband and father, right? They – "

"Don't talk to me about my family. You don't know them and you don't know me, anymore. This is our business so leave me alone."

"So that's it? So what's the plan? You come out here with your little gun and do the deed? Then what?"

"Leave it alone, Jesse. It's none of your – "

"Yeah, I know, it's none of my business. Except, you know what, it IS my business, Rudy. Growing up, you were the closest thing to a brother I ever had and you and Loreen have always had the kind of marriage I hoped I might have some day. So, you can tell me to go away, but you can't stop me from caring about you. Whatever you do up here on this mountain, you will always be my friend – my brother."

Jesse knew he was taking a chance, pushing so hard, but his instincts told him that Rudy was not going to be sweet-talked into anything. If he was going to talk him down from this ledge, he was going to have to take some chances.

"Brothers, huh? Is that why I haven't seen you in how long? Oh, wait, I saw you last summer, but you didn't have time for me. Yeah, brothers; I forgot how close we are."

"You're right. I deserved that," Jesse said.

"So, where you been, bro? While I've been here, going nowhere, needing somebody, anybody, to understand what's going on, where you been?"

"Well, I –" Jesse started.

"I know where you been. You been off getting rich and famous and forgetting about all of this. You used to say these mountains were your home – the only place you felt alive. Now, you don't come near. We are not even a speck in your rear-view mirror."

"So this – whatever it is – is my fault?" Jesse said. "If only I had stayed here everything would be alright?"

Rudy spit on the ground and his tone became much darker, "No, man. This isn't about you. It's about me, or what's left of me. I'm just fading away. No work, no prospects, no reason to think anything will change. I died a long time ago but I'm just too dumb to know it. That's why I came up here – to finish the job. So why don't you turn around and head back down the mountain so I can get on with it."

"Look, Rudy, I get it – you're going through a tough time. But you have never been that guy who gives up, and I don't believe you're going to start now."

"Don't tell me what I'm going to do," Rudy snapped.

"OK, so what are you waiting for? You've been up here since yesterday, plenty of time to 'do the deed', but you're still here," Jesse answered.

"Who do you think you are to talk to me like that?"

"Rudy, I'm just the guy who cares what happens to you and wants to help. Let me try, Rudy; let's see if we can get through this together."

"And just how is that supposed to work? We gonna have heartfelt long-distance phone calls once a week?" Rudy said.

"Maybe," Jesse answered, "but I'll be here, too, I promise. I will come every week and we'll hang out and work on making things better. Don't give up on me, Rudy. More importantly, don't give up on yourself. You have so much to live for, so much life ahead of you, and you have a wife and family who love you.

I've been thinking about you and Loreen, lately. Do you have any idea how lucky you are? I would give anything to have what you have. You see, I met someone, Rudy; someone I was starting to think might be my Loreen. But then I blew it, and I lost her. That's what I'm doing here this weekend, trying to fix it and maybe hold on to the possibility that she and I might make a life like you and Loreen. I don't know if we can or not, but if we did that would be something worth living for, worth fighting for, worth holding onto until my last dying breath. And if I had your boys, well…" Jesse's voice choked with emotion.

Rudy lowered the rifle and leaned against a snow-capped boulder, "I don't want this, Jesse. I just want to stop hurting and feeling like I let everybody down. Loreen and the boys deserve better than that. They deserve better than me."

"There is no one better than you, Rudy. You are the man – their man – and you are going to get through this." Jesse walked over and put his hand on Rudy's shoulder, "I'm going to tell them we are coming down. OK?"

Rudy nodded his head without looking up.

Jesse reached for his com-link and found the switch open, "Base, do you copy?"

"I'm here, Jesse," Leah said.

"We're coming down. Ask someone to call Loreen and have her meet us at the trailhead."

Leah answered, "Will do."

Jesse turned aside and said softly, "So, was my com-link on the whole time?"

"Yes, it was," Leah whispered.

"And you were there all the time? You heard everything?" Jesse asked.

"Yes."

Jesse heaved a sigh, "OK, then. I guess we should talk when I get back."

"I'll be here," Leah said. "Jesse, I'm not going anywhere."

Chapter Twenty

Jesse and Leah tried to talk back at the Priory, but in all the hubbub, they never had a moment to themselves. They were swept up in the good feelings of a successful search and seeing Rudy and Loreen reunited. Sheriff Hansford joined in the celebration telling Rudy about a possible job opening with the county.

"Skeeter Manfred is retiring next month and I'm pretty sure they have money in the budget to replace him. Rudy, you did logistics in the Army, right? So purchasing and fleet management should be right up your alley. I'll find out who is doing the hiring and get back to you next week."

"You can use me as a reference, Rudy," Brother Clement offered. "I still have some friends at the County office building."

"Thanks, everyone," Loreen said seeing that Rudy was having trouble finding words of his own.

The long drive back to Boston gave Jesse and Leah plenty of time to talk, but neither of them knew where to start. They passed the first hour and a half in silence.

Finally, Leah spoke, "Well, this weekend turned out to be quite a surprise."

"Which part?" Jesse asked.

"Pretty much all of it," Leah chuckled. "The Priory, finding out about our ancient history, seeing you and the others on a real search, meeting Rudy and Loreen and the boys – I could not have imagined any of it."

"So, after all of that, what do you think? Now that you know just about everything, what's the verdict?"

"Jesse, did you mean what you said to Rudy up on the mountain? What you said about you and me? Or were you just trying to –"

"I meant every word. I don't understand it, myself. We haven't known each other very long, but being with you feels right. I don't really understand it but I know I want to be with you."

Leah nodded, "I know what you mean. I'm very cautious about relationships but with you it just felt like we were meant to be, right from the start. I don't put much stock in fate, but when I saw that picture of us as children, the hair on the back of my neck tingled and I got goosebumps. Maybe it's just one of life's quirky coincidences or maybe it is something more. I mean, just because we have a past doesn't mean we have a future."

"I remember Sister Miriam used to say, 'The past is history, tomorrow is a mystery' – "

"And today is a gift, that's why we call it the present," Leah said finishing Jesse's sentence. "My Grandmother used to say the same thing."

"So we have a past. I hope – I believe – we have a future. But right here, right now, I want to spend this day with you. This day and the next and the next and all the days I can imagine to come."

Jesse kept his eyes on the road but held out his hand to Leah. After a moment's hesitation, Leah took his hand in hers and squeezed.

"So how is this going to work?"

Jesse answered, "I don't know. The logistics could be a challenge with you in New York and me in Massachusetts."

"Don't forget what you promised Rudy."

"No problem – I just have to figure out how to be in three places at once," Jesse laughed. "I don't know how, but for you and for Rudy I will make it happen."

Leah appeared lost in thought for a while then said, "My internship at the magazine is up in May. I don't know what I will do then. I'm hoping to land a real job but that could be anywhere: New York, Chicago, Los Angeles – "

"Even Boston?" Jesse added.

"I suppose so, but that would take another intervention by fate or our guardian angels or whoever it is that's pulling the strings on our relationship."

"Like we said before, the future is a mystery," Jesse said. "For now, it's one day at a time. OK?"

"As long as we get to spend that one day together it's OK with me," Leah said still holding Jesse's hand.

The next few weeks passed quickly. Leah was back working in New York during the week, but they were together almost every weekend sometimes in Boston, sometimes in New York City and sometimes at the Priory. Jesse kept his promise to Rudy talking regularly on the phone and making weekly trips to the mountains. To make time for so much travel, Jesse backed off on some of his teaching commitments. He did, however, return to his role as an active SAR team member and de facto team leader.

In mid-March, Jesse meet Leah in New York for the weekend and found her especially excited. She had an advance copy of the magazine.

"We got the cover, Jesse! I knew they were thinking about it, but I never expected them to give it to a story by an intern. And my story survived almost intact. The editors polished up my writing, thankfully, but the pictures I chose – every one of them – are there!"

"Congratulations! Your first byline, your first feature and your first cover all in one issue – that's got to be some kind of record, right?"

"I don't know about that but it feels so good to see my work in print. It will certainly buff up my resume when I get serious about looking for a real job."

"I'm happy for you, Leah. We should celebrate, do something special this weekend," Jesse said.

"Jesse, there's one more thing. They want me to do a follow-up piece. I told my boss about our ancient history and she thought it might be a good angle for another story if the public reaction to this article is as good as they expect. They want me to write it from a personal perspective. It would just be a short human interest piece and they might not even run it.

What do you think? Would that be OK with you? I mean, I would have to include some of your story, maybe not the whole thing, but I would have to write about the Priory. If you want me to say no, I will."

Jesse did not answer at first then said, "Sure, Leah. Whatever you think. I know you will handle it right. It's time I stopped avoiding the past. It is what it is and I can't be embarrassed by it."

They spent Saturday celebrating. Leah took Jesse to a new exhibition at the International Center for Photography and then to view the "artsy" photography at the Museum of Modern Art. Leah knew both places like the back of her hand, but Jesse had not seen either collection before. They ended the day with a quiet dinner at a small Greek restaurant near Washington Square and splurged on a taxi instead of taking the subway back to Leah's apartment.

At the door Jesse said, "It's late, Leah – I should be going. I'll come by after church in the morning."

When he bent close to kiss her goodnight, Leah turned her face away putting her lips close to his ear, "My roommate is away for the weekend. Why don't you stay and we can go to church together in the morning?"

"Are you sure?" Jesse asked.

"I'm sure. All the hotel stays are getting expensive and – "

Jesse interrupted, "That's no reason – "

"I know," Leah said. "I'm nervous and I'm new at this kind of thing. What am I supposed to say? I don't know how to be seductive and sexy. I just know I want us to be together and whenever we say goodbye at night I feel so empty inside."

Jesse smiled, "I thought I was the only one feeling that way. We don't need seductive and sexy. Knowing that you love me is enough; more than enough. All I want to do is be with you."

"So stay," Leah said with more urgency. "Stay."

Jesse paid the driver and together they stepped inside.

Three weeks later the magazine hit the newsstands and Jesse found himself being treated like a celebrity. He did several interviews with newspapers and Leah brought him stacks of mail from readers. But when the follow-up article was published a month later telling more of Jesse's personal story, the reaction was overwhelming. Jesse was inundated with requests for interviews and invitations for speaking engagements, most for worthy causes. The mail piled up and the email response swamped Jesse's inbox to the point that he had to establish a new account for his work-related communications.

Against his better judgement, he agreed to do a segment of the television show, *Up Close and Personal*. Jesse was leery of so-called television news magazines as it seemed to him they were more about sensationalism than news. Still, he hoped that by doing this one interview, the other programs who were relentlessly pursuing him would be less interested.

The interview went as he expected. Suzanne Amodeo skimmed lightly over the details of his SAR work and quickly zeroed in on his personal story, hoping for the emotional response that was the holy grail for every UCP segment.

Near the end of the interview, the camera zoomed in, filling the screen with the director's requested "money shot". The extreme close-up had become the trademark of *Up Close and Personal;* a shot so close viewers could count the freckles on the young man's cheek. However, counting freckles was not the point.

The unstated, but accomplished, objective was to capture the first tear as it formed on his lower eye-lid and then slowly trickled down the side of his nose.

"I suppose it is ironic, isn't it? I mean, what I do – searching for people who are lost and here I am, like some pathetic lost boy myself. I don't know who my parents were, I have no family, and my best friend is my dog. I have a nice place to live, but it seems like I'm never there. We are on the road so much of the time, now, trying to help others find their way home that I'm seldom home myself. The Bible speaks of the blind leading the blind; I guess my version of that passage is 'the lost seeking the lost'.

I'm not complaining; I've been blessed in so many ways. I do wonder, though, if my own story has something to do with why I do what I do. I wonder if helping others who are lost somehow makes up for being lost myself. Does that sound crazy?"

Suzanne Amodeo smiled a scripted smile as she brushed an unscripted tear from her own eye and shook her head, "No – that doesn't sound crazy at all."

Gradually the media moved on to other more pressing stories and Jesse's life began to return to normal. He and Leah spent much of their time together going through the mail that continued to come. Some were from media junkies who obviously chased after the celebrity of the day, whoever they were. A number of other letters, however, came from people with stories to tell. Stories of personal experience with searches and rescues, both successful and failed. Some even wrote to tell Jesse their own stories, thinking something in their lives struck a chord with Jesse's own experiences. He insisted on reading each letter and personally responding to many of them.

The weekend after Easter, they were going through the week's mail when Leah held up a letter and said, "Well, here's a first. A letter from the warden at the state prison in New Hampshire. He's forwarded a letter from an inmate, there, a Malcom – "

"Yeats," Jesse finished. "Malcom Yeats is on death row and I guess I helped put him there."

"What?" Leah said.

"He's a bad guy; a serial rapist and murderer. I was part of the team that rescued Miranda Curtis a few years ago. Remember that case? She is the only one of his victims who survived to tell about what he did. Her testimony put him where he is today. What in the world does he want with me?"

"There's only one way to find out," Leah said as she handed the envelope to Jesse.

Inside he found a letter typed on the formal stationery of the Department of Corrections folded about a smaller envelope with his name scrawled in somewhat erratic handwriting. The letter read:

Dear Mr. Tobias:

I am writing to you in my capacity as Warden of the New Hampshire State Prison at Avondale. Enclosed is a letter one of our inmates, Malcom Yeats, has written to you. (All outgoing mail is read by prison staff prior to mailing.) Yeats claims to have some information that would be of interest you.

As I believe you know, Yeats is currently on death row having been convicted of multiple abductions, rapes and murders. You assisted in his capture with the rescue of Miranda Curtis. The State Police believe Yeats is linked to several other unsolved crimes but he has not been forthcoming. While we do not know what Yeats wants to tell you, if you meet with him it is possible that he might reveal information useful in their ongoing investigation.

If you are willing to meet with him, please call my office at the number below to arrange your visit.

Jesse refolded the warden's letter and picked up the second envelope. The letter from Yeats, scrawled on a single page of lined paper was far more succinct.

Dear Jesse:

As soon as I saw the article I knew it was you. I have information about your mother and father. Come see me – let's get reacquainted. Any day is good for me – they are all the same here. Just don't wait too long.

Jesse put the letter away and then said, "Yeats wants to meet with me. He claims he has information about my parents."

"What? What could he know about your parents?" Leah said. "What does the warden say?"

"He wants me to meet with Yeats. Apparently, they think he may tell me something that might help resolve some outstanding cases."

"What difference does it make? If he's already on death row, why do they need more cases?"

"They connected him to five or six murders, as I remember, but they think there may be more. I don't imagine they care about more charges against Yeats but there are still families out there wondering what happened to their loved ones. If they can close more cases, maybe recover more bodies, it could mean a lot to those families."

Jesse sat quietly looking at the papers in his hand for several moments then said, "I guess I'm going to New Hampshire."

Leah came over and put her arm around his shoulders, "Are you sure, Jesse?"

Jesse nodded, "I think so. I need to hear what he has to say, for me and for those families. Maybe it's nothing, or maybe…"

"OK, but I'm coming with you," Leah said and before Jesse could object she added, "We're a package deal now. Where you go, I go."

Two days later Jesse and Leah sat uncomfortably in the warden's office, waiting. Everything about the prison seemed designed to intimidate. The tall gray concrete walls topped with razor wire, the guard towers with tinted glass secreting who-knew-what, the enormous metal door that clanged shut behind them with heart-stopping finality, the institutional paint and lights, the sparse furnishings and every person in the place, except for Jesse and Leah in easily identifiable uniforms. There would be no mistaking prisoners for guards or staff; even the warden wore the distinctive gray trousers and shirt that marked him as staff. The only concessions to his authority were the military necktie he wore and the braid on the shoulders of his jacket. Jesse made a mental note never to end up in a place like this.

"Mr. Tobias, I'm sorry I kept you waiting. I'm Daniel Wagstaff," the warden said as he shook Jesse's hand but looked directly at Leah.

"Warden, this is Leah Madison my, uh, friend," Jesse said before adding quickly, "and the author of the magazine article that caught Yeats' attention."

"Ms. Madison," the warden nodded in Leah's direction, "I wasn't expecting the press."

"I'm here as Jesse's friend," Leah offered, "for moral support."

"Still, I can't allow you to meet with Yeats," the warden said.

Jesse answered, "No, that would not be good given his violent tendencies with young women. I will meet with him, alone."

Leaving Leah to wait in the warden's office, the two men walked down a long hallway, up a flight of stairs and across an open catwalk to another section of the complex. As they walked, Warden Wagstaff explained his plan to Jesse.

"You will meet with Yeats in a small conference room separate from the usual visiting area. The room is wired with hidden cameras and microphones so that everything Yeats says or does will be recorded. Yeats will be manacled the entire time and two corrections officers will be outside the door. If you feel unsafe at any time, call for the guard and they will be in the room in seconds.

Yeats would not tell me what he wants to say to you but we are hoping he might divulge information about open cases. Anything you can do to encourage him to talk about what he has done would be helpful."

Jesse said, "Won't he know what I am trying to do?"

"Yeats is not stupid. He will know, right away, that the room is not the usual place for visitors and is more like the interrogation room where he has been questioned by investigators. Don't think you are going to trick him into saying something that he doesn't want to say. The thing is, I think he asked to see you because he wants to say something, but on his own terms. I don't know his motives. It could be his conscience, it could be him showing the police that he is in control, not them. Or it could be more sinister. Since you had a role in putting him here, maybe he thinks he knows something that will be hurtful to you, as some kind of payback. Whatever he has to say and whatever his reason, try to keep him talking. The more he says the better the chance we will learn something helpful."

Jesse sat in the conference room for several minutes waiting for Yeats. The only furniture in the room, a metal table and four straight-back chairs, was bolted to the concrete floor. He glanced around the room looking for hidden cameras but could not be sure exactly where they were. Once more the setting seemed intended to intimidate and Jesse could testify to its effectiveness.

Finally, two burly corrections officers led Yeats into the room, his rolling gait resulting from a distinct limp. He shuffled along with heavy shackles on his feet; his hands held waist high by the handcuffs clipped to a leather belt around his waist. They sat him down across the table from Jesse and chained the restraint belt to the chair.

"We'll be right outside if you need anything," one of the guards said to Jesse as they exited the room.

Yeats looked older than Jesse remembered from the press coverage of the trial. If Jesse did not know what Yeats had done he never would have taken this slightly built, gray-haired old man for a dangerous criminal.

Yeats looked long and hard at Jesse for several moments, then he nodded his head slowly as if satisfied by Jesse's appearance.

"I was pretty sure it was you when I saw the magazine articles. Now, I know; it's good to see you again, Jesse."

"I don't know what you think you know, Mr. Yeats, so why don't you tell me why I am here," Jesse said.

"Right to the point, huh? Look, I don't get many visitors so let me enjoy this a little, OK? Besides, aren't you supposed to humor me – get me talking so I end up telling you what they want to know?"

"They?"

"Don't be coy, Jesse. I know they are listening, probably watching too. So let's not pretend this is just a friendly visit."

"No, this is not a friendly visit," Jesse said with an edge in his voice. "We are not friends – never have been and never will be. I am here for only one reason: you claim to have information about my family. Personally, I'm betting this is a waste of my time. I don't know what you are up to, but I don't think you know anything beyond what was written in that magazine article."

Yeats chuckled, "And still, here you are."

"Here I am, but not for long. If you have something to say, say it. Otherwise, we're done."

Yeats expression darkened, "Don't push me too hard, Jesse."

"You have ten seconds to get my attention," Jesse said.

Yeats stared at him and then said, "What did Brother Clement tell you about the day you were left at the Priory?"

"You tell me," Jesse said. "This is supposed to be about what you know."

"OK, you doubt me, I get it. What if I were to tell you that I know all about that day, because I'm the one who left you there."

"Well, that would be a good story if you could prove it."

"I think I can. Clement told you that you were left on the steps of the Priory, wrapped in some old clothes, right?"

"That much was in the article, Yeats."

"One of the rags you were wrapped in was a remnant of a green plaid flannel shirt. Did he tell you that?"

"No, why would he? And if I asked him now, why would he remember? That doesn't prove anything. You're bluffing, Yeats," Jesse said.

"Did he tell you that you were left with the afterbirth still attached? That wasn't in the story, was it?" Yeats snapped. "Judging by the look on your face, he never told you that, did he?"

Jesse wanted to knock the smug smile off Yeats' face, but his mind was racing, trying to remember if Brother Clement ever said anything about the afterbirth.

He tried to stall, "I, uh – "

"Now I've got your attention, don't I, Jesse? If you still don't believe me, call him. I'll wait. I've got time, plenty of time. Call Clement and ask him, then maybe we can get on with this."

The guards came as soon as Jesse called them, "I need to make a quick phone call."

As if they expected him to say that, one of them stayed with Yeats while the other led Jesse down the hallway to an office with a telephone. Brother Clement answered on the second ring. After a few words of greeting, Jesse got to the point.

"Brother Clement, do you remember that first day when you found me on the steps of the Priory? You said I was wrapped in rags – do you remember the rags? Was there a part of a flannel shirt?"

Clement took a moment to respond, "I don't know, Jesse. That was a long time ago; what's this about?"

"I'll explain everything later, just try to remember."

"Jesse, I'm sorry, but I don't know."

"OK – I figured that was a long shot. One more thing, though, what about the afterbirth? When you found me was the afterbirth still attached?"

"The afterbirth? Jesse what is this about?"

"Please, Brother Clement – was the afterbirth still attached or had the umbilical cord been cut."

"No, there was no afterbirth," Clement said. "I know that for certain."

Jesse sighed with relief, "No afterbirth. Thank you Brother Clement. I'll call you later and explain the whole thing."

"Jesse, wait!" Clement said. "When I found you, Sister Serena had already cleaned you up some, like one of her puppies. There were teeth marks on your umbilical cord. I've never told anyone this – I didn't want anyone to think Serena might have harmed you. When dogs clean up their young, sometimes they eat the afterbirth. Since she had bitten through the umbilical cord she might have…" Clement's voice trailed away.

Jesse's head was swimming, "Thanks, Brother Clement. I'll call you later."

Jesse tried to piece together what was happening as he walked back to the room where Yeats waited.

When Jesse sat down, Yeats said, "You still think I'm wasting your time?"

Jesse put on his best poker face, "I don't know. Brother Clement did not remember the shirt and he said when he found me, there was no afterbirth."

"He's lying!" Yeats shouted. "It was there. You wouldn't stop squirming and I was afraid I would cut you so I left it attached. When I left you on the steps, when that dog came after me – "

"Dog? What dog?" Jesse said.

"I don't know, one of those dogs they raise at the Priory, the yellow ones with the big heads –". Yeats stopped in mid-sentence, then continued, "The dog! The dog must have found you and eaten the afterbirth! They do that, right? That explains it; the dog did it."

Jesse was stunned. When he had tried to imagine all the things that Yeats might tell him, he had never even considered the possibility that somehow Yeats was there when he was born or that Yeats was the one who left him at the Priory. He had always assumed it was his mother who left him there.

Yeats was looking at him again, "You look like her, you know. You have the same eyes and nose. Your mother was quite pretty in her own way."

"Is that what this is about, Yeats? You want me to know that you know my mother? OK, I'll bite – who is she? Where is she? Is that what you're dying to tell me?"

"Easy boy, take it easy. If I left you at the priory when you were only a couple of hours old, then I guess it's safe to say I knew your mother," Yeats paused for a moment. "Her name was Julie. Julie Crandall."

"Was?" Jesse said. "Her name *was* Julie Crandall? Are you telling me that she is dead? So what happened Yeats? Was she one of your victims? Did you kill my mother?"

"Slow down, Jesse. Your mother died in childbirth. Your mother died giving birth to you. It all happened so fast; I don't know what went wrong. One minute she was going into labor and the next you were born and she stopped breathing. Such a shame, a young woman like that gone so suddenly."

Jesse looked at Yeats. Something about the story, and the way he told it, did not ring true.

"I'm not buying it, Yeats. Young women don't die like that in childbirth anymore; maybe a hundred years ago, but not now with modern medicine. If she died where is she buried?"

"What is it going to take to get you to believe me, Jesse?"

"I doubt if I will ever believe you, but let's start with the name of a cemetery. If my mother died, like you said, where is she buried?"

"If I tell you and you see for yourself, will you stop all this and believe me?" Yeats asked.

"Try me," Jesse said. "What cemetery?"

Yeats did not answer right away, then he said, "She's not in a cemetery. I buried her in the mountains not far from the Priory. She liked it there and besides it would have been, uh, awkward to report her death to the authorities."

"Awkward?" Jesse said. "You buried her in the woods because it would have been awkward?"

"Let's just leave it at that, for now," Yeats said.

Jesse shook his head in disbelief. "Where? Tell me where she is."

Jesse wrote down the directions and sketched a rough map as Yeats described the location. It sounded plausible, but finding the grave after all these years would be a longshot.

"So when you find her, you'll come back, right?" Yeats asked. "I mean, we have so much more to talk about."

"There's more?" Jesse said.

"Oh yes; much more."

Jesse could not imagine what else Yeats could have to tell him, but the way he said it made the hair on his arms stand up.

After a quick debriefing session with the warden, Jesse and Leah drove home while Jesse told her about his meeting with Yeats. They stopped at a small diner for an early dinner and Jesse called Rudy Talltrees.

"Rudy, I need your help," Jesse said and then he told Rudy what Yeats had said. "I'll be there tomorrow; can you meet me?"

"I'll be there, Jesse. If she's out there, we'll find her."

Chapter Twenty-One

  The search for Julie Crandall's grave went on for three days. It began with Jesse, Leah, Rudy Talltrees, most of the members of the Priory community and Sheriff Hansford with two of his deputies. By Saturday, the third day of the search, word had spread and more than two hundred volunteers converged on the heavily wooded area at the foot of Giant mountain.
  They organized the search grid like a search and rescue operation with Brother Clement coordinating the effort. Jesse brought Sacha and both Brother Marcel and Brother Reuben brought dogs from the Priory although they were not trained for this kind of search. As if to prove that point, late Saturday afternoon a specially trained cadaver dog, on loan from the State Police, indicated strongly in a spot that Jesse and Sacha had cleared only minutes before. Searchers on their hands and knees scraped at a twenty-foot square patch of ground for nearly an hour before one of them found the first evidence of human remains. By dusk, they had unearthed most of a skeleton wrapped in plastic sheeting just as Yeats had described.

Brother Clement called in the searchers and asked them to assemble outside the command tent. When they had all gathered, Sheriff Hansford announced that a body had been found. He explained that formal identification would take some time but, based on the information at hand, they believed it was the body of Julie Crandall and so the search was officially suspended pending final resolution.

Brother Clement then spoke, "Thank you all for your help and for the compassionate way you conducted this search. If you are willing, I would like to invite you to join me in an attitude of prayer."

Most of the searchers bowed their heads, some removed their caps and still others simply stood silently as Clement prayed.

After most of the others had departed, Clement found Jesse kneeling just outside the crime scene tape that boxed off the shallow grave where Julie Crandall's remains were found. The County Medical Examiner was still collecting physical evidence and documenting the find with numerous photographs.

Clement rested his hand on Jesse's shoulder, "Dr. Chavez says he needs another hour then he will take the remains back to the morgue. Before the search began, Sheriff Hansford accessed a copy of Julie's dental records so, with a little luck, they should be able to confirm her identity."

"It's her," Jesse said. "Yeats described the location and the plastic sheeting. It's her; it's my mother."

"Be patient, Jesse. Let Dr. Chavez be sure. I don't know what is motivating Yeats, but just because he probably left this body here doesn't prove it is Julie Crandall. Even if it is, it doesn't prove that Julie was your mother."

"Why would Yeats make up a story like that? Besides he knew too much about the day I was left at the Priory. Anyway, we'll know soon enough. I gave Dr. Chavez a DNA swab. So, we'll know..."

"Jesse, I understand this is hard for you. You didn't know her, but still..." Clement left the sentence unfinished. "You are not the only one hurting, here. You probably don't know this, but Brother Reuben knew Julie Crandall, in fact, they were quite close."

"Reuben?" Jesse said.

He got to his feet and scanned the area, spotting Reuben standing nearby. Rudy Talltrees had his arm around Reuben's shoulders, but when Jesse approached Rudy stepped away.

"Reuben – Brother Clement just told me that you knew Julie Crandall. I'm sorry for acting like this was all about me. I never stopped to think that other people might have known her. Are you OK?"

Reuben nodded his head slowly, but did not look at Jesse. After a few seconds he wiped his sleeve across his face and spoke in a voice not much more than a whisper.

"I tried to persuade myself that somehow she got away from him, forgot about me and made a new life for herself. I didn't believe it, though; she would never have left me..." Reuben's voice cracked as he looked Jesse in the eye, "We were going to run away together."

Jesse felt his own eyes filling up as Reuben wiped away another tear, "Someday – not today, but someday – would you tell me about her? Just whatever you remember, so I can know something about my mother..."

Reuben nodded his head and the two men embraced as if to hold one another up in their shared grief.

Jesse and Leah remained at the Priory to wait for Dr. Chavez's confirmation. They did not have to wait long. Monday afternoon, Dr. Chavez arrived at the Priory with Sheriff Hansford. They met with Jesse, Leah, Reuben and Clement in the chapel and Chavez confirmed the results of his examination.

"Dental records were conclusive; the remains belong to Julie Crandall, age 22," Chavez said. "I sent the DNA off to the lab.

It will take a while to get those results, but that is just a formality. I'm sorry."

Sheriff Hansford said, "Jesse, tell me again what Yeats said about how Julie died. Tell me everything…"

"He said she died in childbirth. I was being born and suddenly she stopped breathing. That's all he said. Why?"

The Sheriff nodded toward Chavez who said, "After so many years, I can't tell about death during childbirth. But Julie had other injuries that, in most cases, would indicate she was murdered. Her left occipital bone was shattered and there is a fracture to the base of her skull that would most likely have been fatal."

"So Yeats killed her!" Jesse seethed. "I knew he was hiding something."

Leah tried to comfort him, but Jesse's anger erupted. He jumped to his feet and charged out of the room. Leah started to follow, but Clement gently took her arm.

"Let him go, Leah. Give him a little space."

Leah paced the room for nearly a half hour then turned toward the door.

"Try the chapel," Clement said. "That's where I would usually find him."

When Leah's eyes had adjusted from the bright sunlight to the dimly lit chapel, she saw Jesse sitting in the front pew. She went to him slowly and sat down close enough to hear his deep breathing.

"I don't understand," he said without looking up. "For all these years, I lived without knowing her; truthfully, without thinking of her much at all. I came to accept that my life was different from everyone else's. I didn't have a mother and father but in many ways what I had here in the Priory was an amazing substitute. Sure I wondered what it would be like to know my mother and whenever I did think about her I struggled with how anyone could abandon their own child, but for the most part I was content with my life.

Now, I feel like a gaping hole has been ripped open in my gut. I didn't just appear here by some act of God. A living, breathing human being gave birth to me and lost her own life in exchange. Almost as if she was punished for having me; almost as if Yeats – "

Leah cut him off, "Jesse, don't do this to yourself. Malcom Yeats is a sick man. What he did is on him; it's not your fault."

"She deserved to live; she was younger than you are now. She had so much to live for but because of him her life ended before it ever began. Yeats made that decision as though it was his choice not hers. And now he's making decisions about my life, too. Even in prison, waiting to die, he's still pulling the strings of other people's lives."

"So, don't let him, Jesse. Don't play along with his game. Don't give him the satisfaction of playing out whatever he thinks he is doing to you. He can't hurt you unless you let him – so don't let him!

Jesse, I love you. These past four months together have been the best of my life and I hope they are just the beginning of a long life together. I don't care where we go or what we do as long as I am with you. Forget about Yeats; let him rot in that cell. Don't let him do anymore to ruin your life, our life."

Leah leaned in and kissed him on the cheek and tasted the salt of his tears on her lips. She pulled him close and they held a long embrace.

Without letting her go, Jesse said, "I love you, too, Leah and there is nothing I want more than to make a life with you. But you've got to understand why I can't let this go. I have to finish it with Yeats. I can't let it end with him calling the shots. He has to live the rest of his days knowing that he did not win; that, whatever it is that he has planned so carefully, it did not work. He may think he can decide what happens in my life, the same way he decided for my mother, but he is wrong and I'm going to make sure that he knows he is wrong."

"OK, Jesse," Leah said, "We'll do it your way. But we'll do it together. Like I said before, we are a package deal, now."

It took several weeks, but Jesse waited for the DNA results to come back before going to see Yeats again. They met in the same conference room at the prison so everything could be recorded on video.

Yeats came in wearing a smug expression that seemed out of context for a man in chains wearing prison orange. "I wondered when you would be back. I knew you were coming but – "

"I don't really care what you think you know about me, Yeats," Jesse said.

"Why, Jesse, I'm surprised."

"Not as surprised as I was when I found out you lied about my mother. Although, I should have expected it from someone like you."

Yeats leaned back in his chair, "Lied? What do you mean? You found her body, just like I told you. I saw the news coverage. It wasn't on TV but I would bet the farm that you did a DNA test to confirm she was your mother. Am I right?"

Jesse nodded, "DNA confirmed Julie Crandall was my mother."

Yeats smiled slightly, "Just like I told you. I didn't lie – "

"You said she died in childbirth."

"She did!"

Jesse sneered at him, "Was that before or after you caved-in her skull?"

Yeats did not answer at first then he said, "You mean she died from hitting her head, not from childbirth?"

Jesse looked at him closely. Yeats appeared to be genuinely surprised.

"So, did you enjoy it, Yeats – beating a pregnant woman to death? Did it make you feel strong and powerful?"

Yeats reacted angrily, "I didn't beat her to death. I hit her once and she hit her head on the table as she fell. She was still alive, kicking and screaming at me, when she went into labor. Then it happened just as I told you: you were born and she stopped breathing. It all happened so fast..."

An uncomfortable silence hung between them for what seemed to Jesse a very long time. Finally, Yeats spoke softly.

"I didn't mean to kill her; she wasn't like the others. I was just so angry about her and the pregnancy and everything. It must have been the hormones because she seemed to get more determined, more resistant with each month that passed. She was out of control. No matter what I said, she wouldn't listen to me."

"So you killed her," Jesse fought to keep his voice from trembling. "What I don't get is why you didn't kill me, too. It would have been easy just to let me die."

Yeats shook his head, "No – I couldn't do that. Once I knew that she was gone, I knew I couldn't keep you but I couldn't let you die, either. Not you, not my own son..."

The words exploded inside Jesse's head. He felt the room spinning out of control. He grabbed onto the edge of the table as he felt the air being siphoned out of his lungs. For what felt like an eternity he floated, not moving, not breathing, until his vision blurred and he felt certain he would pass out.

Suddenly other people were in the room and Jesse felt hands on his shoulders shaking him. With an explosive cough, Jesse gagged then sucked in a deep breath, gagged again, and then drew several short gasping breaths. When his eyes came back into focus, he was still sitting at the table but Yeats was gone and one of the prison guards stood over him. Moments later Leah and Warden Wagstaff hurried into the room followed by one of the prison EMTs carrying an oxygen bottle.

They all gathered around him but Jesse waived them off, "No, it's alright. I'm OK, just give me a minute."

Leah knelt at his side holding onto his hands as the others quietly left the room. Jesse put his arm around Leah and pulled her close.

Finally, Jesse spoke, "I didn't see that coming. Of all the things I imagined Yeats might try to pull, that one never occurred to me."

"Of course not," Leah said, "why would it? He's lying, Jesse! He's just trying to hurt you. It's like you said before, he wants to be the one in control; he's just trying to manipulate you."

Jesse shook his head, "But why me? Why would he wake up one morning and decide to go after me? Revenge for my role in Miranda Curtis' rescue? That hardly seems enough of a reason to dredge up a nearly thirty-year-old crime.

No, I think he is finally telling the truth. I think he raped his niece Julie, who knows how many times, and then when she got pregnant he felt like he was boxed-in. Finally, he struck out at her and whether accidentally or intentionally it really doesn't matter, he killed her and was left with this baby – his baby.

Now here he is, facing his own death and he decides he wants to have some kind of twisted family reunion. So here I am. Funny, I always wanted to know my mother but I never really thought much at all about my father. Maybe somewhere, deep inside, I knew it was better not to know."

"Jesse, I will love you always no matter what comes out of this, but I just can't believe that Yeats is your father. You are nothing alike; there is no family resemblance, at all. When I look at the picture Sheriff Hansford gave you of your mother, I can see her face in yours. But there is nothing, nothing of Yeats in you at all. Nothing."

Leah climbed onto Jesse's lap and they held each other quietly. Moments later Warden Wagstaff came back into the room.

"I did not mean to eavesdrop," he said, "but the cameras were still rolling so I overheard your conversation. There is an easy way to find out if Yeats is lying, or not. We have his DNA results on file; they were part of his trial record. You just had your DNA done to confirm Julie Crandall's relationship to you. Comparing your results with Yeats DNA record would be quick and easily done."

It took only three phone calls and a couple of hours for the answer to come. Jesse held the FAX in his hand when he walked back into the conference room where Yeats waited.

"How are you feeling, son?"

Yeats saccharine tone and confident smirk made Jesse nauseous but he kept his voice level, "I'll admit you had me going for a while, Yeats. Every step along the way this trip has gotten stranger and stranger. Each time I said to myself it can't get any worse but, sure enough, you found a way to make it worse than I could ever imagine. First, you tell me I have you to thank for my arrival at the Priory. Then you lead me to Julie Crandall's body and it turns out that, yes, she was my mother and what's more you killed her. All of that was bad enough, but the thought that you could be my father – well that hurt more than anything else. That was the last straw."

"Ouch," Yeats said sarcastically. "I'm not all that bad, Jesse, once you get to know me."

Jesse said, "No, you are that bad which is all the more reason I have no intention of getting to know you or even seeing you again."

"You mean you would abandon your own father – the father that refused to abandon you all those years ago?"

"No, I won't abandon my own father," Jesse said firmly, "but I will abandon you – you lying, murdering son of a bitch. You are not my father!"

Jesse slid the FAX across the table so Yeats could read the brief message EJ Carlson had forwarded from the FBI Crime Lab: "*After comparing the DNA of Malcom Yeats with that of Jesse Tobias it is 99.4% conclusive that the two individuals are not biologically related.*"

Jesse watched Yeats expression fade from victory to defeat, then he stood up and walked out of the room without saying another word.

Chapter Twenty-Two

Jesse and Leah went off the grid for the next two weeks, as young lovers sometimes do. Cocooned inside Jesse's house they switched off their cell phones and shut out the rest of the world. They spent the days soaking in the perfect joy of being together and they spent the nights exploring ways to express the love they felt for each other. When they spoke their conversation betrayed a new intimacy. In their new and deeper connection, they withheld nothing of the lives they lived before and they fearlessly dreamed aloud of the life they would make together. Neither of them mentioned Malcom Yeats nor any of the recent events that he had precipitated.

At the end of the second week, as they sat together over coffee and fresh baked croissants, Leah said, "I suppose this can't go on forever."

"Why not?" Jesse said with a smile. "Every couple of days I can make a midnight grocery run to the 24-hour market on the corner. No one needs to know except the cashier, and not even her if I use the self-checkout. We can hold out here indefinitely."

Leah laughed, "Jesse, you know what I mean. We have to go back to the real world, someday. All those dreams and plans for our life together aren't going to happen magically. We have to work at them, if we really want them to come true; if they are more than wishful thinking."

"I know," Jesse said, "but these last few days together have been the best days of my life. I don't want them to end."

"They don't have to end. They can be the beginning for us, for our new life. Besides, everyone else must be wondering what happened to us. Brother Clement, everyone at the Priory, Rudy Talltrees – you promised to see him every week, remember? And my parents must be out of their minds by now. I talk to my mother three or four times a week. I bet my voice-mailbox is overflowing with messages from her. Besides, I've got to find a job now that my internship is over. I don't like being unemployed."

"We can live on love – and the income from my annuity," Jesse said.

Leah shook her head, "I still can't believe you have all that money in the bank."

"I never really felt right about taking the money from Andy Griffis' father."

"So you just ignored it?" Leah said.

"Sort of; Archer Blake set up this investment account so I didn't have to do anything but sign the tax papers at the end of the year. I figured I could decide later what to do with it; keep it or give it away or something.

I live a simple life, Leah, and my income from training and consulting is enough to support me. My work has never been about making money. I would do it even if I had to pay for the privilege."

"I feel the same way, Jesse. I want to work because I am a photojournalist – not because I want to make money by taking pictures. It's a good thing, too, because photojournalism is not exactly the fast track to riches. I hate to disappoint you, but if you're thinking I will be able to support you in your old age you've picked the wrong girl."

They both chuckled and then were silent for a few moments until Leah said, "Before we reconnect with the outside world maybe we should decide what happens next, for us, I mean. We both want to be together but we haven't talked about how that will look or work. When I call my mother and you call Brother Clement what do we tell them? How do we describe who 'we' are now and who we intend to be together?"

"First things first," Jesse said. "You have met my so-called family, but your parents probably don't even know I exist. Right?"

"Not exactly; I've told my mother about you – about us – and I would bet she's told my father," Leah said.

"Oh?" Jesse said. "When did all this happen and what did you tell your mother about 'us'?"

"Like I said, we talk several times a week, so she knows pretty much everything up until we unplugged a couple of weeks ago," Leah answered.

"Everything?"

"Well, no, not everything," Leah laughed. "She knows the G-rated version that most girls share with their mothers, but I wouldn't be surprised if she has guessed most of the rest."

"All the more reason for me to meet them in person, before they come to too many conclusions about me from incomplete description and innuendo," Jesse said.

"Right. So one step in our 'next steps plan' is for you to meet my family. Then what?"

Jesse took a deep breath and said, "Then I guess we need to decide where you will work and where we will live after we get married."

Leah looked away from Jesse, bowed her head and didn't say anything.

"OK," Jesse said, "maybe that was a little sudden. I really didn't think it through all the way; it just kind of came out. I've never done this before so I'm not sure...it's just...well, I never really believed it happens like in the movies so... Help me out, Leah! I'm dying here. If you don't want to... OK, I'm going to shut up now and hope you will say something..."

"Don't want to what, Jesse?"

"What do you think? Get married!" Jesse sputtered.

"How can I answer that, Jesse? Of course, I want to get married someday, but I can't answer that now."

"Why not?" Jesse said.

"Because no one's asked me," Leah said with a look that displayed equal parts humor and seriousness.

"Right," Jesse said. "I guess that wasn't much of a proposal. Like I said, it just kind of came out. So, consider that a warning shot. Unless you wave me off right now, someday soon – very soon – I plan to ask you, the right way. When I do, I hope you will be prepared with an answer."

"Thanks for the warning," Leah said. "Until then we just tell people we are together and trying to figure out where this is going."

Jesse leaned in and kissed her softly, "I think we know exactly where this is going. All we need to do is figure out how we get there."

"Jesse, there is one more thing that has been on my mind. I know we said we weren't going to talk about the whole Malcom Yeats business, but –"

"Yeats has nothing to do with us, anymore. He is nothing more than a smudge on the rear-view mirror of my long ago life," Jesse said.

"I agree, and believe me, I couldn't be happier about that," Leah said. "Just thinking about him gives me the creeps."

"Then don't think about him," Jesse said.

"I don't," Leah answered, "but the whole business with him left one big unanswered question: if Yeats isn't your father – and I am thrilled to know that he's not – then who is?"

"I don't know," Jesse said. "For some reason I have always wondered about my mother and seldom even thought about who my father might be. Now that I know about my mother, maybe that's enough."

Leah took his hand, "Maybe in other circumstances it would be enough. But, Jesse, it seems so close, unless you don't want to know."

"I'm not following, Leah," Jesse said. "Of course, I want to know, but where would we begin? How is it so close – I'm confused."

Leah smiled at him, "Jesse, you know how babies are made, right?"

"Yeah, I know," he chuckled. "It's got something to do with what we were doing last night – oh, and there's a stork, right?"

"Jesse, I'm serious. Julie Crandall – your mother – became pregnant the old fashioned way, right? And we now know that Yeats was not the father. The fact that he thought he was means that he assaulted her at least once, probably more often, and that other than himself, he did not think that Julie had been with any other men. Clearly, he was wrong but I would bet the ranch that Julie had only one other lover, someone she loved and someone that Yeats tried to keep her from seeing."

"Reuben!" Jesse said as though the name suddenly appeared in the air before him. "Of course! Why didn't I think of that? I was so caught up, so afraid that Malcom Yeats would turn out to be my father that I never even thought…"

Leah squeezed his hand a little tighter, "We can't be certain, but it makes perfect sense to me. You said they were in love and planned to run away together. After Julie disappears, Reuben ends up working at the Priory. You and he have a special bond that everyone can see, and when Reuben officially joins the Priory he becomes something of a surrogate father to you. Maybe he knew; maybe you just filled a hole in his life; only Reuben can tell us.

But, Jesse, this is all speculation. It is a question that can be answered, however. So, do you want to know?"

Jesse nodded his head, "Yes, I want to know, but does Reuben want to know? If he suspected all along, why wouldn't he have said something? If he didn't suspect then, he must suspect now. I mean, if you figured it out surely he would."

"Thanks a lot, Jesse," Leah said feigning insult. "You sure know how to make a girl feel special."

Jesse hugged her, "That didn't come out right but you know what I mean. Once he got over the shock of Julie's death and we proved Yeats wrong about being my father he must have started wondering. So why hasn't he said anything?"

"Maybe he's been trying."

"What do you mean?"

"Jesse, we've been incommunicado for two weeks, ever since you debunked Yeats' claim of fatherhood."

"Right," Jesse said, "so maybe we need to reconnect with the world and check voice mail."

Leah's phone showed nearly a dozen messages from her mother and another ten work-related messages. Jesse had two messages from Brother Clement, one from Mr. Carlson and one message and eleven missed calls from Reuben.

Leah looked over Jesse's shoulder at his voice mailbox and said, "He knows."

Jesse and Leah had a second cup of coffee and came up with a plan for the next few days, knowing those days would impact the rest of their lives. First, a visit for Jesse to meet Leah's parents, then a heart-to-heart with Reuben at the Priory and somewhere in between they hoped to sort out a few pesky details: little things like where they would live, where they would work and what their life together might look like.

"Details, details, details," Leah scoffed.

A long weekend in Abbottsville, Virginia, accomplished their first task. Leah's parents seemed happy to finally meet the man she had been telling them about. Phone calls, texts and social media posts had prepared the ground, but meeting face-to-face completed the puzzle.

From Virginia, they drove straight to the Priory. Eleven hours on the road gave Jesse time to think about the conversation with Reuben. Leah wanted to help but she knew that Jesse needed to do this alone. Besides, what did she know about how it felt to discover that a long-time trusted friend was actually your father. Talk about a life-changing conversation…

As they drove deeper into the Adirondacks Leah asked, "Are you ready? Have you decided what you want to say to Reuben?"

"Not really. He and I have always been able to talk to one another. I'm hoping that once we are together we will find the words."

"Jesse, you are incredible. If it was me, I would be so stressed out, worrying about finding the right things to say, wondering how he felt about discovering he had a child after all these years, being afraid that this news might change everything – and not for the better."

"Thanks for that, Leah. None of that had occurred to me. Now I have a whole list of things to worry about," Jesse said and then smiled when Leah looked like she took him seriously. "I'm kidding! Of course, I wonder about all of that but I trust Reuben like he was, well, my father. In many ways, he's been a father-figure to me for as long as I can remember. I don't really think this will change much between us. I don't want anything from him that he hasn't already been giving me for as long as I can remember."

Leah smiled at him sweetly, "There are so many things that I love about you."

When they arrived at the Priory, Brother Clement greeted them and helped them settle into their rooms. Although he knew they were living together, they would have separate quarters at the Priory.

"Reuben is anxious to see you, but he thought he should stay away and give you time to settle in after your trip."

Jesse nodded, "It's been a long day on the road. Maybe we could meet in the morning."

Reuben appeared in the dining hall the next morning as Jesse and Leah finished their second cup of coffee. Jesse thought he looked terribly vulnerable.

After they exchanged hugs, more tentatively than usual, Leah said, "I've got some things to do, so I'll let you two talk."

"Let's walk while we talk," Jesse said. "Sacha needs some exercise; he's been cooped up too much lately."

They walked together over the familiar trails of the Priory grounds. Jesse told Reuben about his confrontations with Yeats about Julie's death, Yeats' claim that he was Jesse's father and the DNA testing that proved him wrong. Then he stopped talking and they walked on in silence for several minutes. Finally, Reuben motioned to a large boulder and they sat down together.

Reuben spoke slowly and quietly at first, "Julie – your mother – and I met in high school. I was older and after I graduated we didn't see each other for quite a while. Several years later we met up again and I knew that, although I had forgotten her once, I would never forget her again. Her mother was dying of cancer and Julie spent most of her time caring for her so we didn't go out much, but we were together nearly every day. When we were apart I felt so empty; I couldn't wait to see her again."

"Tell me about her; tell me about my mother," Jesse asked.

"She was the most authentic person I've ever known."

"Authentic? What do you mean?"

"Julie was Julie. She never tried to pretend she was anything else. Other girls may have been prettier, but Julie took my breath away. I could sit and look at her for hours. Other girls may have been smarter, but Julie knew things; she understood the things that matter in life. You know how some people say someone is 'wise beyond their years'? That was Julie. Maybe because of what happened to her mother or maybe it was just her, but she had a kind of depth and understanding about life that you don't find in someone that young. Most of all, if Julie told you something you knew it was true. She never lied; she never made promises she couldn't keep. That's why I knew something was terribly wrong when she promised to meet me and then didn't show up."

"What happened?"

"It all started to come apart after her mother died. Malcom Yeats was Julie's uncle by marriage; her father's brother-in-law, but I hardly ever saw him until Julie's Mom died. After that, he seemed to take over everything. He treated Julie like his personal servant and he did everything he could to keep us apart. Actually, I don't think he even knew who I was; all he wanted was to have Julie at his beck and call.

We still managed to sneak off and see each other. Julie was also taking care of her grandmother who was slipping into Alzheimer's disease. Whenever Julie went to her grandmother's house, I would be there. We pretended it was our house and we dreamed about the day when we would have our own place, far away from Yeats."

"Did he," Jesse hesitated, "abuse her?"

"I don't know. I was sure there was something she wasn't telling me, but anytime I would try to talk to her about it she would shut down and refuse to answer. A couple of times she had suspicious looking bruises but she always had a story about how she got them."

"Yeats claimed to be my father, so he must have..."

"I know, but I can't let myself think about what he must have done to her. If I had any idea, Jesse... If I had known that... I would have ripped him apart with my bare hands."

Jesse thought how much out of character that sounded. Reuben had always been one of the calmest and most gentle men he had ever known.

"Maybe that's why she didn't talk to you about it – to keep you from doing something that might have ruined your life."

Reuben said bitterly, "So instead, he ruined her life. If only we had gotten away like we planned."

Jesse said, "You were going to leave?"

Reuben nodded, "I was saving every penny I made so we could run away. We still didn't have enough money, but Julie said we couldn't wait any longer, we had to go. The night we were supposed to go, she disappeared. I never saw her again."

"When was that? I mean – "

"I know what you mean. I've been doing the math, myself, ever since I heard the news. It was about 5 months before you were born. She must have known she was pregnant when she told me it was time for us to go."

The two men sat drinking in the quiet of the forest. After a long while, Reuben looked Jesse in the eye for the first time since they sat down.

"Jesse, I'm your father. That's the first time I have said that out loud," Reuben paused thoughtfully then continued, "but there is no other explanation that makes any sense. Julie and I were lovers. She was not with anyone else. We dreamed about marrying and having a family. I thought all of that was lost long ago, but here you are – evidence of the love we shared. In case you have doubts, I did a DNA swab for Dr. Chavez so it will be easy to prove."

Jesse nodded his head slowly, "It's funny, but somehow I feel like I knew it all along; not consciously, but on some deeper level, beneath the other truths of my life I knew this one unspoken truth. I always wondered about my mother, but I never thought the same way about my father. Maybe because something in me knew my father was right here, all the time."

Reuben smiled at him, "Watching you grow up, grateful to be part of your life, I used to think to myself, I wish I had a son like you."

"I know what you mean. I always thought of you as a kind of surrogate father. My pretend family in my imagination included Brother Clement as my grandfather, Sister Miriam as my grandmother, Brother Marcel and Brother Adam were my kindly uncles, but I always imagined you as my father. Funny, though, I was always waiting for my imagined mother to come home for me. Now, she has."

"So what do we do now?" Reuben asked.

"Well, Dad," Jesse paused dramatically, "I probably ought to tell you that I'm about to get engaged."

"Does Leah know about this?"

"Yeah, sort of," Jesse chuckled. "I kind of proposed a couple of weeks ago. It was pretty clumsy and not well thought out, at all. She essentially said I should get my act together and try again sometime. I'll get it right this time and I'm pretty sure she will say, 'Yes'."

"I'm happy for you, Son," Reuben replied. "Isn't it interesting how your entire life has revolved around this place. For a 'little lost boy' you found a family here to love you, roots to your biological family and now these mountains have even introduced you to your bride. After all, you met Leah here for the first time when you were just children."

"All the more reason for us to start the next chapter of our lives here in this place."

The next day, Jesse and Leah left right after breakfast. They packed a lunch and headed off into the mountains for a day hike with Sacha. The mountains percolated with life, again, after another hard winter. Jesse led the way over familiar trails that climbed slowly but steadily toward the crystalline blue sky. They talked sparingly, content to be in one another's company and soaking in the wonder of the day.

When they stopped for lunch, Jesse picked out a flat-topped boulder to serve as their table. The sack Brother Seth packed for them provided a true hikers' feast: thick, over-stuffed sandwiches on fresh-baked multi-grain bread, tangy coleslaw, pickles, and oatmeal cookies still warm from the oven.

When they had eaten, Jesse said, "You don't remember this place, do you?"

Leah looked around and then said, "No, I don't. Should I?"

Jesse shook his head, "You were too young. But I will never forget it. I found you right over there, crying and shivering under a tree."

"Here? This was where you found me?"

"Maybe not this exact spot, but pretty close. It was all covered with snow that day, but I remember seeing you with the Hurricane Mountain fire lookout tower behind you, just as it is now. I'll always remember that day."

Leah scoffed, "That sounds a little creepy, doesn't it? I mean I was only seven."

"Yes and I was twelve, but you were my first."

"What?!" Leah said.

"My first rescue! Jeez, come on! Sara and I came over that ridge — we left before the others and took a different route. Looking back, it was a stupid thing to do, but we made it. The others found your parents, but we found you.

So, I'm thinking, what better place could there be than where we first met, so long ago."

"Better place for what?" Leah asked.

Jesse knelt down in front of her, "Leah, I didn't know it back then, but I know it now: we are meant to be together, forever. Will you marry me and give me the chance to love you for the rest of my life?"

Leah took Jesse's hands in hers, kissed them and softly said, "Yes. But you should know that if you hadn't asked me, I would have asked you."

For the next few minutes they sat together holding hands, sharing an occasional kiss but not speaking, as if they were both savoring the moment. Finally, Leah broke the silence.

"I'm glad you met my parents last week. At least, they will know who you are when I tell them we're getting married."

"They already know – or I should say, they know I planned to propose." Jesse saw Leah's surprise, then continued, "I asked for their approval when we were there visiting. They were very gracious, considering they had only just met me. But you should know they have complete confidence in your judgment. They said if you said 'yes' they would know we were meant to be together."

Leah smiled, then said, "What about your family? Who should we tell?"

"Reuben knows I planned to propose today. We can tell the rest at dinner, if that is OK with you."

"Jesse, I have a thought. What if we get married, right here, in October on the anniversary of the first time we met? I know that's pretty soon, but if we just invite family and close friends it might work. What do you think?"

Jesse smiled, "Perfect. Exactly what I would have suggested if I was smart enough to think of it. Just as long as it doesn't snow this time."

Epilogue

Jesse and Leah married on October 5. The wedding was held in the Priory chapel, a concession made when EJ Carlson agreed to be Jesse's best man. EJ swore he would put knobby tires on his wheelchair and go off-road for a ceremony on the mountain, but the chapel provided a good compromise. Brother Clement performed the ceremony and Brother Seth outdid himself preparing the reception dinner.

After the wedding, life began to settle in to a new and comfortable routine. They set up temporary housekeeping in Jesse's home outside of Boston until they could find a place of their own. Leah's new job with an up and coming internet-based news service allowed them great flexibility since she worked from home. She covered the New England and Mid-Atlantic regions, except for Washington DC which was handled by the political desk. Her travel kept them apart more than they wanted but they made the best of it; sometimes Jesse traveled with her.

They spent their first Christmas with Leah's family and brought in the new year at the Priory. Wherever they were, they seemed to move about in an aura of blissful happiness. Everyone commented that they had never seen two people more in love.

They did not plan it but neither of them was surprised when Leah announced on Valentine's Day that she was pregnant. Ironically, her doctor estimated her due date to be October 5.

Jesse said, "That date seems to be our destiny."

Leah's pregnancy passed without incident for eight months. Then, just after Labor Day weekend, she began to have pain and discomfort off and on through the day. Leah had stayed with her doctor in New York City, wanting someone who knew her and whom she trusted. So Jesse, Leah and Sacha traveled to the city a few days later. Leah's mother had both of her children come early and Leah feared it might be something hereditary. Dr. Stern was not overly concerned. The baby showed no distress and was already over six pounds. Still she advised Leah to stop working and to avoid strenuous activity, including travel.

They decided to stay in New York for a while, just to be safe. EJ Carlson had loaned them his townhouse in Brooklyn and was happy to have them stay there while he was on assignment somewhere he could not talk about. EJ was now working out of the FBI's New York field office on a project to disrupt money transfers of criminal enterprises using off-shore banks. Some of those transfers apparently routed through computer servers on U.S. soil, so the FBI could claim jurisdiction.

"I could tell you more –" EJ started.

"I know," Jesse chuckled, "but you would have to shoot me."

EJ shook his head with a scowl, "No, Jesse. We, G-men, don't work that way. I was going to say 'I could tell you more but I would have to report it to the CIA – and who knows what those guys would do. Maybe a trip to a room without a view somewhere in a jungle?"

EJ promised to fill them in once the operation concluded but, in the meantime, his flat in Brooklyn was all theirs. They did not have to wait long. On September 11 at 5:15 in the morning, baby Julie Lynn Tobias came into the world and announced her presence with authority – Julie for Jesse's mother and Lynn for Leah's mother. She was a bit early, but weighed in at six pounds eight ounces, a squirming pink bundle of everything a parent could hope for. Jesse held her moments after her birth while Leah insisted on counting her fingers and her toes. The three of them, together, radiated pure joy spiced with a tinge of first-time parent jitters.

They were sitting together, still basking in the glow of Julie's arrival when, shortly before 9:00am, Jesse's phone rang. He had set it to block all but emergency calls and he recognized immediately the ringtone he had assigned to the SAR team dispatcher.

He looked at Leah, "Sorry, she must have forgotten that I am out of town."

Answering the phone, he heard a breathless voice ask, "Jesse are you alright?" Before he could answer the dispatcher continued, "You're still in New York, right? When I saw the news I panicked. We are doing a call-out but then I realized you are there so – "

"Slow down, Roberta, what's going on?"

"You haven't seen the news?"

"No. The baby was born this morning – Julie Lynn – and we are at the hospital."

"Jesse, get to a TV! An airplane hit the World Trade Center a few minutes ago! One of the Twin Towers is on fire!"

Jesse went to the window. He did not need the TV – he could see the smoke billowing high above the city.

"We are in a hospital in Brooklyn, but I can see the smoke over Manhattan. What are they saying about causalities?"

Roberta settled down into her usual professional demeanor, "Nothing yet. First reports were that it was a small, private plane like a Cessna or something, but now we are hearing it was a passenger jet. Jesse, thousands of people work in the Twin Towers – this is going to be bad, very bad."

"Has New York asked for us to respond?"

"Not yet, but – " Roberta gasped, "Oh no..."

They saw the second plane at the same time; Roberta on television and Jesse watching out the window. Although it was far away and it happened quickly, there could be no doubt. A second airliner had crashed into the World Trade Center.

"Roberta," Jesse said calmly, "Send the call-out message, again – all hands on deck. Don't wait for New York to ask for us. Send everyone who can go. I will coordinate from this end; tell them to have their comm-links on when they approach the city."

Leah was sitting up in bed, rocking Julie in her arms and staring at unimaginable images on the television. Tears streamed down her cheeks.

Jesse sat next to her for a moment in silence, then said, "Leah, I – "

"Go, Jesse," she said. "I know you have to go but you come back to us, you hear? I know other people need you right now, but we need you, too. So, go, help them – but make sure you come back to us!"

In less than an hour, Jesse and Sacha arrived at the police barricade a few blocks from the scene. The South Tower had collapsed moments before and the immediate fear was that the North Tower would collapse as well. Evacuation efforts in the tower and surrounding buildings were still underway so all they could do was wait. Minutes later, Jesse watched as the North Tower fell and a blizzard of dust billowed into the sky, blocked out the sun and then fell back to earth covering everything in a muted gray shroud.

The days that followed were filled with heroic rescue efforts fueled by courageous desperation. Everyone, including Jesse and Sacha, worked relentlessly searching for survivors but with very few successes to show for their efforts. Despite the long hours and desperate measures taken by thousands of rescuers including hundreds of urban search-and-rescue dogs, only eleven survivors were found. The evacuation had saved thousands of lives but of those who could not be evacuated few survived. When the mission officially changed from rescue to recovery, Jesse and Sacha went home.

∞

Weeks later, family and friends gathered at the Priory once more to celebrate Julie's baptism. In the peacefulness of the chapel, Brother Clement placed baby Julie on the altar, just as he had placed baby Jesse years before; just as he had placed every baby baptized since Jesse.

"In our baptism," Clement said, "God claims us as beloved children, so it is altogether fitting that this child, like her father before her, should be placed upon this altar in dedication to the God who created her, the God who claims her in love, the God who will be her constant companion in life. In this child, in this new life, we find proof of God's abiding love and hope, not only for us and for our lives but for this troubled world."

Jesse looked around the chapel and found himself overcome with emotion. He looked at Leah standing next to him, radiant and perfect in every way. He saw her family, now his family too, and felt love for them taking root in his heart. He felt Reuben's hand on his shoulder and smiled, knowing that even as baby Julie would teach him about being a father, his own father would be sharing that learning experience with him. In the members of the Priory community he saw his true family more clearly than ever. He had come to this place as an abandoned child but he was lost no more. In his abandonment he had been welcomed with unconditional love into this place – this place that in every sense had become his home.

Jesse snapped back to attention when he heard Brother Clement say his name.

"Jesse, wants to share a story with us," Clement said.

Jesse cleared his throat, took a deep breath and spoke, "As you know, Julie was born on September 11th, a day that for most people will be remembered only for sadness and suffering. But for us, it will always be the day that love became real for us with the birth of our Julie.

Later on that day, the first of many that Sacha and I spent at Ground Zero, as we searched for survivors in a scene of pure horror I constantly felt surrounded and upheld by something I can only describe as God's love. Searching for life in the midst of overwhelming destruction and despair, I sensed an undeniable sacred presence there on that pile of debris, as if we were treading on holy ground.

We worked through the day and deep into the night until neither Sacha nor I could stand any longer. The subway to Brooklyn was operating again so we took the train back to EJ's townhouse. On the subway, people sat and stood in almost complete silence; like they were in church or at a funeral. When we got on, still wearing our Search and Rescue gear and covered with dust, they stepped aside, making room for us; a woman even stood up and insisted I take her seat.

Grateful, I sat down unable to hold my head up; Sacha collapsed at my feet. I pulled out my cellphone and began looking at pictures of Julie that I had taken that morning. As I scrolled through the pictures they seemed to come from another place, another time, lifetimes ago. I didn't realize it, but tears began to leave dusty tracks down my cheeks.

The woman who had given me her seat put her hand on my shoulder and asked, 'Are you OK?'

I nodded but could not find my voice to answer.

She noticed the picture of Julie in my hand and said, 'What a beautiful baby – boy or girl?'

I cleared my throat and managed to say, "A girl; her name is Julie – she was born this morning."

'This morning?' she said and then she took my phone and held it up for others to see. 'Hey, everybody," she shouted, "look at this! On this terrible day something good actually happened! A new baby – a little girl, Julie – was born this morning!'

People began to applaud and call out congratulations. Others crowded around to see Julie's picture and to pat me on the back and shake my hand.

Soon everyone was talking to one another, telling stories about their own kids, when they were born or what they were doing now. In a heartbeat this subway full of people, many of whom were wearing the same gray dust as me, were called back from the edge of the abyss by the notion of new life in the world.

I will never forget that moment. I will think of it every time I look at Julie."

When Jesse finished, no one spoke for what seemed a long time. Finally, Brother Clement nodded at Sister Adina.

Adina began playing softly, at first. The music filled the chapel and surrounded them all as they sang together:

> "Amazing Grace, how sweet the sound,
> that saved a wretch like me.
> I once was lost, but now am found,
> was blind but now I see."

Acknowledgements

    The seed that germinated into this story was sown by my son Michael and his dog Seven. Michael and Seven are an explosives detection team, not a search and rescue team. Still, their relationship and dedication to their work inspired me to write about the world of SAR and the incredible women, men and canines who inhabit it.

    Good fiction usually finds its roots in truth. The story Jesse tells at the end of this book was inspired by a blog entry posted by Michael Daley of the NY Post, January 13, 2011. Daley recounts the true story of Michael Slater who found inspiration in the birth of his daughter on September 11, 2001. As one who will never forget that day and how it changed my own life, I am grateful for the uplifting events and experiences that helped all of us get through some terrible times.

    Finally, as always, the patience, support and encouragement of my family are a great gift to me. I could not immerse myself in the process of research and writing without them. Thank you!

Also by William Delia

Healing River
(Westbow Press, 2012)

Healing River is a story of healing, faith, doubt and hope. Here is a brief excerpt:

"It all began innocently with a dying man grasping at faith, hoping to steady himself for whatever came after death. What happened next was beyond anyone's imagination.

At the age of fifty-seven, Luther was diagnosed with pancreatic cancer and given only a few months to live. Family members say he took the news as though it was a message he had been expecting for a long time, the inevitable outcome of a hard life. He never talked about his years away from Jericho Falls, leaving everything open to speculation. Apparently, he had lived a mostly solitary life. His hands were calloused and his shoulders slightly bent as if from years of hard labor. He smoked a little, drank a little, smiled sparingly and spoke even less. From all indications, Luther had never been a churchgoer. Still, it was understandable that, facing such a bleak prognosis, he might begin to ponder his life and his rapidly approaching death. Perhaps it was too late to make amends for the life he had led but maybe it was not too late to seek God's mercy."

Healing River invites the reader to think about what it truly means to be healed. Healed, not only from illness but also from the many forms brokenness takes in this life.

Home to the Mountains
A Fawn for Christmas
(CreateSpace, 2015)

Home to the Mountains tells a heart-felt story about home and family, perhaps the two most important things in any life. Rafford Brown is empty, alone, and haunted by the death of his four-year-old daughter when he seeks refuge in the Adirondack Mountains of upstate New York. Looking only for a place to camp for the night, he meets an elderly widow named Abigail Sherwood and her family and to his surprise Rafford finds a second chance at life; a life he was sure had passed him by. In the wonder of an Adirondack winter, with the help of a rare winter fawn, they discover what family and home truly mean.

A brief excerpt from Chapter 20: [*Rafford Brown says*] "The Adirondacks saved me. One day in sheer desperation, I packed my camping gear, drove to Old Forge, put my canoe in the water and paddled away. I didn't know where I was going or what I was going to do, but I was determined to find some answers in the mountains. If not, I was ready to use the pistol that I carried in my backpack to put an end to my misery. I was running away but, thank God, I ran to the one place that had always been a touchstone for me; the one place where I felt I really belonged. I know it sounds trite but the mountains became my sanctuary."

Home to the Mountains invites the reader to consider the meaning of home and family in his or her own life - a notion worth considering.

Coming in 2017
Truth, lies & consequences
a new novel by William Delia

Conor Jamison, sitting vigil at the bedside of his dying grandfather, realizes how little he knows about him. As his grandfather passes in and out of contact with reality, he tells Conor a tale of a life rooted in Eastern Europe, resurrected from the ash piles of Auschwitz and rendered unlivable by the threats and deeds of the criminal underworld until it is reimagined in the love of a good woman.

Conor cannot decide how much to believe of his grandfather's ramblings. When his own investigation begins to lend credibility to the old man's story, Conor comes to understand that all things in life, both truth and lies, have consequences; consequences often visited on generations that follow.

ABOUT THE AUTHOR

    William Delia is an accomplished writer, songwriter and public speaker. Born in Connecticut and educated in California, he enjoyed a lengthy career as a non-profit executive and in the ministry. He has composed nearly 100 songs, both words and music. I Once Was Lost is his third published novel.
    He lives and writes in the foothills of the Adirondack Mountains of upstate New York. For more information about Delia and his books, go to www.wmdeliabooks.com.

Made in the USA
Columbia, SC
05 October 2022

68529945R00171